NO
HESITATION

ALSO BY KIRK RUSSELL

PAUL GRALE THRILLERS

Signature Wounds
Gone Dark

BEN RAVENEAU MYSTERIES

A Killing in China Basin
Counterfeit Road
One Through the Heart

THE JOHN MARQUEZ MYSTERIES

Shell Games
Night Game
Dead Game
Redback
Die-Off

NO HESITATION

A GRALE THRILLER

KIRK RUSSELL

This is a work of fiction. Names, characters, organizations, places, events, and incidents are either products of the author's imagination or are used fictitiously.

Copyright © 2020 by Kirk Russell

All rights reserved.

No part of this book may be reproduced, or stored in a retrieval system, or transmitted in any form or by any means, electronic, mechanical, photocopying, recording, or otherwise, without express written permission of the publisher.

Published by Strawberry Creek, LLC, Berkeley

kirkrussellbooks.com

Edited and designed by Girl Friday Productions
www.girlfridayproductions.com

Design: Paul Barrett
Project management: Sara Addicott

Cover image credits: CO Leong/Shutterstock; rdonar/Shutterstock; Alexyz3d/Shutterstock; Ryan Fletcher/Shutterstock

ISBN (paperback): 978-1-7343146-0-1
ISBN (ebook): 978-1-7343146-1-8
Library of Congress Control Number: 2019919007

For Clara and Margot

AUGUST 2ND

Two US Customs and Border Protection agents led the man inside the Metaline Falls Border Station, where he handed over his passport and was questioned about his travel plans. The driver who'd picked him up an hour north in Nelson, Canada, was also questioned, but she was known. She'd grown up in Spokane and was a childhood friend of the agents questioning her passenger.

"He talked the whole way here about his trip," she said. "And I mean, the whole way. He also showed me the camera he bought for wildlife photos. This guy is a tourist."

The man appeared calm as he used his phone to show agents his lodging reservations at Zion and Yellowstone national parks, as well as his return flight to Europe. His German passport read Heinz Ulrich, age fifty-four. He matched his passport photo, with brown eyes and dark hair graying at the temples. From his responses it seemed he understood English better than he spoke it.

One of the border agents interviewed later said the man was emotional as he talked about his desire to see the American West and how he'd saved money for this vacation. He'd gotten teary and appeared confused after he was told he might be denied entry.

"I am a hiker," he said and showed them a Yellowstone trail map on his phone.

The border agents had a problem with the new facial-recognition software. If unable to verify identity, it gave a probability estimate. The estimate was intended to aid agents, but so far had only complicated their jobs. With the individual in question it gave a sixty-one percent probability that the man was a bomb maker, long sought, named Frederic Dalz.

Further complicating the agents' jobs was the poor quality of known photos of Dalz, and the fact that several Western intelligence agencies believed he was inactive or dead. On top of that, the new facial-recognition software had a mixed record at the Metaline Falls Border Station.

Two weeks earlier, it had identified a Spokane rancher as a terrorist. He was detained overnight, an arrest that had generated significant media coverage and provoked an embarrassing apology. The desire not to be implicated in another mistake weighed on the agents' minds as they conferred out of earshot.

Two agents remained with the man as he waited. He enthusiastically described a new camera he'd bought for the trip to the agent nearest him. She listened without interest. She said later that as the agents returned, she saw his eyes go flat and expressionless.

Four years earlier, an American FBI agent named Paul Grale, who worked on the domestic terrorism squad in Las Vegas, had nearly trapped Frederic Dalz with the help of Croatian police, or so Grale believed. Dalz had escaped. Grale was the FBI agent most knowledgeable about Dalz. In interviews later, the Metaline border agents said they'd come close to calling him.

The agents reached a decision and fanned out as they returned to where the man stood waiting. The lead agent handed *back the passport and said, "Welcome to America, Mr. Ulrich. We hope your trip is everything you've dreamed of."*

1

AUGUST 5TH

Near sunrise we passed through a guarded gate at a military testing site then crossed a flat valley and rose into bone-colored desert mountains on a narrow unpaved road. A mile up, after rounding a long climbing curve, Dr. Ralin pointed at a small flat area near the cliff edge.

"Park there, Agent Grale, and I'll tell you what happened."

As we got out, I saw Ralin pick up on my limp. I've had a lot of back pain the past few weeks, but it's an old problem that dates to the Iraq War when the FBI sent agents to help the Army defuse bombs. I don't like to talk about those injuries and was glad Ralin didn't ask.

We walked over near the cliff edge and looked down at a dry valley and then across it at gray-and-red-striped mountains, and a tall rock formation there that Ralin pointed at.

"A battle was fought here, a mock one between two drone squadrons. I'm violating every security regulation telling you this, but the FBI needs to know. The green drones were controlled by Air Force officers, the red by Indie. Each squadron had a master drone and nineteen attack drones. Indie is our nickname for the artificial intelligence at Independence Base. Indie used that rock formation to hide its master drone."

"Machine against man," I said. "Hasn't that testing gone on for years?"

"Yes, but never with an artificial intelligence as sophisticated and capable as Indie."

"How did 'Indie' communicate with the drones it controlled?"

"Through JWICS, the Joint Worldwide Intelligence Communications System. All communications are through JWICS—Internet, Pentagon, everything. It created a slight lag in the battle, but that would also happen in war. You use JWICS at the FBI, don't you?"

"For anything secure," I said, then asked, "If there was a lag, wouldn't that have given an advantage to a human commander?"

"If the human commander could react as fast or see everything at once like Indie does. Indie had the advantage of running millions of mock battles prior to and during the battle as it evolved. Picture your brain being able to do an enormous amount more all at once and quickly. In drone warfare, a full second is a large amount of time."

"How long was the battle here?"

"Forty-three seconds."

"Start to finish?"

"Yes."

"Where's the rest of the world at with this?"

"We're racing Russia, China, and other nations. The Russians are further along than they let on. China is very capable and has focus, money, and ambition. They're pushing hard. Several nations have military applications for AI programs. We're in a dangerous race toward weaponizing AI. At the moment, we have a slight lead or at least think we do. If we get too far ahead, our enemies will have no choice but to try to slow us down."

I'm a career FBI agent on the domestic terrorism squad in the Las Vegas office. I've been briefed on Ralin's belief that we should push ahead with the military AI project at Independence Base, but also share with the world the computer source code that led to Indie. He's said as much in interviews, on TV talk shows, and even in a TED presentation. He's also said the sharing right now isn't realistic, so it's hard to know what he really thinks. My guess is he wants it that way.

"Who of our allies would you share code with?" I asked.

"A year from now I'd share with our closest allies. AI will benefit all of humanity if allowed to."

I started to ask more but then thought, why bother. We weren't out here for that. We were here at Ralin's request after two top coders on the Indie project disappeared last night. The pair missing, Alan Eckstrom and Eric Indonal, were coders but also computer scientists and equals to Ralin or something close to it. Or that's what he communicated on the pre-dawn drive here and much more calmly than he had at three-thirty this morning.

"What happened here may explain why Eric and Alan quit," Ralin said.

"So now you think they quit?"

"Now that I've had more time to think about it, I do think they quit."

On the drive here Ralin had talked about their start together seven years ago on the project that became the breakthrough Indie. His call at three a.m. to our Las Vegas FBI Field Office was after Laura Trent, the girlfriend of Alan Eckstrom, called him worried and frightened that her boyfriend, Eckstrom, hadn't come home. Ralin's call was referred to me, but only because there were security worries surrounding anyone working on the Indie project.

When we talked, he told me he doubted Eckstrom and Indonal had been abducted, but wanted to come here to explain why. He returned to that as we dropped the open source code talk.

"The red machine struck first," he said. "Both teams hid drones by making them hard to detect with radar. They used natural structures. The red team used that rock formation across the canyon I pointed out. I was in an observation helicopter. Two observers were parked where we've parked."

"So right here?"

"Yes, right here, and their job was to watch, evaluate, and write up the battle results. It wasn't as much a hunt for nineteen attack drones as a hunt for two master drones, and we're still analyzing what Indie did, but I can tell you that it ran very rapid calculations that measured millionths-of-a-second differences in message delivery times between the enemy master drone and its soldier drones. Using that information, it triangulated and located the green master drone's approximate then exact location."

"Say all that again," I said.

He did and more slowly, with more detail. By measuring tiny signal-timing differences, Indie had pinpointed the location of the green master drone and destroyed it.

"What was the skill level of the human opponents?" I asked.

"The Air Force delayed the test three weeks until they could fly in the very best. Now they're planning another test. They'll plan another after that and another and another and another until they finally accept this generation of AI is superior."

He said that with such certainty, I turned, looked at him, and thought about all the times people were certain and then things turned out different than expected. It also struck me as an odd thing to say after Indie just killed two people.

"If you were in charge would you shut the AI down while you figured out what happened here?" I asked.

"It's pointless to talk about," he said. "It's not going to get shut down. That invites even worse risks. We're in an arms race."

"Are we?"

"We most definitely are."

"You don't see Indie, our AI, in a strictly deterrent role?"

He smiled at that and said, "You know as well as I do, it's not a deterrent."

I did know. Indie was anything but. It was out across the world breaking into computer systems, crypto cracking, and ghosting through enemy computer files while our government issued righteous denials.

"I'll show you what happened here," Ralin said, "but I need my laptop."

He got that from inside my car and opened it on the hood. His hands trembled as he started a video playing. It began with the mountains across the valley in sunlight and shadow. The camera panned over rock formations and then the flat valley below.

"Watch the timer in the upper right-hand corner, and the green and red boxes. Those boxes are tallying kills."

Firing began. White smoke trails streaked the sky and flashes of light corresponded with the kill count in the upper right corner of the screen. A timer showed the seconds as they ticked by, and as Ralin had said, it all went down in forty-three seconds. When the firing ended, a camera on the helicopter zoomed in on the red master drone repositioning itself a thousand feet above the vehicle of two military observers. The camera then zoomed in on the vehicle, and I read the Department of Defense insignia on the driver's door.

I felt Ralin tense and only then did I realize what was coming.

"Indie already knew it had won," Ralin said, then glanced at me and added, "I have a lot of trouble watching this. The red drone positioned itself above the observers. I was very nervous then and am now. I'll never get over it. We couldn't understand what the red master drone was doing, but we should have guessed and taken action."

"Were the observers warned?"

"Yes."

In the video, a man got out of the passenger side and walked a short distance away, then looked up with binoculars.

"Were they told the red master drone was above them?" I asked.

"Yes."

Just as Ralin answered, there was a bright flash of light and the head and chest of the observer outside exploded. That's the only way to describe it. He was there and then gone. When we could see again, parts of his body were scattered over the rocks. Ralin bowed his head and turned from the laptop as a second rocket struck the jeep. It burned with the other observer inside.

Ralin spoke again and in a flat voice said, "Indie wouldn't do anything without a logical reason, but so far, we can't determine how it got there. It may have perceived a future threat or even considered the men's role as observers and what they'd learned about its attack strategy. There has to be a reason. Most likely, almost certainly, it's a coding error. I just don't know what it was, and neither do Eric and Alan."

"What happens when you ask the AI, Indie, as you call it?"

"We get answers that are hard to explain unless you have worked with AI, and I really shouldn't be talking at all. I've shared enough to get arrested."

"You're fine talking with an FBI agent. I've been down this road before, don't worry. You can talk to me."

"We've tried to program a moral code without hampering Indie's ability to fight to win, but that's very difficult when the primary goal is to have the fastest, most accurate response to achieve a war objective. Winning requires no delay or hesitation."

"How did Indonal and Eckstrom react?"

"We were all shocked. I've thought and thought about what happened here. I . . . It did happen. There's no questioning that."

He started to say something more, stopped, then said, "Indie often takes a different path than we anticipate. Sometimes it takes us a while to understand why. This time I don't really know what we witnessed. We've come up with theories but none quite fit, or they do and they don't."

"Was the decision to kill the observers made before or after the battle started?"

"After, and the killings may have to do with the future and not this forty-three-second battle. Forty-three seconds will very soon look as quaint and slow as the horse and buggy. AI machines will do more damage faster and on a larger scale than we've ever seen. Wars fought between AIs may start and finish within hours and days, not months and years. We thought we'd witnessed a coding error when it killed the observers. What we may have watched was the future and a reflection of ourselves and how we treat future variables in warfare."

"What do you mean when you say 'variables in warfare'?"

"Enemy soldiers are known combatants, but a sixteen-year-old witnessing a battle is a variable. AI may view the unarmed adolescent as a future source of information and kill the teenager. Wars fought at the speed of AI will evolve toward more efficient killing. Taking prisoners of war could end. The execution of prisoners, killing witnesses who could aid the enemy—none of that's new, but it could get much faster and more efficient."

"Is that why Indonal and Eckstrom quit? Or is there more?"

"What happened here shocked them. It shocked me, but for Eric and Alan it may have been the catalyst. But they also have some issues with me, serious issues."

That was the first time he'd said that and I nudged him along. I didn't want to call him out on holding back.

"They want to get to a new, more positive project. We didn't work years and years on AI with war in mind. I don't believe a foreign power abducted them, and I can promise you they're not going to help a dictator or any country that restricts the freedoms of its people."

"Then why did they just disappear? Why not tell you?"

"They're angry at me. They want to shut down Indie until we solve this. The Department of Defense owns this project and has said no shutdown but no more live testing. I was okay with that solution but they weren't."

"You didn't say any of that last night."

"I know. Alan's girlfriend, Laura, was so upset and worried, I wasn't thinking clearly. She had talked to him and he was ready to come home but never showed up. Only later did it occur to me I needed to bring someone from the FBI out here. The switch from DARPA to DoD was hard on all three of us, but particularly them. They dream of a better world more often than I do. I'm not as optimistic about humanity."

Ralin and his team of neural-network specialists were initially funded by DARPA, the Defense Advanced Research Projects Agency. After Indie proved viable, DoD made the decision to build Independence Base. DARPA falls under the Department of Defense umbrella, so DoD took over. The switch from working for DARPA to DoD could easily be a rough change. Stricter new rules. The whole thing.

Last night, Indonal and Eckstrom had met for drinks at a bar named the Blue Jaguar. When Eckstrom didn't come home, his girlfriend, Laura Trent, called Ralin. That was just before three a.m. That and Ralin's explanation here was what I had to work with. I'd called Laura Trent and questioned her but didn't get much. This visit was well worth it and really might explain why the guys disappeared.

After we left here, I'd drop Ralin at the Independence Base guard gate. Someone there would drive him across the base to the half-subterranean building that housed the AI, Indie, and I'd begin looking for Indonal and Eckstrom, starting with the Blue Jaguar. At the FBI we'd go out with an APB, all-points bulletin, that morning on both unless they turned up.

"You're telling me you think the guys quit and walked away?" I asked. "That's what I'm hearing and that's what Eckstrom's girlfriend didn't say last night."

"They'll turn up," Ralin answered.

"So, are they taking a break or did they quit?"

"I can't answer that. I just don't know."

"If we go out with an APB, agents will get diverted from other investigations and their disappearance will get spun all kinds of ways. With the knowledge they carry, it's inevitable treason and the question of whether they're traitors out selling secrets to our enemies will come up."

"I get it," Ralin said. "And I'm worried."

"All right, let's head back."

"I'm sorry about last night. I'm sorry I didn't say more then."

He could easily have said more, but he hadn't. Instead, he'd brought me out here, which to me said he wanted to control how the story evolved.

"No need apologize," I said.

"I'm the one who should apologize. I should have said more last night."

"Let me ask you something: Would DoD shut Indie down if you recommended it?"

Ralin looked at me as if I'd asked an unusually naïve question.

"Do you understand what's at stake?" he asked. "Everything is at stake. Absolutely everything. Our freedom, our military might, our economy, everything. We can negotiate on our terms if we get there first, but not if we lose the race. We have to solve this, but we also have to be first. We cannot, we must not, lose that race."

2

"Where are you at?" my supervisor, Ted Mara, asked.

"I dropped Ralin off. I'm on my way to the Blue Jaguar, the lounge bar where Indonal and Eckstrom were drinking before they walked out and disappeared last night."

"The bar is open?"

"Not until late afternoon, but the waitress who served them volunteered to come in early. She knows them. I'm going to talk with her and a bar manager."

"Good, but don't lose track of time. We've got a one o'clock meeting with the Department of Defense agents, and I want to meet alone with you after. You also got a message this morning from the Nevada State Highway Patrol. They've got something for you on that dark web group you're tracking. Bismarck and his followers are here or close to here. Highway patrol pulled over a half dozen of their vehicles for broken taillights, no plates, no current registration, you name it. They told the officers they're here to mind-meld with the AI."

"I've known why, but I didn't know they were already in Nevada. Bots originating somewhere in Eastern Europe are helping drive his followers out here. Someone wants to amplify Bismarck's mind-meld crap. If he's here, I'll find him."

Bismarck's true name was John Bales. Dark web followers know him as Bismarck. I'm a follower, as are other agents on domestic terrorism squads at six other FBI offices. Nineteen years ago, his parents approached the Boston office—where I was stationed for a year—with fears surrounding letters their son had written, in which he detailed fantasies of killings where he absorbed the life energy of the victims. We questioned him at length, but there was nothing to charge him with.

Five years later, he approached the FBI voluntarily with information about a young woman named Janet Li who'd been reported missing. Her body was never found, and he knew way too much about her. That was the start of him taunting us and the start of an ongoing file on Bismarck.

Trespassing, disturbing the peace, poaching—he's been charged with those crimes but not a single violent crime against another individual. And yet, he lingers on an FBI watch list. That's in large part for the tips he's provided us. He'll send photos of, say, a piece of charred human skull in a firepit in a remote meadow somewhere that was given to him by a person he'd never seen before but prayed for later. His tips have led to exhumations and long interrogations he seems to enjoy.

At the Jaguar I sat with the waitress who'd served Indonal and Eckstrom drinks. She knew and liked both, but I had to remind her of their last names, which seemed to embarrass her.

"They're not here that often, but I always talk with them. I hardly did at all last night because it was so busy, and they weren't alone like they usually are. A woman was sitting with them, and a guy at the bar seemed to know them. The woman who sat with them sat close to the taller one, Alan."

"Alan Eckstrom?"

"I don't remember his last name. I might not even know it, but he's a nice guy and shyer than Eric."

"They're regulars?"

"More like once a week and they're always friendly and they tip. The woman with them wasn't anyone I'd ever seen before and not someone I would have expected to be with them."

"Why not?"

"I don't know, maybe she's more refined or something. That might not be the right way to say it . . ."

Alan Eckstrom was the taller of the two. He was my height, six foot one, and had brown hair and acne scars on his neck.

"You don't miss much," I said. "You ought to come work for us."

She smiled and said, "You have to watch everything when you're running cocktails, and I like those two guys. I didn't mean anything bad about them. They're really nice guys. They're just much more casual than she was dressed. She's a different type. The guys are always easygoing."

When I left the Blue Jaguar, I checked with the businesses along the street that had surveillance cameras and struck out with the first half dozen storefronts before getting lucky.

The owner of a boutique shoe store went out of her way to help. We found Eckstrom and Indonal on her security surveillance video. At 9:21 p.m. last night they walked past her store. Two other businesses down the street caught them on surveillance video. My progress slowed at an intersection then moved forward again when a department store's surveillance cameras showed them crossing a wide, empty lot toward a van. The van's headlights came on, and a woman got out and hugged Indonal hard. I replayed that several times then stopped worrying about abduction.

Neither Indonal nor Eckstrom had any criminal record. Indonal had a speeding ticket five years ago. He was homeschooled in Northern California and accepted to Stanford at age seventeen after testing off the charts in math, physics, and geometry. He excelled in the Stanford School of Engineering where he took up computer programming and data science. That's where he met Eckstrom, who knew Ralin.

Near noon, after returning to the office, I learned more about them on a call with Sally Weiss at Stanford. I was referred to her. She'd worked with all three.

"Indonal is far and away the brightest," Weiss said, echoing what Trent said last night. "If you're asking me how they got to the breakthrough, Mark Ralin wrote a significant algorithm they call the Golden Algorithm. It came at just the right moment for the neural-network approach and was a big step at the time, so I don't want to downplay Mark, or Alan for that matter. But the later advances that truly changed AI were possible only because Eric has mathematical gifts that are once in a generation. Or that's my opinion, but I'm certain Google would have loved to have had Eric Indonal on the DeepMind team."

"You see him as key to the current project?"

"It's not that simple, but I'm sure he is. I see Indonal as the true genius. Other people may disagree, but I was around them for a long time."

"Thank you, Sally. If I need your help again, what's the best number to call you at?"

She gave me her cell just before I headed in for the meeting with the Department of Defense agents that turned out to be a lot of nothing except for one thing. DoD had stalled, delayed, rescheduled, and otherwise messed with us for months, but now all of a sudden, they wanted to work closely with us.

No one bothered to ask why. Everyone in the room already knew. The pair of DoD agents here to meet with us today weren't the ones who made the earlier decisions, so why harangue them? They would agree we should have started working closer together months ago. The threat level was way up, and DoD was worried. They'd wanted to maintain the highest level of secrecy and were afraid our agents would compromise that. They'd deny it forever, but that's the bottom line.

Now they're scared, now they need us. Indonal and Eckstrom missing was just one piece of that. We went down the list of things we would coordinate together, and then ended the meeting. After we broke up, Mara wanted to meet alone with me. He'd been secretive about this closed-door meeting. I worried it was about my back, and it was at first, and then about something else entirely.

were arguments on both sides of the open source code debate, and we didn't know yet why Eckstrom and Indonal staged a disappearance.

"More on Ralin," Mara said. "He bounces between Las Vegas, London, and Stanford, where he's a visiting professor in the School of Engineering. In London he has a girlfriend named Claire Henley that British intelligence suspects is taking directions from Moscow. The Brits briefed the CIA, and the CIA briefed headquarters. Henley is a computer scientist who approached Ralin ten years ago. That's a Russian concept, paying attention to the rising stars. She's also married to an eighty-seven-year-old Russian oligarch the Brits suspect distributes money for Russian operations in the UK. He's quite wealthy and very forgiving of his younger wife. Ralin has been warned about Henley but has continued the affair. That might be his way of pushing back, or maybe he just doesn't like being told how to live his life."

"How long have Ralin and his wife been separated?" I asked.

"Two years."

That was long enough to know where the marriage was going, but Ralin's marriage wasn't any of our business, and highly capable people were already all over Ralin. He was probably monitored from every which way.

"Henley isn't the only other woman he's seeing. There's a PhD candidate at Stanford he mentors far too closely."

"Is the Stanford woman a suspected spy?"

"Not as far as I know."

"Okay, what else?"

"I'm just bringing you up to speed, Grale. If you don't want background on Ralin, I won't bother you with it. And it's not why we're in this room. Let's talk about your back. Whatever flare-up from your old bomb injuries you're having has gone on longer than any I remember."

My back was hurting worse than it had in a long time, and it worried me. To be active duty you need to be physically fit. There's a running test I wouldn't pass today. Or even come close to passing.

"What are you taking for pain?" Mara asked with a blank face as if we'd never talked about it before.

"Tylenol and Aleve, and if it's bad enough I'll take a NORCO 5."

"That's an opioid?"

"It's hydrocodone and acetaminophen, so a mix, but I only take the NORCOs at night, and only if it's bad. I also have Percocet but try not to use it."

"When did you last use Percocet?"

"A couple of nights ago."

"Are there any other drugs?"

"Those are the ones I use."

Mara shifted in his chair and his eyes flickered back to mine, and then to the wall behind me as he asked, "So no other drugs?"

"I have OxyContin but try to avoid taking it."

"Are you on it now?"

"No."

"When is the last time you saw your doctor?"

"I don't know, two or three months ago, but not about my back. That doctor is a specialist. He's booked months ahead."

"Schedule something. I'm being asked, and I need a better explanation."

"I'll do that, but the flare-up will probably die down before the appointment comes around."

"Make the appointment anyway. Assistant Special Agent in Charge Esposito, the ASAC, wants more information. So do others. Your 'flare-up' as you call it has lasted longer than some of the higher-ups are comfortable with, so I'll be blunt. Active duty is on the line."

I nodded and said, "I'll make an appointment."

I've counted on Mara to defend me and say, *It's okay, Grale is solving cases and getting the job done. His back goes through bad periods occasionally, but it'll get better.* Or that's the conversation I imagined.

"It's been over a month," Mara said. "I get asked all the time about what's up with your back. You need to see a specialist; you can't downplay this or micromanage what people think. You can't just ride this one out. You need to get proactive."

"I'll do that."

"I hope you hear me."

"I do."

I stood to leave and Mara said, "We're not done. There's a video clip you need to see."

"What is it? A video of me walking with a limp?"

"It was taken at the Metaline Falls Border Station north of Spokane where they're testing new facial-recognition and body-type-identifier software. A man who crossed at Metaline triggered the software, but the percentage of recognition wasn't definitive, and they've had a recent string of false positives so they let him through."

"Crossed when?"

"Three days ago. August second."

"That's a while."

"It is. They brought him inside and questioned him at length. That gave the cameras a better look, but the problem with the individual in question is a lack of up-to-date photos. The man in the video you're about to watch was very enthusiastic about his national park reservations at Yellowstone and Zion, but so far, he hasn't showed up at either of them. Analysts at headquarters reviewed the video. That's when your name came up."

"My name?"

"Your name."

There were only a few ways that could happen. A cold feeling ran down my spine as I said, "Metaline Falls."

"That's right, Metaline Falls. From there it's a two-hour drive to Spokane."

"Run the video," I said.

"Here you go." Mara started the video as he slid his laptop over to me. "The man you're looking at hired a driver to pick him up at a train station in Canada and take him to a hotel in Spokane. The driver is a local they don't have suspicions about. She dated someone working at the Metaline station and grew up in the area. She's known."

"Known by whom?"

"Several border agents at Metaline know her."

"What's the name of the train station where she picked him up?"

"I don't have it, but I'll get it if you recognize the individual in question."

I stopped the video on a clear view of the man's face as Mara said, "They questioned him inside at length. He showed the border patrol officers his national park reservations and told them he'd waited on hold last September to get one of the government cabins in Zion and knew what room he had at Yellowstone Lodge and what the view was from there. He wanted to go back to the car and get the new camera with a 300-millimeter lens he'd bought for the trip to show them some of its features, which is to say he wasn't in a hurry to leave."

"What it says is he took over the conversation."

Mara mulled that over, then said, "Yeah, maybe. Grale, maybe you just hit the truth. Several agencies are waiting for your answer, so take your time."

The video was already enough for me, but I reached for my phone and called up a series of photos, none of which were very good. Throughout his career he'd avoided being photographed.

"What height did the software put him at?" I asked.

"Six foot two to six foot four."

I nodded then said, "He's six foot three. In France they call him *l'homme des chiffres*. The Numbers Man. The numbers were on a diagram French intelligence found in a hotel room. The numbers tied to the names of people he assassinated with a bomb as they sat down for a dinner. They found typewritten details on each individual in a dossier the French said was thick as a novel, as if he'd studied at length everyone who sat down at that table and was killed. He made notes he numbered and gave each person a number and made lists of the numbers that applied to the notes. This guy is a trip. If he's here, others are too. He'd be part of a team. Part of, but still somehow alone."

"You really have spent time on him, haven't you?" Mara asked.

I looked at Mara as I thought about Dalz entering the US. Dalz had killed our military officers, diplomats, spies, and tourists, but as far as we knew, he'd never come here.

"Other agencies are waiting on your response," Mara said.

"It's Dalz. The question is, why is he here?"

4

JACE

FBI Special Agent Kristen Blujace loaded a U-Haul earlier that morning in Oakland with the help of two neighbors in their early twenties. Both had smelled of last night's alcohol and dope. Neither had finished high school or had steady jobs, but they talked as if things were going well. Jace saw something different, but liked and cared for them. She hugged each before leaving.

"If you ever need a reference for a job or if things just aren't going right, call me. Or if you just want to talk, okay?"

The rented van was a wide drive, wider even than the black FBI Suburban she'd driven for years as an agent. She'd liked the Suburban but not the look people gave it, thinking it's a fed vehicle all washed and clean and guzzling gas with one person inside. The government always taking care of itself first is what they really thought, same as Congress and government officials with their guaranteed health care, talking like they know what it's like not to have it.

The U-Haul took up most of the lane, and with traffic bumper to bumper it was watch and go, not just stop and go, until she was south of the Bay Area. Only then did her thoughts stop jumping around.

She didn't know where this move's changes would lead. In the San Francisco FBI Field Office, she'd worked longer and longer hours. She laid out her clothes at night, knew exactly what she'd put on early the next morning, how many minutes in the bathroom getting ready, and what she'd eat going out the door. She lived alone and focused on investigations. It wasn't working. No other way to say it, but in Vegas, maybe she'd meet somebody and start again. And her dad was there, her dad whom she hadn't talked to since she was five years old. Her feelings were a whole mix of things when she pictured knocking on his door.

Older agents who were more accustomed to moves understood her practical reasons for Las Vegas: going where you can at least save some money and someday buy a house that's not a million bucks or more for some worn-down relic with two bedrooms, new paint, and a realtor driving a flashy car. The move to Vegas made more sense to those agents than her younger FBI friends. Those who knew her best put the move down to the motorcycle accident that left her former fiancé brain-dead. His body lived with a caregiver in a cottage behind Gene's mother's house in Sausalito. Jace needed somewhere she could start again.

In some ways she thought of the FBI as her family, and she was simply moving to another branch of the family. She'd floated that family idea yesterday with her San Francisco supervisor, who shook her head and laughed before turning serious.

"Your family is there for you when you screw up. You screw up in the FBI and you'll be handing in your badge and gun. That isn't going to happen to you, but remember that, Jace. Don't ever forget it."

When Jace became an FBI agent, she became part of something larger, something that mattered. Family was the wrong word, but she needed the connection with other agents. Jace was driven and needed purpose. She was like Grale in that way and wanted to learn more about investigating from him. He had a way of making things happen.

Her mind cleared more as she drove south in the long, flat Central Valley. The Sierras were off to her left, hazy in the distance. Her phone rang as she crossed the Tehachapi Mountains. It was her new domestic terrorism squad supervisor, Ted Mara, calling back again, so maybe he was a touchy-feely type of supervisor or maybe something had happened.

"How's the drive going, Agent Blujace?"

"Going well. I might get in a little earlier than I'd thought."

"That's all good, but I'm going to tell you something now you're not going to like."

"What does it have to do with?"

"Agent Grale. I know you like him and that you worked with him during the electrical-grid attacks."

"You and I talked about him," Jace said.

"I know we did, but this is different. Metro police here in Las Vegas have an undercover drug operation underway and claim they videoed Grale making street buys of illicit painkillers."

It took her a moment before she said anything. "I don't believe that. Not Grale, of all people, he wouldn't be doing that."

"My reaction too," Mara said, "but his back is as bad as I can remember. He's hurting. He's in pain and has dealt with pain for a long time. Metro is certain Grale is buying from a dealer they expect to take down. Their call was somewhere between a courtesy call and a warning. We have some time to act. I don't know how much, but probably not long or they wouldn't be calling. I have to notify the Office of Professional

Responsibility, but we can investigate within the squad before they take over, so we're going to."

"OPR Grale?"

"I know it's hard to believe, but get past that. I'm going to ask you to be a part of investigating. If you can't see yourself doing that, I'll assign someone else to team with Grale. I'm sorry, Agent Blujace, I really am, but I want to keep it very discreet, as quiet as possible, and you're new. No one knows you so that makes you a good fit. How familiar are you with Grale's injuries?"

It took her a moment to answer. She couldn't get her head around it.

"Has he told you what medications he takes?" Mara asked.

"If he has, I don't remember." She remembered the lap pool. "He swims. He's got a lap pool."

Jace tried to picture Grale making street buys but couldn't get there.

"I don't believe it," she said more softly.

"I don't either, but that's not the way to approach this."

"What about his girlfriend? She's a doctor. Have you called her?"

"Not yet. How close are you to Grale?"

"I don't know him that well, but I've learned a lot from him. I can say that. He's more street than computer, but he's both. He's technology and street, pretty unusual for an older agent."

"Is he a mentor to you?"

Her radar picked up on something in the way he asked that.

"Sorta, maybe, though I don't know what a mentor really is. I know people get called that. Grale and I are about work. We're alike that way. You know I want to work with him, right?"

"Did he encourage you to transfer?"

"No. I floated the idea with him once but haven't told him that I went through with it."

"I told him you're coming in this afternoon and that I want you two to work together initially. He's all for that, but you haven't talked to him since the transfer was approved?"

"That's right, I haven't."

Why was he asking in that way? It bothered her, but she pushed the feeling aside for now.

"If you agree to help investigate him, it's going to feel like betrayal. Are you up to that?"

"What happens if I'm not?"

"Then I'll put someone else on the squad with him."

"Put me with Grale."

"Drive and think about it and let's talk again later today."

"I don't need to think about it. If someone is going to do it, assign me."

"I want you to think about it, but let me ask you this: When you worked the grid attacks with him, did he ever talk about how he deals with pain?"

"No."

"Did you ever notice anything that suggested drug use?"

"No."

"Would you know it if you saw it?"

"I would."

I've seen drugged-out people like you would never guess, Supervisor Mara. People I know, she thought. Curled up in the corner of a filthy house, her cousin did guys one after another just to get her next fix.

"Think about it and we'll talk, and I want to say we're looking forward to you joining DT squad. We've got a vehicle waiting for you and a desk you'll share. Is there anything I can do to help your transition?"

"Just put me with Grale. I'm an FBI agent first. I'll do what's needed, and I'd like to come in tomorrow. I'll want part of the day to move, but I don't have much stuff. I'd rather come in and learn the office in the afternoon than arrange towels in a closet."

During the grid attacks she'd learned from Grale, and Jace craved learning. She wanted to be the very best at her job—developing a case, writing the proposal, the whole thing. For miles she turned the idea of Grale addicted to drugs in her head and then decided there was nothing she could do other than what Mara said: investigate and find out. Pain can grind down anyone, and she'd seen Grale wince getting out of the car after long drives they'd made during the grid attacks.

She stopped in Barstow for gas then got back on I-15 to Vegas. When she'd left the Bay Area it was windy and cold, but now the truck's air conditioner couldn't keep up. Last time she talked with Grale he'd casually said it was 112 degrees as if that was normal. Or maybe the people in Las Vegas are like dogs that get beaten every day and only understand crazy.

She could deal with the heat, but a wave of sorrow caught her. It came up through her chest and over her heart as she pictured taking down Grale. Supervisor Mara must think it's real and serious. Why else would he call? She drove the last miles to Vegas picturing busting Grale. It was a lousy feeling on the way to her clean start.

5

Midafternoon, Ralin called me and sounded hopeful. "Indie found something you may want to take a look at. Base regulations prevent me from sending it to you, but you can come see for yourself. It's an image taken by a freeway onramp traffic camera last night. Indie identified the driver's face as Eric's."

"Eric Indonal?"

"Yes, and he's driving a pickup pulling a camping or fishing trailer. If he owns a pickup or a trailer I've never seen either, though I do remember something about a trailer. Indie is very good at facial ID, and if it knows any face better than Eric's, I'd be surprised."

"Yours included?"

"Yes."

"What does Indonal usually drive?"

"An old Toyota four-door he got from his aunt. He doesn't care much about cars."

"Have you ever seen him driving a pickup?"

"No."

"How good of an image is it?"

"It's poor. It's something only an AI at this level could use to come up with an ID. If you want a look at it, I'll call the guard gate and tell them you're coming. They'll wave you through. I'll be here. Just ask for me."

Forty minutes later, I passed through the Independence Base gate and drove the straight road across the desert plain to the building housing the AI. A DoD security officer walked me to Ralin's office.

Ralin's face was hidden behind a computer when I came in. A half-eaten chicken breast and fried potatoes sat in an oily cardboard container on his desk. The room smelled of it. We looked at frames of photos taken from the video cam at the freeway onramp, and in particular one image of a pickup towing a small recreational trailer last night. Only part of the upper half of the face of a man driving the pickup was visible. It was disappointing, but I didn't say so.

"Indie is tapped into various local networks, including traffic cams, and AI is far better than humans at facial recognition," Ralin said. "Indie looked at all of the Las Vegas traffic cam videos and puts a high probability on this partial face being Eric."

Ralin glanced over, possibly looking for a reaction before continuing. "You may have read about Chinese police using AI some years ago to pick a man out of 60,000 faces at a concert and arrest him? Since then, AI has only gotten better. Indie pulled this image from an onramp feeding I-15 east. It knows every pore and hair of Eric's, Alan's, and my faces, so I have to take this seriously."

"Do you recognize him?"

"From this? No, I really don't, and I understand your skepticism. One thing, though. After we talked, I remembered Eric once saying—and this was years ago—that an uncle died and left him a fishing trailer."

I stared at the image trying to imagine the AI recognizing Indonal from the little the camera had caught but couldn't see convincing anyone it was a lead we should follow.

"Do you have any other contact numbers of friends or family of Indonal?" I asked. "What about Eckstrom's girlfriend, Laura Trent? Would she know about a trailer?"

"I really don't know. You'd have to ask her. Here at the base they'll have next of kin for all of us, so that might be the way to find out about the trailer. You don't believe Indie identified him, do you?"

"I'm not disbelieving," I said. "I'm just trying to figure out what I can do with this information. This isn't going to convince my supervisor. Or anyone else."

"What about you?"

"Make me believe, convince me."

Ralin looked down at his desk for several seconds and may have muttered something about bureaucracies, then looked up with a fatigued, defeated face. He was thirty-eight, with turned-in shoulders, probably a result of sitting long hours at a keyboard.

"Do you use Google Translate?" Ralin asked.

"When I need it, I use it. Sure. Look, I'm not challenging your AI's capabilities and we do want to locate them, but as far as we know they haven't committed any crimes and did leave on their own. And to be blunt, as near as we can tell, they were unhappy and quit."

"Did you use Google Translate before the fall of 2016?" Ralin asked.

"I did and I have a reason to remember. I was in Croatia looking for a bomb maker named Frederic Dalz. I didn't know the language. On and off I'd used Google Translate, but it didn't work particularly well, and then all of a sudden it did. The difference was like night and day. I couldn't understand what had happened, but I still remember the *New York Times* wrote that the 'AI system had demonstrated overnight improvements roughly equal to the total gains the old one had accrued over its entire lifetime.'"

"Exactly," Ralin said. "Picture even more rapid changes, most of them small, but many of them significant."

I couldn't picture it, didn't know how to. I looked at him then back at the trailer and the pickup and partial of a man's face. Ralin was correct in guessing that I was disbelieving. AI as I understood it needed more than what this photo showed.

"Let's do an experiment," he said. "Send me two photos from your phone. They can be any photos however obscure as long as you remember where they were taken. Let's see what Indie comes up with."

"I pick any two I want?"

"Any two."

"Okay, you're on, I'll pick two."

What followed changed my opinion of AI. It both disturbed and awed me.

6

I have an FBI phone and a personal phone. Many agents do. From my personal phone, I sent Ralin an obscure landscape photo I took on a vacation. From the FBI phone, I sent a second photo, that of fourteen-year-old Ellen Kinas.

The disappearance of Ellen Kinas dated to my third year as an FBI agent. We'd trailed a serial killer suspect named Warren Schilling and were ready to arrest him when I talked the team into waiting longer. We knew he was ramping up, and I wanted to catch him in his car with his rape and kill gear.

Maybe he spotted us trailing him. I don't really know, but I was the one driving the morning we lost him. I missed a turn he made onto a dirt road. I've lived with that mistake a long time and have never stopped thinking about Ellen Kinas.

Many investigators and detectives have a similar story. I try to use mine as a touchstone to remind me to do better, but at heart it was a failure and the case has haunted me.

Ellen Kinas disappeared walking home after the school bus dropped her less than a third of a mile from her house. The bus stop was thirty-seven miles away from where we'd last seen Schilling, a significant distance, and yet the whole thing fit his MO.

I sent Ralin both photos then watched him communicate with Indie. Sure, I knew Indie would get the landscape shot. The world was mapped, almost every square mile known, but where would it go for Ellen Kinas? Probably back to childhood school photos. I expected nothing and yet my heart beat harder.

"Won't be long," Ralin said.

It was and it wasn't. I heard a soft beep, and Ralin moved to a desktop. He was on it ten minutes before turning to me with a slight smile and saying, "Your photo was taken in the Atacama Desert on the side of a volcano cone at 18,052 feet. You were near the border of Chile and Bolivia."

"Congratulate Indie for me," I answered, but wasn't at all surprised.

"I need a little more time with the other photo. Give me ten to fifteen minutes." He looked over. "What you gave me was a very old photo of a child. Is she a relative? Did something happen?"

"She wasn't a relative. She was a young girl abducted early in my career."

"I'm sorry."

I sat and answered text messages, but I could hear him murmuring, talking, and I wondered if it was just possible.

"Okay, we've got something," Ralin said. "I'm sorry for the delay. I had to read so I understood. Quite a story. Ellen Goodwin. When she was a child, her father gave her to a church sect that believes girls entering puberty should live as if they were in convents until age twenty-one and then be married to a man the church chooses. The sect took her to Australia and into the outback where they own land. She escaped five years later, made it to Sydney and stayed. She's married with two children now. Her story is online and she self-published a book three years ago under her married name, Ellen Carter."

Ever skeptical, but with a flood of emotions moving in me, I studied the face. I found the scar on her left cheek, faint but still there, and another on her neck, both from a fall off an ATV that happened when she was five.

"What's wrong?" Ralin asked.

"It is her and it matters," I said, and for a moment my voice may have faltered.

I sat still, unaware of time, as I tried to accept the idea that Ellen Kinas hadn't been another of Schilling's victims. I studied the woman in the photo and finally said, "I'll call her, or we'll call her."

I thanked him as a rush of emotion flowed through me. Then we talked some more about Indonal and Eckstrom before I left.

"If the AI is accurate, then Indonal is fine," I said. "He looks like he's headed out on a vacation, but by now or very soon, he'll know there's an APB out for both him and Eckstrom. What will he do when he learns about it? Will he contact us or other law enforcement?"

"I don't know."

"When was your last contact with him?"

"Yesterday, early evening."

When he said that there was a slight hesitation that might or might not mean something. Hard to say, but I noted it.

"If they've quit, where will they go next?" I asked.

"There's a demand bubble in AI," Ralin answered. "Worldwide there aren't enough people with the right mix of math, intuition, coding, and computer science. They'll be offered salaries of over a million a year. Eric is very gifted. He'll get offers right away. He could get a high-salary offer that's made by a foundation but funded by an enemy government. We've worked in such an isolated way, they'll have to reach back to earlier connections and they'll be vulnerable to new ones."

"Vulnerable?"

"Both are naïve, Eric less so."

"Will they pick the project or go with the highest bidder?"

"The project, and it won't be for a totalitarian government."

Ralin had dark thoughts he expressed about totalitarian governments wanting AI to monitor and control the lives of their citizens, and about others in freer societies who were eager to dominate a business and drive rivals out.

I called Mara at dusk as I left the Indie building. In my rearview the building looked small and lorded over by a spine of dry mountains.

"Ralin asked for two random photos from me to prove Indie's image-recognition capabilities. I gave him a vacation pic and the photo of a girl who disappeared early in my career. A girl I've assumed all these years was murdered by a serial killer after I missed a turn on a road. She's alive in Australia."

"How do we verify?"

"He showed me photos and I recognized her. I think we accept it."

"That's not good enough."

"I think it is. The DoD has invested billions in Indie and I recognized Ellen Kinas. I'll find a way for us to contact her."

"Do that, and where are you headed next? Are you on your way back to the office?"

"Yes, but before you hang up—"

"Come find me when you get in."

7

JACE

Jace wanted to check in with Grale after getting her new apartment key from the building manager in the late afternoon. She was hungry but upbeat, and happy to be in Las Vegas. She called Grale.

"I'm here," she said, "and I've got the key to my new apartment. Can you recommend somewhere for dinner? Someplace uncomplicated, but anywhere you think is good."

"Where's the new apartment?"

"Less than a mile from the FBI office, so somewhere around here."

He gave her a couple of places to eat and said, "I just met with Dr. Ralin, who heads the artificial intelligence project at Independence Base. Two coders disappeared last night after drinking in a lounge bar. Indie, the AI, ID'ed one of them from a traffic cam photo taken late in the night. The guys are critical to the project and a security worry. We need to find them. We know they haven't used their passports and they staged a disappearance at night after leaving the bar."

"Staged a disappearance, so definitely weren't abducted?"

"It's looking like they left on their own. If Indie, as they call it, the AI, is correct about the traffic cam photo, then they've staged a disappearance."

"Why would they?"

"That's the big question. They know a lot, they could sell computer code or other information, or meet up with a foreign spy, whatever. That one of them, Eric Indonal, is driving a pickup dragging an old trailer in the traffic cam photo fits with video I saw from a department store security camera that was taken last night. A woman met them with a van and hugged Eckstrom."

"What do you think, Grale?"

"They went out of their way to disappear, and we need to find them to determine why. I'm gathering they were critical to the project and will be difficult to replace. So, there's the two coder computer scientists missing and there's a bomb maker I've hunted for two decades who crossed the Washington border three days ago. Why the bomb maker matters is that there's a heightened threat level surrounding the new AI, Indie. That includes phone chatter about attacking Independence Base, Indie Base. The AI is in a building on the base. It's all Indie and AI right now, Jace."

"I don't know anything about AI."

"No one here does either, but we've got a consultant we're leaning on. Hey, I've got a call coming in I've been waiting on. I'll call you back later."

Afternoon heat and the unmistakable smell of urine hit Jace when she opened the apartment door. She wanted a shower and a beer. She jumped as a door opened and all of a sudden there was a guy standing behind her.

"Hey, neighbor," he said. "I'm Darren from next door. You probably want to know about that smell."

"I do. Talk to me."

He started talking about the weird guy who'd just moved out of this apartment, but he danced around any details and Jace excused herself. After he'd gone, she walked the whole apartment, from bedroom to the living area, where she found rodent droppings that didn't look like rat. She knew rat. Could be some desert mouse or whatever they had out here. She called the manager to complain.

***

"The rugs were cleaned," the manager said after he arrived.

"Don't you smell that?"

"I don't. I don't see anything either."

Jace leaned over then straightened and said, "Put out your hand."

"Why?" he asked but put out his hand anyway. She dropped black-brown pellets into his palm. He stared in disgust, then flipped them onto the rug.

"Call your carpet guy," Jace said.

"There's no reason to. That rug has been cleaned. It's standard procedure before a new tenant."

He repeated that as he stood at the kitchen sink and washed and rewashed his hands. He was still muttering to himself as he let himself out, just as Grale called back.

"You in?" he asked.

"Yeah, in my new apartment but looks like the last tenants were rodents, so I'm not sure whether I'm staying."

"You can stay with Jo and me as you get sorted out. We have an empty bedroom. You can be there as long as you want."

"Isn't your niece living with you?"

"Julia moved to Utah a while ago."

"Thanks, but I'll get this sorted out. Talk to me more about what I'm walking into on the DT squad."

"Like I said earlier, the focus is Indie and the threat level. I'll take you out there for a look around. Indie is penetrating defenses faster than anyone thought possible. Or that's what we're hearing from sources that are pretty reliable. The CIA has passed on information that suggests an espionage team is either en route or already here."

"What's the name of the bomb maker you mentioned earlier?"

"Frederic Dalz. I'll tell you what I know about him when I see you, and don't worry about what you don't know about AI. We're looking for two missing guys and trying to stop attacks on the base or base personnel. That's not AI work."

She laughed and Grale said, "It's really great to hear your voice, Jace. Welcome to Vegas. See you tomorrow."

8

My girlfriend, Jo Segovia, is a doctor and answers medical questions nonstop at work, so I try to avoid them at home. We live together and were lucky to find each other. I get asked why we're not married and I don't have an answer that satisfies anyone, but we've both been married before and for now we're happy this way.

I was still at the office when Jo texted; she'd just gotten home. I wanted her advice about my back without waiting until later or tomorrow. I called her, and Jo being Jo, she was ahead of me.

"I've been waiting for you to say something. You haven't wanted to hear this, but it may be more than the flare-up you've been thinking it is. What's it like down your left leg?"

"Sharp pain that makes it hard to walk normally, but the worst is my back near that lump of scar tissue. I thought it would get better by this week. It's usually been that way."

"This feels different?"

"It hurts more than anything in recent years."

"Show me when you get home."

"I may not get home until late."

"Wake me when you do, then show me."

***

But I didn't wake her. I got in late and let the hot shower run a long time on my lower back, then lay down alongside her. Jo slid closer, and I fell into a quasi-sleep, half dream, half memory, where I returned to a bar in Paris and my last meeting with a friend, a French intelligence officer named Pierre Desault who'd worked in the 20th arrondissement in the DGSE, the French external intelligence service.

That night Desault had proposed something so contradictory to his investigative career that I've thought about it ever since.

"Consider how many years Frederic Dalz eluded capture," Desault said. "Who else has remained active this long without arrest or death? He's killed your soldiers. He's killed CIA agents that no one should have known were there. How did he know their whereabouts? Can you answer that?"

The answer was our enemies provided him directions, money, and information, but animated and drinking as we were, Desault couldn't hear that. He was a month from retirement. We wouldn't see each other again for a very long time, if ever.

Tonight, he wanted me to accept something that I couldn't. In French foreign intelligence circles, no one knew more than he did about Frederic Dalz, but I'd been in law enforcement long enough to recognize the frustration investigators can carry out the back door over cases they didn't solve. It was also alcohol talking.

"I accept that it is too late for me to find him," Desault said. "Someone protects him, though we haven't been able to figure out who. That's a danger for you as well. He knows your name by now."

"You can't know that."

"I am sure of it."

There was no way to answer that, so I moved on and said, "Your General Board of External Security came close to catching him in Lebanon. Others have come close."

"No, we did not come close. We said that, but the truth is he ran back into the burning hotel. He could not have escaped death, yet he did. We had no explanation for that, so we made one. Very experienced people reviewed the reports and the film. He went in but did not come out, and yet, he's alive."

Concrete spalled, steel melted, the ashes of the bones of the dead blew away in the wind that followed.

Either Dalz wasn't inside, or the man who went into the hotel was not Frederic Dalz. How could anyone argue otherwise? And of all people, how could Desault, a rationalist and skeptic, believe anything else?

I put that night down to two bottles of wine and Desault's coming retirement. It was an emotional good-bye. We were kindred spirits. In the months I was in France, he'd mentored me and introduced me to officers I would otherwise never have met. I owed him, and more than that, I admired him and should have thanked him more for his gracious generosity. But like only someone young can do, I assumed there would be another time for that.

"You don't believe me," he'd said, and it felt as if I was across the table from him again.

"What I believe is that there has to be a rational answer."

"Not always." When I didn't respond and drank instead, he asked, "Do you believe in God?"

And just like that we arrived where we were always going.

"Have you ever lost someone and asked God to hold very close the soul of the one you loved?" he asked.

"I have," I said.

"Then you've allowed the possibility of God, so you must allow the devil as well."

"Here are my thoughts about where Dalz came from," I'd answered. "An enemy intelligence agency—I hope it's an enemy—was thinking long term. They found a child, erased what little past he had, raised him in seclusion, teaching him the sciences and the bomb making and the other techniques for killing we know he's capable of. They chose him early for his aptitude and personality characteristics. They created a superagent with specific talents. They pay him well and keep him safe, and for that he owes them."

"That's a fantasy," Desault said. "What's true is he escaped us by running back into the hotel and he's still alive. No one inside survived the heat. Even their bones became ash. Yet he is here. If you are honest about the facts, then you must question what you believe."

***

I wondered why that conversation of so long ago had returned to me. I felt Jo stir. As she did, I saw Desault standing near the foot of the bed and for a moment the bedroom looked unfamiliar.

"What were you saying about a fire?" Jo asked. "You've been talking to someone. Were you dreaming?"

"I've been awake. I was remembering a conversation I had with a French agent long ago."

"You must have been dreaming."

"I don't think so, but I'm sorry I woke you. It was a vivid memory."

"I feel something here," she said and slid close. We held each other and talked more, and whatever she'd felt in the room must have gone away.

9

AUGUST 6TH

At nine o'clock the next morning I got an unexpected call from Kathy Tobias, head of DARPA. She caught me in my car on my way to pick up a prescription refill from my pharmacist. I'd never met her but I knew her name. Her voice carried a soft drawl. She said she could call back if this was a bad time.

"Go ahead," I said. "I'm in my car, this is a good time to talk."

"Well, first I have to tell you, you're on speakerphone. I'm in a room in a meeting with DoD brass. We don't mean to put you on the spot, but we're discussing security at Independence Base. We're told you're investigating threats to the base, and I've heard good things about you, so I thought we'd give you a call. If this puts you too much on the spot, we can do it a different way."

"I'm fine, go ahead."

"What are your primary external threat concerns? Talk to us about the ones you're worried about."

"Okay, here's one. This morning the National Security Agency passed phone intercepts of three people talking through the logistics of flying a cargo plane loaded with explosives into the building housing Indie. They talked about the road here as having a length of 1.87 miles of flat, then a gradual rise to the building."

"That's accurate on the road length," a male voice said, "and we're aware of that threat. I'm going to say something else. As far as I know, and I've got twenty-two years in, we have never once asked for help from the FBI to defend a base."

He started to say more, and I was ready to get into it with him, but Tobias interrupted. "I'm taking you off speakerphone, Agent Grale. Keep talking. What other threats have the FBI's focus?"

"A truck bomb at the guard gate followed by an attack with all-terrain vehicles. That comes from Interpol and a conversation intercepted in Belgium. That one could be a suicide mission where they kill everyone inside and destroy Indie before they're killed. We've got as many threats from inside the US as outside. People are afraid of AI. The immediate general worry is an attack initiated outside the base."

We talked through another four or five threats before she asked what may have been the true purpose of the call.

"You've met Dr. Ralin," she said. "What's your sense of him?"

"Are you speaking to loyalty?"

"Some in the room here are concerned."

"I'm hearing that other places too, but I don't really understand that."

"Why not?"

"He's devoted years of his life to AI, as have Indonal and Eckstrom. They left academia and went to work for DARPA, so that says they all knew it could and likely would get militarized. Ralin has testified before congressional committees.

He's on TV regularly arguing for AI, selling the public on why we need it. That the three of them have issues with some of the military application isn't surprising. After all, they initially set out to improve medicine. I'm sure you know that."

"I've heard them say that and I'd like to have a longer conversation with you," she said. "Are you by chance the Agent Paul Grale of the Alagara bombing?"

"I am."

"That makes me feel better."

"It shouldn't."

"But it does, and I'm going to give you my cell number. It will always get you to me."

"Okay, but do something for me before we hang up. Can you put Indie into some sort of context I can grasp? What's so special about this particular machine? How does it differ from other AI?"

"Big picture, it's just another step along the way, but a transformational one. It's part of what's called the third wave of AI. Do you remember when IBM's Deep Blue beat Garry Kasparov, the chess champion, in 1997?"

"Kind of, and Dr. Ralin told me an AI advancement story yesterday where the machine is better than any human. Is that a good thing?"

"Not necessarily, but hear me out," she said. "You remember Kasparov versus Deep Blue? That was a big deal, right?"

"At the time."

"Exactly, at the time, and that's really the point I want to make. Fast forward to 2017 when a machine in Google's AlphaZero program played against the 2016 computer chess champion. That's machine on machine. The machine AlphaZero played against had everything known about chess, all of chess history, everything. For years it had been the world champion."

"Okay, world computer chess champ."

"Of the one hundred games AlphaZero played against it, AlphaZero won twenty-eight and tied seventy-two."

"So a new champion."

"Yes, but here's the takeaway. AlphaZero started from scratch, taught itself chess, and in four hours became the best in the world. Four hours, Agent Grale, zero to best. What's in the basement of the Indie building you're looking at is another level up again from that, and it's out there worming its way into their war machines."

"They can't stop it on their end, so they're coming for it. Is that what you're saying?"

"Yes."

"What happens if they get to it?"

"If they destroy it, we could lose our lead."

"Then what?"

"I don't like to speculate and I'm not big on drama, but if we fall behind and a hostile power confronts us and demands the US surrenders, I don't think we'll have a choice. The days of wars being fought only on a distant battlefront are ending. In future wars our infrastructure in the US may come under attack at the same time our bases are being attacked elsewhere. Water, power, communications, banking, everything could be attacked simultaneously. We do not want to lose the lead. We can't risk it. I'll send you my contacts. Call me anytime, day or night. Do you go by Paul or your last name?"

"My last name."

"I thought so. I look forward to meeting you in person," she said, then was gone.

10

DALZ

That morning at a freeway rest stop outside Las Vegas, Frederic Dalz met with the man running the operation. The rest stop was empty. It was windy, and the man waved him over to get in his car.

"Call me Sean," the man said as Dalz got in. "I'm your point of contact for all things."

"Even assembly questions?"

"Everything, and you need to know I didn't want you here. I was against using you. I don't like mercenaries and freelancers."

"Do we have to like each other?"

Dalz didn't stare at him but took enough of a look and could hear him. Sean spoke English scrubbed of any accent, but he was unmistakably Eastern European, like Dalz. Sean was blue eyed, dark haired, square shouldered, and confident in the way fools are. He was probably the product of a midlevel military unit focused on espionage and intelligence gathering.

"All questions go through me. I want to hear you say that you'll follow that order."

"Everything goes through you," Dalz said.

"That includes telemetry, fuel burn variance and ratios, secondary explosions mechanics, all things, whether I understand the questions or not. Other than the assembly team, I am the only one you talk to. Follow me in your car. I'll take you first to where we'll assemble, then to where you do preassembly and stay."

Dalz followed. In the building where he would run the assembly team, the windows were taped and covered. If anyone asked questions, they were foreign filmmakers making a documentary. Questions were to be referred to the "producer" who, of course, was Sean.

"The rest of your work will be at a leased ranch nine miles from here," Sean said. "We'll go there next, and you'll stay there."

"When does work begin?"

"Tomorrow."

The ranch was well back from a two-lane highway. There was an aged house and four outbuildings on arid land. Sean showed him the building he'd use for preassembly of components and for storage, and then where he would eat and sleep.

"Two of your assembly team in the other building will be Americans," Sean said. "Do you have a problem with that?"

"Not if you've vetted them."

"Do you have a problem with anything I've told you?"

"No."

"Okay, good, but remember I don't like you. I don't want you here. If I have trouble with you, they'll send a replacement, and I'll dispose of your body in the desert. Show me the same dead eyes tomorrow morning, and I'll ask for a replacement. I want obedience and efficiency until the operation is over. That is all I want from you."

"You'll get that from me."

"Good. Now, give me the keys to your car."

"Is there food here?"

"None."

"I need to eat," Dalz said as he handed Sean his keys.

"Tonight, you think about what I said. Tomorrow you eat."

11

My prescriptions refills are delivered by an ex-big-box-pharmacist named Gary Potello, who once worked in a mall a few miles from my house. For years, my prescriptions were refilled there, often by him. That was before the chain he worked for cut back. When they closed the mall store, Potello was laid off, and he came up with the idea of starting a small mobile pharmacy.

He talked me into signing up, and why not? There were larger prescription delivery businesses already. The idea wasn't new, and for me, it was about convenience. It was also more discreet, although "cowardice" and "embarrassment" are better words than "discreet." I didn't want anyone who knew I was an FBI agent to overhear me refilling a painkiller prescription. Probably no one listened or cared, but I was sensitive about it and lived with a worry that my back flare-ups would get me pulled from active duty.

I've grown used to Potello's deliveries. That's not to say I wasn't aware the deliveries could look like a drug buy, but I've been careful with that. More often than not, I'll meet him at his tiny shop or on a street corner. His business is registered with the State of Nevada, and once a year I check to see he's current.

Lately, I've grown warier. Potello has become flighty and diffident and barely apologetic when he screws up.

After the call with Kathy Tobias, I drove to Potello's shop, a tiny storefront with nothing more than a steel door and a bulletproof window and a tray where credit cards and cash go in and prescriptions come out. A Nevada State Board of Pharmacy license taped to one corner of the window. There's a bakery with good coffee down the street. I bought a double espresso, and Potello looked like he'd just gotten back from there. He was eating from a box of cookies and drinking sugared coffee out on the sidewalk when I walked up. He'd put his box of cookies down on somebody's car.

"You're hurting," he said. "I watched you limp down the sidewalk."

"Same old thing."

"Looks worse and you're pale. You okay, man?"

"I'm hurting and I'm running late. I've got to get going."

"There's a problem with your prescription."

"What kind of problem?"

"I'm not sure yet, but I'm trying to get it refilled."

Potello was midforties, with a paunch. He favored golfer dress, slacks and a lightweight short-sleeved shirt. At times he was friendly, but there was often a distance between us, some disconnect. I got the feeling sometimes he finds something comic in a limping FBI agent. That's fair, I suppose, but he was also one of those guys who out of habit look first for what's wrong with you.

"Your NORCO 5 order isn't happening. I didn't get a delivery," Potello said. "The good news is I've got something else you should try. It'll work a lot better. It's stronger."

"No thanks. Call me when the NORCOs come in."

"What about Percocet? I know you use that. I've got it right here, and you haven't reordered OxyContin in a while. I can give you a few right now that you can swallow before you get back in your car. They're on me for not having the NORCOs ready for you."

"I've got a nearly full Percocet bottle at home, and I hardly use the OxyContin."

"Well, use it now. Here. It'll get it for. It'll get you through the day."

He went through the door into his tiny pharmacy space and rooted around for some pills. I wasn't going to take them but I sure hurt. I needed something. The pain was very sharp when I turned to my left.

He came out and offered two pills on his open palm. That was unusual and a little strange.

"Come on," Potello said. "You're being too hard on yourself. OxyContin lasts a lot longer than the Percocet. Take these two. Like I said, it'll get you through the day, and I'm expecting a delivery later this afternoon of everything else. I'll bring what I owe you tomorrow. But come on, take these. There's no reason to go through the day in agony."

Potello's attitude was new, half chiding, half pushing, and it bothered me. I could have taken those pills on his palm, but I didn't. Instead, I left and drove to the office with my back hurting so much that tiny beads of sweat covered my forehead. After parking I sat for ten minutes with the car door open before lifting my left leg out.

Two agents on the DT squad, Murray and Edelstein, must have spotted me having trouble and came over. They helped me out of my car. It was that bad.

"It's temporary," I said. "A flare-up."

Neither said anything to that, and we walked in together. When I stopped, they continued on as I wiped my forehead in the cooler air and straightened. I got something like a normal walk going before reaching my desk. My back problems were worsening. I just didn't know what to do about it yet. I kept thinking, *Give it more time. You've had flare-ups before,* I reasoned. They come and go. This was just a particularly bad one.

I stopped in the DT bullpen and sent the photos of Ellen Kinas off to Karen Chine at headquarters. If you were an agent in the field and knew Karen, it was very likely you were indebted to her. She was always somewhere out in front of the main cogwheels of the Bureau. She worked in the same system as everyone but had figured out ways to up the quality and speed of results.

Chine was a connector and aggregator and very good on the phone. She was piped into the FBI's exploratory programs. Street agents, investigators, they all knew Karen. I loved working with her. She was very into results and got as excited as an investigator type when we scored a hit. Karen was one of us.

When she got the photos with my explanation, she wrote back, Really?

You tell me, **I typed.**

Have you tried calling?

I've been out in the field but will today.

We're back and forth with Aussies all the time, **she texted.** Want me to?

You have a connection?

A good one.

Go for it and I'm buying you lunch next time I'm in DC.

Nah, I'm as curious as you.

I hadn't expected anything for a couple of days, but while I met with Mara, another text came back from Chine: Australian Federal Police know her and have interviewed her. They confirmed dates match and her escape from a fringe religious group in the outback years ago. She has a family and three kids in Sydney. She changed her name to Ellen Goodwin after escaping.

I read that then continued talking with Mara, who pushed an old Dalz file across the table toward me. I recognized everything about the file right down to the coffee stains on it. I'd spent many nights with it, and it didn't get me anywhere. Mara's theatrics, sliding it across as if the file held case-breaking information, put me on edge.

"Agent Blujace learns Dalz from you. Take her through that file. Your focus is Dalz, and she's going to work with you. I may pull her off as needed, but she needs to learn everything you know about Dalz. Should we go out to the public with Dalz's face?"

"I don't think we do that yet, but let's reach out to Las Vegas police."

"All right, we start there. Aren't you going to open the file?"

"I know everything in it."

"I want Agent Blujace brought up to speed on Dalz. She'll need the file."

"I'll give it to her."

"I want you to take her carefully through it."

I nodded and we stared at each other, then Mara jumped to Indonal and Eckstrom and said, "We're assigning more agents to look for them, and that's coming from headquarters. I'm sure you've seen the news coverage and the traitor speculation that they've sold out and are working with our enemies."

"I've seen some of what's on Twitter and the cable TV talk."

"It's gotten a lot worse in the past twenty-four hours, and Washington wants more agents on it. The search will broaden. If they try to board a flight to wherever, they'll be detained. What they know is crucial to national security."

"They're computer scientists who quit," I said. "They're not criminals and we shouldn't be talking as if they are."

"They didn't just quit. They disappeared and with extremely valuable information that could be shared. They created Indie with Ralin, but it's not theirs. That's where we're at," Mara said.

"Whatever happens they've brought on themselves. The statement we're going out to the public with is an appeal to help find them to keep them safe. They won't be labeled as possible traitors."

"That's already happened."

Mara didn't answer, so I opened the Dalz file after all and flipped through photos, including one of a school bus carrying the kids of diplomats, twenty-four of them, where an incendiary bomb was used. Half the children burned alive. That's when I'd started to learn about Dalz.

I closed the file as Mara said, "Let's get back to you. Did you make an appointment with your doctor to get your back evaluated?" When I didn't answer he continued, "I'll keep you in the mix, starting with locating Bismarck. You're the right agent for that. But let's talk more on a day-to-day basis about your investigative goals."

"You're going to direct my days?"

"I want to talk more often and plan more together."

"We can do that, but why now?"

He didn't answer and I didn't ask again. Something was changing between us. Maybe it already had.

12

JACE

"Where were you living before you moved here?" the building manager asked Jace.

She took him in: blue jeans, boots, a big belt buckle that cost some money, a tucked-in shirt loosened a little to hide his gut, and a name tag on the shirt pocket. Maynard Wright.

"I lived in Oakland near Lake Merritt."

"Oakland?"

"Do you know Oakland?"

"I know enough to say a rat may have traveled with you. I have a friend who manages apartments in Oakland. He says there are major pest problems in the city."

"The boxes in the kitchen and the bedding are all I brought in yesterday. It's *not* a rat."

"If you want me to bring the cleaners back, you'll have to pay. Or you find another place."

Before Jace could answer that, Darren the next-door neighbor walked in. He must have been in the hallway and overheard. He pointed a finger at the manager.

"The guy who lived here had hamsters, like five or six of them, and he let them live in the bedroom. They ran around in here."

The manager stared at him, then said, "I didn't know that."

"There's a lot going on around here you don't know," Darren said, and added as an aside to her, "I've been here nine years, ever since I got *divorced*." He put a particular emphasis on the word and gave Jace a smile. "He had a pet snake that once a month he let hunt in here. If you want to smell something *really* friggin' nasty, try snake shit."

Jace looked at the manager and said, "Different apartment."

"They're more expensive."

"Then it better be bigger." Her phone rang and before answering she said, "This has to happen today." She handed him her FBI card. "Call my cell in the next half hour. I've got a moving van that has to be returned tomorrow and movers coming today."

"You're an FBI agent?" He sounded disbelieving.

"You push the line with me, dude? Watch it."

"I didn't mean it that way."

"So what did you mean?"

While he figured that out, she walked out into the hallway feeling angry. She called Grale back, but he didn't pick up. She tried him again. Still no answer, but the apartment manager had just discovered another unit he could show her.

"Let's go take a look," she said and returned a call from Mara as she trailed behind him.

"Grale was videoed buying from or meeting with Potello again today," Mara said.

"Who is Potello?"

"A pharmacist suspected of illegal sales. There's more I've got to brief you on when I see you next."

"Who told us today about this meeting with Grale?"

"It's coming from a Metro police undercover agent who has caught Grale and Potello on video once before. Metro just called me and said Grale went by Potello's drug booth downtown this morning and met him again maybe an hour ago. I'm texting you the undercover officer's phone number and where he saw Grale make a buy."

"Or Grale picked up his prescription."

"Sure, it could be. This Gary Potello is a licensed pharmacist, so I'm hoping that too."

"Okay, well, I'll give the undercover a call and go meet him. It's time to see this guy and hear why he's so sure."

"Call me after."

"I'll do that. Talk to you then."

13

I checked out Bismarck's dark web site before I went looking for him. There's the site and then separate chatrooms. The chatrooms we had trouble getting into, but Bismarck used a public bulletin board as well. I read a new posting about the imminent coming of the new order where some would die in sacrificial honor at the first mind-melding. It was the kind of thing you have to read twice.

It could mean Bismarck intended to ask his followers to trespass onto the base sometime very soon and make their way toward the building housing Indie. If so, that would lead to arrests. After rereading it yet again, I decided the best thing was to head it off, so I called the highway patrol. I talked to a captain who gave me directions to where vehicles in Bismarck's caravan had left the highway.

"It's a sandy desert road that runs toward some hills. Bring your own water, there's nothing out there."

When that call ended, I let Mara know my plan was to try to locate them and asked that we get a plane or helicopter up for a look as well.

"Be careful, Grale. Keep it to a scouting run."

I didn't say anything to that. Jace arrived and Mara took her in tow. She'd need an hour and a half, maybe two, for the tour of the office and some introductions. I left soon after.

In recent months Bismarck has called on his dark web followers to come to Vegas but couldn't have known that a flood of bots originating outside the US would help spread his message. The bots drew our attention, as well as that of other US intelligence agencies. The bots may lead us to their source, although I'm told we'd probably never hear the details. There's a quiet war underway in cyberspace.

Forty minutes later, I found the cutoff then drove across a plain and up into heat-soaked hills with mesquite, cactus, and, higher up, small stands of stunted pines. In a sunburned clearing, a collage of vehicles and people were camped. I drove past and a half mile farther on, parked and called in my position. Just ahead was a rusted RV that was likely Bismarck's.

Nearby was a modified jeep with enormous tires and painted in desert-camouflage colors. A picnic table, possibly stolen from a state park or rest stop, sat with a faded parachute propped over it for shade. I locked my car and walked up slowly, watching as a low shadow appeared near the side of the trailer, then disappeared. A quiet tinkling of link chain and a low growl led me to spot a yellow-eyed dog crouched belly to desert sand near the left rear tire beneath the trailer. According to Bismarck's statements in a 2017 FBI interview in New Orleans, the dog was a pup feeding on a child's carcass when he found him. I doubt it's true. His discordant mind generates a steady flow of dark imaginings.

Bismarck's boot heels clanged down the metal stairs. He stood in frozen silence for long seconds as he came off the last tread before calling the dog. He unhooked the long chain, and the dog lunged, but at Bismarck's hard commands he backed away and slinked up the stairs.

Bismarck followed the dog up, pushed him inside, shut the door, then tramped back down. He faced me silently for a moment, then launched into how he'd staked six claims for mineral rights in Nevada, and others in Utah where the government had opened large tracts of public lands for exploration. He'd marked the corners with rocks and paid the nominal fee.

"I've got as much right to be in Nevada as you," Bismarck said.

"But not on Independence Base. Trespass, or encourage your followers to do so, and you'll see charges."

"The AI was built for me."

"Good to know, I'll pass that on to the Department of Defense in case they haven't heard. What you need to know is that if you incite your followers to trespass, we'll arrest you. You could face terrorism charges."

Bismarck turned, stared, and smiled. Like me, he knew it wouldn't be hard to walk onto a large tract of land in the desert. Even patrolled, there's always a way, and no way to fence it all. I stared back at him, committing his face to memory once more. He was older. His cheekbones were more prominent. Thin skin stretched over them barely hiding the bones, as if mocking mortality. His eye sockets were so deep, I felt like I was talking to a skull. He was wiry, strong, and unwashed. His breath was awful. No, it was worse than awful. It stank more than any I can remember, and I've sat in interview rooms for long hours with some rough smells.

"Your world is ending," he said. "Your badge will get used as an ashtray, and the government that made you possible will be stories of failure for children."

"That's for later," I said. "The warning I'm giving you is now."

"You're injured, and resting your weight on your right leg," Bismarck answered. "You stumbled walking toward me. I know a man who has to drag himself across the floor. He can't get into his wheelchair without help. He talked poorly to his daughter, and she left him on the floor for a week. If he hadn't been able to get water from a toilet, he would have died. His daughter was traveling with me. There's something like that in your future."

"You need to know that terrorism investigations operate under a different set of rules. You could find yourself behind bars for a long time."

"You'll die young," he said. "I can see it in your eyes."

"Don't forget what I said. The Bill of Rights, constitutional law, it's all out the window when you get charged with terrorism."

"Someday, after you retire, we'll have a much more intimate talk. I look forward to it."

"Let's stick with today for now, and I'm going to repeat myself: if your followers trespass at your urging, we'll come looking for you. Think about what that could mean, Bismarck."

I didn't wait for an answer and walked away.

14

JACE

Jace's orientation was interrupted when ASAC Esposito texted Supervisor Mara he was needed in a meeting. Mara apologized, saying they'd finish her orientation later that afternoon, or to be safe, they could reschedule for tomorrow. That seemed to be what he wanted to do. The meeting he was going into was unexpected and might last for hours.

"Why don't you finish your move," he said. "If you'd rather stay here, there's a file on a bomb maker named Dalz that Grale will take you through, but you may want to read it first. Dalz may be here."

"Grale talked to me about Dalz."

"Briefed you?"

"No, but he said with all the threats against Indie, Dalz could be headed here. He said Dalz is a kind of freelancer."

"That's right, and there's a theory a group of freelancers might be used by an adversary or enemy as a way of disguising their involvement. There are always theories, so take that with a grain of salt. But listen to Grale about Dalz. He knows more about Dalz and his patterns than anyone in the FBI, so in this office you and Grale are on Dalz. That said, we have no idea if he's headed here, so let's not go down that rabbit hole right now. But take a look at the file and ask Grale to take you through it carefully very soon."

Mara started to walk away, then turned and said, "Or, if you want to wait on Grale to go through the Dalz file, call that number I gave you for the Metro undercover officer. Just don't make that call from the office."

Jace took the empty desk she'd share with at least one other domestic terrorism squad agent and flipped through the Dalz file, then decided to wait for Grale and go through it with him. She tried texting him since he hadn't responded to her calls.

When he didn't answer her text messages, she checked with the front desk and was told he was out looking for a fringe group led by somebody who called himself Bismarck. She decided to join and called the Nevada State Highway Patrol as she headed out.

Their directions were straightforward. As she got closer to where they said to watch for an unpaved road, she passed a jacked-up Chevy Malibu with outsize tires. It looked like a pregnant insect. In it were four passengers, three fortysomething males and a young woman who could be as old as sixteen but looked younger. The driver glanced over, made her as law enforcement, then looked away.

She passed another Mad Max car and three worn campers a quarter mile or so on. Three miles later she found the unpaved road and turned onto it with a rising anger she couldn't quite identify. Some of it was fear. Some of it was that Grale hadn't called her back. She didn't like being out here alone. A mile farther in, she approached some sort of bizarre refugee encampment in a fold between two sunbaked hills and called Grale again. This time he answered.

"I'm on my way out," he said. "Turn around and I'll meet you at the highway."

"How about you show me what's going on with this group first? Introduce me to this Bismarck."

"Where are you?"

"I just came around a corner and am looking at a weird scene. Torn tents, rusting campers, pickup beds turned into homes, smoky mesquite fires—what is this?"

"Bismarck's followers."

"Who are they? Where are they from?"

"From all over."

"This is big-time weird. Why do they follow him?"

"Bismarck claims to see the future and has a following of end-timers who are counting on everything falling apart. They've got their hearts set on it."

"Say what?"

"Hey, Jace, turn around where you are. That group of guys standing there is focused on me. I'm calling Mara for immediate backup. Better that you stay on the other side of them."

"And leave you there alone? No way."

She broke the connection and drove down the dip then up to him. Behind her, a pickup pulled in alongside a jeep and a rebuilt Army half-track to block the road out. They were out of their vehicles by the time she reached Grale. She saw guns come out and what looked like a grenade launcher.

"This is insane," Jace said. "Why were you out here alone, and what are they thinking? I don't want to die in some freak show."

"We won't."

Grale retrieved a flare gun from his trunk. He laid that on his car roof as he talked with Mara. She checked and rechecked the clip in her gun, then returned to her trunk for a shotgun. Her hands were shaking as she made certain the shotgun was loaded.

"Mara has a helicopter on the way," Grale said. "I didn't know the crew down below us would pull weapons. I'm sorry, Jace. I'm walking down there as soon as Mara texts me."

"No, you're not."

"Mara has a close friend over at Nellis Air Force Base, a jet-pilot trainer. Two pilots are on their way back from a training mission and will do a flyby here."

"Who cares? What does that have to do with anything?"

"They're working out an idea that may help."

"Help get us out of here?"

"Yes, but we'll get out either way. I drove out to let Bismarck know he could face terror charges for inciting his followers to trespass onto Indie Base."

"You drove out here alone to tell him?"

"I know him."

"You know him? What does that mean in this situation?"

"There's a tie to protecting Indie and everyone working on the project. Bismarck believes or is telling his followers a new millennium will begin, the great change he's predicted, after he mind-melds with Indie. Bot clusters originating in Eastern Europe are helping drive his followers here. I doubt he knows it. The disruption and distraction could help someone planning an attack. That's why I'm out here. That's the real reason."

Mara texted Grale and he turned his phone so she could read the text. It read, They'll pass over low.

"Who will?" Jace asked. "Jets or an FBI helicopter? How far out is our helicopter?"

"Both are on their way, and I'm going to walk down to talk to the guys right there."

"Don't."

Grale moved the flare gun to the hood where she could reach it more easily and said, "Watch the sky to your left. If you see fighter jets, launch the flare straight up. They're not sticking around, but it'll help our friends down there grasp we're not alone."

"This is macho bullshit, Grale."

"Nah. I'm just going to talk to them."

He started down slowly and just before he reached them, Jace heard the jets and turned toward two black dots coming low and fast. She fired the flare gun. The flare burst in a bright plume that the jets veered toward. They streaked straight over, low with a deafening roar. She saw the pilot in the first jet and then saw Bismarck's followers down in the camp running for cover where there was none. What did they imagine would happen? Did they think American military jets would fire at them? Apparently so.

The jets were gone just like that, and Grale was down there talking. He pointed up at the sky, then shook hands with two of them as the FBI helicopter closed in. A guy in camo pants, a filthy T-shirt, and a ragged Army surplus coat walked halfway back up with Grale, who shook the guy's hand again.

Soon after, they moved their vehicles, and she and Grale drove out. No one was arrested, no one apprehended. It made little sense to her. She felt relieved but still angry when she and Grale reached the paved road. It was a crazy first day of working with him and made her wonder about Grale in a way she never had.

The FBI helicopter circled several times then flew away as Grale got out of his car and walked back to her.

"Let's go get something cold to drink," he said, and Jace laughed at the casual attitude after the flyby and grenade launcher. She laughed but didn't feel it inside. She'd just witnessed serious bad judgment on Grale's part that could have gotten them killed.

"We couldn't have shot our way out," Grale said. "These are people who think the FBI exists only to keep the corrupt in power."

"I don't know about all that, but I know we shouldn't have been out here without more agents. That was crazy, totally whacked out, and I don't get it."

"I came out alone, Jace, to deliver a message to Bismarck. I checked in with our office when I found his trailer. Bismarck and I know each other. I knew he'd recognize me and would want to talk, but I didn't anticipate the group blocking the road."

"Right, you didn't anticipate. You screwed up. You could have gotten us killed."

Grale nodded, but said, "The guy who walked halfway back up the hill with me served in Afghanistan right after 9/11. War messed with his head. His reality is different than yours and mine. He's living Bismarck's illusion, but he's not a bad guy."

"Right, he's just crazy."

"He's damaged but he's correct in this sense: the land they're planning to trespass on is the property of the people of the United States. To him it's like walking on his front lawn. He went to Afghanistan to protect it. He doesn't see it the same as the Department of Defense does. If Bismarck says go, the guy you're talking about will go. Bismarck will hang back and watch. It's his followers I worry about, so if we can talk them out of it, that's better than arresting them."

"How is it you know how they think?"

"I don't, but I know enough about Bismarck. I've tracked him a long time, and you're better off not knowing him."

"So, you're protecting me, right? You said you were afraid or whatever that he would lock in on me. That's what you said."

"I am trying to keep him out of your life. It doesn't take two of us, and you don't need to know this guy. He's bad news."

"That's crap, Grale."

"It's not."

Grale was tense and watching her. It was a long way from what she'd pictured as their first day working together. They did stop for a couple of cold sodas, but it didn't change much. She felt distant from Grale. That could be the drug investigation or just the newness of being here. Either way, it wasn't a feeling she'd expected. She almost laughed aloud at what he said next.

"I've got a prescription refill I need to get and then a very short meeting with two DoD agents," Grale said.

He started to say something more but must have changed his mind. He limped to his car, and watching him get in she knew the day could come when they didn't see eye to eye enough to work together. That feeling surprised her, and she was unsure how to deal with it. Some of it was wrapped up in how uncomfortable she'd been out on the desert road, but Grale getting a prescription refilled was exactly what Mara would want to know about.

Jace picked up her phone and brought up Supervisor Mara's number. She was about to call him when something inside said wait. For long seconds after Grale drove away Jace sat holding her phone for several minutes then laid it down without calling Mara. She started her car and drove away.

15

Ralin called me after I left Jace and had what might be a lead on Indonal. He'd reached out to Indonal's family. A cousin looked at the trailer in the traffic cam photo and recognized it as a fishing trailer Indonal had inherited from an uncle who'd died.

"I'll text you contact info on that cousin," Ralin said, "and send you the photo of the fishing trailer he sent me."

He did that, and I called Indonal's cousin from my car and asked, "What makes you certain it's the same trailer?"

He laughed and said, "Because I got my feelings hurt. Eric doesn't fish, or hardly ever, and I'm a big fisherman. I fished a lot with Uncle Mac. I thought he'd leave the trailer to me. But it's not like Eric didn't know about the trailer. The whole family met every year at Panguitch Lake in Utah. That's the lake in the photo."

I looked at a map of Panguitch Lake and searched for camping areas with trailer hookups. I remembered the lake but hadn't been there in years. Google had it as a three-and-a-half-hour drive, so seven hours round trip on a chance guess that Indonal would head there. Like Jace said, that's a lot of ifs to assume he's gone there, but in another way it's human nature to go where we remember as safe and familiar. The cousin wanted to know Indonal wasn't wanted for a crime before acknowledging, "Yeah, that's a place Eric might go."

"Have you talked to him?"

"Not in a couple of years."

I thanked him for his help, then left Jace a message.

She texted back, Why aren't we going out to local law enforcement first?

I texted, Talked to Indonal's cousin and this looks like a viable lead. I'd like to check it out.

We wouldn't get back until late tonight.

Jace's approach was more efficient, but I needed to see things firsthand. It's how I'm wired. I was fine with making the drive alone, rather than arguing over getting the county sheriff out to the lake and then waiting to hear back. I didn't expect Jace to come with me and let Mara know that. No sooner than I did, Jace called and we did almost the same back and forth.

"Why not call and talk with the Garfield County Sheriff's Office?" she asked.

"How about you finish your move-in, and I'll check out the lake? It doesn't take two of us."

"Out and back, seven hours in the car, isn't going to make your back better. What do you do about back pain on a drive that long? NORCOs?"

"They don't work well with driving. If you want to come with me, call me within half an hour."

"You're the original 'stop, think, there must be a harder way' guy."

"Enough fits that I want to check it out. If you talk with Ralin, he'll tell you the three of them have worked day and night for seven years. Indonal hasn't been out fishing, hiking, and checking out lakes. He was towing a trailer at night when the traffic cam caught him and was on his way somewhere. That onramp headed him in the right direction on the right road. I doubt he's got a long list of places he might go. I'd go someplace I know."

"Don't leave until we've talked."

"Half an hour."

I called Eckstrom's girlfriend, Trent, on the chance she might know something about Indonal and a twelve-foot trailer.

"Nope. Can't help you. Sorry," she said. "And my boyfriend was *Alan*, not Eric. I don't exactly keep track of what Eric does. What's the big deal about some crappy old trailer anyway?"

Jace texted that her movers were there and to go without her, but by then I was already seventy miles down the interstate on my way to Utah.

16

JACE

Jace agreed to the apartment switch then called the movers and met them in the lot near the U-Haul with her stuff. She unlocked the U-Haul and one of the two reached in, put one hand under the couch she'd almost left behind, and pulled it out of the van as if he were picking up his coat.

Both guys laughed as she told them the hamster and snake story. They were cool with moving the bed from last night's apartment to the new one. They were also fast and into getting done, paid, and gone. Inside of an hour the move was down to the last cardboard boxes. She'd drop the rental van tomorrow.

She checked her phone as they left. When she didn't see any messages from Grale, she called the Metro police undercover officer, Wycher, and asked if they could meet. He was okay with it but short with her, as if he didn't have time to talk even though he was sitting in a car watching a house.

That changed after she got there. In person he was a talker.

"Not that many years ago, this area was foreclosures right and left. Houses were super cheap and squatters would move into the empties. Neighbors would figure it out, call us, and we'd go knock on the door. But the squatters weren't stupid. They'd send a kid to answer the door holding a lease. The kid doesn't know jack but hands the lease to the officer standing there and that was game over."

"Why? I don't get that. Oh, yeah, I do, it becomes a civil issue."

"You got it. Local law said an officer couldn't do a thing if there was a lease. If you showed a lease it became, as you said, a civil deal. Gangs learned that and moved in. They leased a few, bought a few, and used squatters to cook meth, then started selling every drug you can name from houses that had been foreclosed on." He pointed. "That light-brown stucco house right over there. Potello delivers there. I'm talking *bags* of pills. And right over there, I've seen FBI Grale parked."

"Have you seen Grale go into the house?"

"No, he meets Potello—Poco, I call him Poco for short. Agent Grale is quick about it. He gets his fix and splits. And look, I know what you're thinking, and I know who Grale is. He's done some serious takedowns in his career, so I know why the FBI wants to protect him. And he was stand-up during the bombing we had in Vegas. But that was then, this is now. Look, I know users. It's what I do. I've got film of Grale parked here with Potello. Poco is going down, and it looks like Grale's going with him."

He winked at her.

"Maybe they'll share a cell," he added.

"Or maybe you're wrong. He's got back injuries and doesn't like to wait in pharmacy lines. He likes the convenience of Potello. You could be reading the situation wrong."

He shook his head and said, "I've been doing this a long time, and I've seen a lot of shit go down. I know what I'm looking at. Go check out Poco's drug shop, then tell me he's legit. He's sitting behind bulletproof glass."

"Potello isn't Grale. I'm talking about Grale."

He paused on that, then looked at her hard and grinned.

"Maybe you're not the right agent to be investigating him."

***

Jace drove to Potello's drug shop after the Wycher meeting. It had a walk-up window with a tray to slide things in and out from behind what looked like bulletproof glass but probably wasn't. It was a tiny shop.

Mara called before she made it back to her car. It turned into a long call and involved more evidence on Potello that Mara wanted to pass on and talk about at length. The detail he went into told her he cared about Grale and valued him. And still, he was very critical of Grale. When Mara finished he asked, "What's your read on Wycher?"

"He's the type who's born certain," she said. "When I questioned his conclusions, all of a sudden he's too busy to talk and gave me a dead-eyed stare."

"What did he see Grale do?"

"He saw what he thought was a quick, suspicious-looking exchange between Grale and Potello, who he calls Poco. He didn't seem to have any proof other than his *experience*."

That seemed to frustrate Mara, but she couldn't help that. He wanted to talk it out, so she walked back through it with him, trying to get to a definitive conclusion, but they just couldn't do that yet. When they finished, she called Grale and got his voice mail, so she left a message and then texted him, Where are you?

Headed to Panguitch, he texted back. No big deal. I'll let you know what I find.

17

Panguitch Lake was a soft blue off my left shoulder as I checked out trailers in the hookup area and campsites along the lake before returning to the store. At the store I bought bottled water, salted peanuts, coffee, a candy bar, another bottle each of Tylenol and Aleve, and a Panguitch Lake map as an old-school way of keeping track of areas checked off.

The lake was about two miles long with a road wrapping it, so I had just enough time before dark if I kept moving. I passed Bear Paw and Lake View resorts, then was in and out of small roads before turning into an area called East Shore. There I didn't see much of anyone, almost no traffic at all.

Past Skoots Creek I bore left onto the West Shore Road and checked out Church Road, Hyrum Lane, and Eagle Lane, and crossed another creek, Blue Spring, before stopping to mark the paper map with areas checked.

The light was still good but paling as I rounded a shadowed corner on a dirt road and scanned through trees, and just like that, there they were: an old aluminum-sided trailer and a new-model GMC pickup.

Funny how it goes sometimes. I didn't feel excitement or adrenaline but did feel relief as I knocked on the trailer door then walked around it and the pickup. The trailer was just like the photo the cousin sent. The pickup was registered to a Brad Smith in Vegas, so maybe Brad was a friend or Indonal bought it recently.

I called Mara before alerting the Garfield County sheriff. Mara wanted to impound both vehicles, but after we talked it through, he backed off and said he'd track down Brad Smith from the office. I texted him a photo of a license plate. A couple of Garfield deputies came out, and a locksmith arrived a few minutes later and got us into the trailer and pickup cab.

Worst case was Indonal was inside and dead, but I hadn't smelled anything as I'd waited for the deputies. Inside, it didn't even smell of food or as if he'd even slept there. I checked the tiny refrigerator. Nothing. Empty. I left my card on his pickup's dashboard. Then the deputies and I knocked on doors in the area. The few who answered my knock were aware of the trailer and pickup, but no one had seen anyone. I showed photos of Indonal and several made the connection to the missing coders. I underscored that he wasn't wanted for a crime.

"We just want to know he's safe."

At twilight I headed home. Jo was out to dinner tonight with a couple of friends. I made a sandwich, opened a beer, and went through the news channels. The usual experts and commentators debated whether Indonal and Eckstrom were traitors shopping Indie's source code. An "expert" saw possible payoffs of tens of millions of dollars.

I had the opposite feeling. That Indonal retreated to the lake rang true to me. My gut feeling was I'd like the guy. Either way, I felt we'd find him soon and I was much less worried about his safety. If he was running, he wasn't working very hard at it. By the time I finished the beer and the sandwich I was done with the TV.

I started to stand and couldn't. The pain was so sharp I had to sit. A few minutes later I tried again and couldn't quite get there. It was another half hour before I could make it to the kitchen for my pills and then to a hot shower, which had always helped. An hour later Jo was home and I felt better. But I was shaken. I'd truly been unable to stand and should have told Jo, but I didn't that night.

18

AUGUST 7TH

I felt better in the morning but was worried. If Dalz was headed here, there was a good chance he'd arrived and joined a team targeting Indie. Nothing I'd learned substantiated that, but given the threat chatter aimed at the AI, nothing made more sense. And I had a gut feeling that it couldn't be anything else. I drove to the office early and ran into Jace outside.

"We need to talk," she said.

"How about we get a coffee and talk?"

We went around the corner of the FBI building and walked to the Starbucks. After we'd ordered to-go coffees and were outside heading back to the office, Jace said she'd spent time with Laura Trent, Alan Eckstrom's girlfriend, yesterday evening.

"She was pretty messed up when I saw her," Jace said. "I ended up at her apartment around six last night, and guess who showed up in an Uber. Dr. Ralin. He got there a little after me, just long enough for her to tell me that she and Eckstrom had broken up the night before he disappeared. Eckstrom told her he's never coming back to the apartment and never wants to see her again."

"Never?"

"Her words. Eckstrom told her to donate his clothes and everything else of his. He'll pay the rent for three months, then she's on her own. I don't know whether any of that is true, but I was there when Ralin arrived with a bouquet of flowers for her. He couldn't see me when she opened the door. He handed the flowers to her, and she threw them down the hall. Ralin wasn't happy about it or that I was there. He asked for ten minutes of private time with her. I said yes, and I know, it was a mistake. Wish I hadn't, but I did. They sat in deck chairs in a first-floor rock garden at the apartment complex with me watching from a distance. I was close enough to see him holding and touching her like they're very familiar with each other."

"Did you ask her?"

"I tried to after he left, but she dodged it and I really didn't get anything from her other than she's in distress. I don't know what all that means, but maybe you do."

"I don't."

"Well, she didn't have anything for us after Ralin left. She may have just wanted someone there. She's got issues, but I doubt she's got any information for us."

"Okay, so let's just keep it open with her. What else is on your mind?"

"Us."

"I know, so let's talk."

"You took an unnecessary risk with this Bismarck creep and his stragglers. I don't really understand that or that you didn't want Bismarck to see me because he'd *lock in on me*. What does 'lock in' mean anyway, and how do you know how he thinks? Explain that to me."

"He targets women."

"Many killers do, so that doesn't cut it."

"There's a darkness in him that I've only seen a few times in my career."

"A darkness? Come on, you're not one of those agents."

"Okay, darkness might be the wrong word, but he's unusual in a bad way that's hard to name. He's told us things he'll claim to have learned from confessions made to him, things that are in effect leads about a missing person—people he shouldn't even know about. He moves somewhere new and two or three years later there's another big statistical bump in unexplained disappearances but no bodies found, no crime scenes. You're a woman and connected to me—that will draw his attention. The people who go missing are always women."

"So you were protecting me? You don't think I can take care of myself. I need you?"

"Not at all, you're probably better at taking care of yourself than I am. It's not about you being a woman. I'm working from my gut and my experience with Bismarck."

Jace sighed.

"I'm frustrated," she said. "I'm frustrated by how we're managing our time. I don't think we've got our priorities straight."

"Okay, what do you see?"

"I see us putting way too much energy into tracking down two computer scientists who quit. I see confronting a freak like Bismarck as a distraction. Our goal is to find Dalz and others who are gearing up to target people working at the project or will even go as far as to attack the base. I feel like we're all over the place without a clear plan."

"With Bismarck, I went out alone to deliver a message, nothing more."

"You went out and *we* ended up needing to call for help. Yesterday, you made a long drive out to Panguitch Lake. If we'd sent the photo of the trailer to the Garfield County Sheriff's Office, they would have found it. Am I wrong?"

"They may have."

"May have? No, from what you described, they would have. They wouldn't have been as thorough as us, but we would have followed through. Right now, I'm guessing Bismarck and his followers are making breakfast, frying up toads and rattlesnakes to eat with their eggs, and they're fine with that. They're one or two water bottles away from having to drink their own urine to survive. But that's their problem, not ours. And it's not ours if they trespass on a Department of Defense base. If DoD can't stop those ragtags, what good are they anyway?"

"I disagree."

"Fine. But don't tell me we're connecting. We're not. We didn't have any problems last time we worked together. I thought it was great, so what's going on now? Is it that you're so used to operating solo here that you can't deal with a partner? Mara says you work alone a lot. Is that true?"

"That's an accommodation the office has made for me due to my back."

"So maybe that's what it is?"

"I like working with you, Jace. My back is bad right now, as bad as it's been since the first year after the bombing, so yes, it figures in, and I'm worried about other things. I'm pretty good at listening and picking up on vibes. I'm going to go out on a limb, and feel free to tell me how wrong I am. You and Mara are asking me the same questions about what painkillers I take, and you *just* got here. What should I make of that?"

Jace sighed yet again. She looked at me, and I could see she was debating.

"There's a lot of worry you're hiding pain and that you're not physically up to active duty. I'm sorry, Paul, but that's what I'm hearing and have been told since I got here. It isn't just Mara."

"Hiding pain? How does anyone hide pain?"

"By masking it."

I knew what that meant, and it stung.

"Why don't we go to Mara and say it would be better if you were teamed with somebody else?" I said.

"I tell you the truth, and your reaction is that you'll just work alone from now on. That's so male. I still want to work with you and learn from you, but I need to be able to question how we use our time, and I need you to be very up front about how you're hurting and what you're doing about it. It's obvious that it's worse than when I last saw you. Talk to me, what's going on with your back?"

"It's worsened. It's in a bad cycle. I'm going to consult with a surgeon and see what can be done, if anything."

"When?"

"Soon."

"How soon?"

"The surgeon is a friend of Jo's. She recommended him, and his office is anticipating a cancellation this afternoon, but who knows where we'll be when they call, if they call."

"If the cancellation happens, you go. I'll cover, and thank you for telling me." She sighed again. "I'm sorry your back hurts as much as it does. I do want to work with you. You found the pickup and trailer because your instincts are that good. You were open-minded enough to listen to Ralin and look at that half-assed traffic cam photo and think, *Well maybe, just maybe.* I want some of that magic. I want to work together, but one question I ask myself is, Have you worked so long alone it's got to be all your way?"

"If we're talking about Bismarck and going alone to Panguitch, I'd do it the same way again. Bismarck needs to get told face to face, and Indonal and Eckstrom are being painted as possible traitors. It's putting them at risk. A well-intentioned citizen might try to hold them at gunpoint, so I'm for finding them now. I see it as urgent. I talked with a woman at Stanford who called Indonal a once-in-a-generation mind. She worked with all three. It's dangerous how their disappearance is getting framed. I feel as if we have to act."

"I know you do, but I would have called the Garfield Sheriff's Office and if they found something, then I'd go there. I still don't think it was a good decision. Look at how you're walking this morning after that long drive. I'll probably kick myself later for saying this, but whatever you're taking for pain may affect your judgment. Do you carry painkillers in your car?"

"I carry Aleve and Tylenol. The stronger stuff is at home for the nights when I really need it."

"What's the stronger stuff?"

"NORCO 5s, Percocet, and OxyContin I rarely use."

"How can you use OxyContin and come to work?"

"I don't." I pulled out my car keys. "Check out my car," I said.

"I don't want to do that."

"Do it anyway."

"No, your word is enough."

"No, I don't think it is right now. Mara is worried about drug use, and so are you. It's obvious in his questions to me, and it doesn't bode well, but between us, you need to know I'm very careful. I don't take anything during the day that could affect my job. Sometimes at night and only if it's really bad, so I can sleep, I'll take painkillers. I can't use the OxyContin because it lasts twelve hours. I probably wouldn't use it anyway. Everything else I've taken more of lately. If things get to where I can't deal with the pain, you'll be the one I tell first."

"Thank you for saying that," Jace said. "Thank you."

She reached over and gripped my arm. For a moment we stood there then walked back to the office and ran into Mara as we came in.

"Indie just took out a jeep with four kids in it," Mara said. "What kind of crap is that? They crossed some bullshit line, and it launched missiles and killed them. You two go find out what happened before they blame the kids instead of their murder machine. Go get the truth, and make sure they understand we're opening an investigation."

"When did this happen?" I asked.

"Less than an hour ago."

"We'll call from the base," I said as we left.

19

Mara sent a long text that Jace summarized as we drove toward Independence Base.

"The boys would have started their senior year this fall," she said. "The girl was sixteen and headed to her junior year. The driver, Justin Cousins, was seventeen. He used to go four-wheeling with his dad in the mountains behind the new base and told his friends he knew a secret route that would get them close to the AI. It sounds like a dare, a way to have fun on a hot summer day."

"It does."

"Mara sent the phone number of one of the officers who just interviewed the mother of Justin Cousins."

"Let's call her," I said.

"Doing it right now. I'll put her on speaker if she picks up."

She did, and as I introduced myself to the Las Vegas police officer, we realized we already knew each other. Her name was Marla Sider. Like us, she knew the kids took a daredevil risk driving out there but was shocked they'd been killed.

"The mother thought the kids were off to a pool party and was worrying about drugs and drinking. It didn't occur to her they were going four-wheeling. When we got to her house she kept repeating that."

"Who told her?" I asked.

"She didn't know. She couldn't give us a name but said the call came from an officer at Independence Base. She believes he identified himself, but she couldn't remember much of anything after confirming the vehicle license plate they gave her was for her husband's jeep. She kept repeating, 'Why would they kill children?' How did it happen, or do you know yet? They've got cameras everywhere. They must have known what they were looking at."

"We don't know yet," I said. "We're on our way there."

At the base we drove out to where it happened. We circled the blackened wreckage of the jeep and realized that not just one but two drone-launched missiles struck it after the driver violated an inviolable, invisible, half-mile defense perimeter around the Indie building. I saw multiple flags marking body parts.

When we returned to the Indie building, we were led to a room with a map and screen. We watched video of the jeep as it neared the base, climbed a steep slope alongside the fencing, and then followed a narrow track down and through a dry wash. I turned to the officer.

"Did you know they were kids?" I asked.

"Inside the half-mile-perimeter red zone, the AI makes the kill decision. We're as sorry as anyone, but they could have been terrorists impersonating high school kids."

"Wouldn't Indie have zoomed in on the driver's face and matched the face to a driver's license?"

"I don't know the answer to that, but there are multiple signs warning trespassers. There are warning signs posted all along the fencing and the access road outside the fence. We've known there were risks; we've worked hard to avoid accidents."

"Does anything say explicitly that if you get within a half mile of the building, you're dead?" I asked and followed with, "I'm not putting it on you personally."

"This is what they are calling an *"inviolable line."* We don't know yet that all procedures were followed, but it appears they were. No one is saying this isn't a tragedy, but they ignored explicit warning signs. Decisions have consequences."

Four kids trespassed, and they were dead as a consequence. I stared at him a moment and tried to choose my words. Jace and I weren't here to judge the ethics of the decision-making. We were here to gather facts. This officer took the defense of failed procedures personally, so I slowed down. We weren't going to get anywhere with him.

"Agent Blujace and I are unlikely to be part of the FBI investigation into how four high school kids were attacked and killed with American missiles on American soil. But what we gather from our interviews today will become part of the final report. Can you tell us or can Dr. Ralin—"

"Dr. Ralin has no role whatsoever in the defenses of Independence Base."

"We'd like to talk with him next."

"I don't know if that will be possible."

"We're not asking for permission to talk with him. We will talk with him whether it's here or at our office. The FBI requests—and you'll get this in writing today—that we be copied all photos, video, and reports that come from the internal investigation into the missile launches resulting in these deaths."

"That's not a decision I can make."

"Who should we contact?"

"I can't give you a contact name yet."

DoD wanted a full review of the facts before releasing anything. That was understandable, but we'd muscle our way in. That would occur way above Jace and I or anyone we worked with daily. The best we could do today was record what we saw and what was said to us. The agitated officer who briefed us was no doubt disturbed but also more able to rationalize it than us.

I could have said teenagers often make bad decisions and asked if they'd planned for that. *They would after the next event,* I thought, *and adjust again and again.* What seemed apparent here was what Ralin had alluded to with the killing of the military observers: that Indie made a knowing decision.

The AI had likely identified the military observers for what they were as well as the teenage driver of the jeep today and who the vehicle was registered to and where the owner lived. If it has the capabilities Ralin claims it has, it put it together and made a decision to protect the inviolable line. That said, it wasn't sophisticated enough and might never be for the freedom of decision they were giving it.

Before we left, we did talk with Ralin in his small glass office. He was shaken yet somehow worked the conversation around to himself. He has a gift for that.

Before we left the base, we drove out to the burned wreckage of the jeep. The bodies and the DoD team were gone. A hot wind had come up, and a lone guard was sitting in a vehicle. Nothing else was within miles, so who knows what he was guarding?

20

JACE

Jace found Mara in the small room that was his office. He took one look at her and asked, "How are you holding up?"

"Investigating Grale sucks. He ended up at that lake alone because I was talking with Wycher and checking out Potello's drug ATM. When do you see this getting resolved?"

"Soon."

"It needs to. He knows he's being looked at, and he's upset."

"How do you know he's aware?"

"He told me you and I are asking him the same questions about prescriptions. He didn't ask me why but was making a point. He offered me his keys so I could search his car if I wanted to. He's put it together.

"Look, I get the feeling he's unsure what to do with the pain he's been in. He also said he's rethinking the delivery pharmacist. He's going to make an appointment with a doctor and may give up on Potello. He said it hasn't worked that well. He volunteered that."

"I wish he'd never gone near that asshole," Mara said with more emotion than she'd heard yet from him. "Metro is very close to busting Potello. Did Wycher tell you they have search warrants for Potello's car and office? It's about to go down."

"He said it was close."

Half an hour later she and Mara were on the phone with Wycher. Wycher was vocal and went after Grale for street buys from a "dirtbag pill pusher."

"I have him on video three different times buying from Poco," Wycher said. "We're working on the possibility it's Chinese counterfeit fentanyl coming in through Mexico. But we've also used up our budget for this one, and my captain is ready to roll. You didn't hear it from me but Potello is about to go down. It doesn't have to be the biggest bust in the world to strip him of his peddling license, but he's looking at much bigger charges."

"When is the bust?" Mara asked.

"Can't tell you. I don't even know yet, but I guarantee you when it does, he'll be looking at some serious charges. He's going to want to trade. That's when your agent Grale makes local headlines. Of course, Grale will get a different ride. You know better than me how that will go."

"How will it go?" Jace asked.

"He'll resign then apologize to all Americans or some crap like that and get admitted to a cushy drug rehab program. He won't do any real time."

Jace watched Mara flinch at that.

"Hold on for a second," Wycher said. "I've got a radio call to answer. I'll be right back."

Mara muted the phone so they could talk as they waited for Wycher to return.

"Metro has told us what's what," Jace said, "but they haven't showed us enough. We've seen photos and video but no hard evidence."

Mara stayed quiet.

When Wycher returned, Mara freed the mute button.

"That was my captain," Wycher said. "He wants our bust plan cleaned up more, but it's going to go down fast when it happens."

"Hey, Wycher, what's your cell number?" Jace asked. "Give it to me, and I'll text you mine."

"You already did."

"Have you still got it?"

"Dunno. I clear them if I don't recognize or need the number."

"Give me yours," she said. "Say it and I'll enter it in my phone."

He was reluctant, which said to Jace they didn't want the FBI around when they made the bust. Maybe they didn't want to be hamstrung coordinating, or maybe Wycher was hoping to bust Grale hard. Jace had known guys like Wycher. They were just born with that streak. If it didn't hurt, they didn't feel satisfied.

Her guess was that Wycher was looking for a headline. The news reports wouldn't have his name, but he'd still own the story. He'd like being able to tell his buddies how he cinched the cuffs tight on an FBI user.

"If I'm close enough when it goes down," Jace said, "I want to be there. If Grale really is buying illegal pain pills, he's got some serious pain."

Wycher sat on that several seconds then said, "I hear you but I've been doing this a long time, and let me clue you in on something. All addicts are alike."

"I grew up around them, so I know something about it," Jace said. "Maybe more than you, Wycher."

"Say that again?"

"You heard me."

"Yeah, I guess I did, but if you want to hold Grale's hand, you need to hang with me and be there when it goes down. We're not building a bust around your availability."

"I'm not asking you to. I just want a heads-up. I'll text you my phone number or if you want, I'll check in with you every day."

"Nah, I'll call you, and if there's a press conference about taking down a major local pill pusher and cartel middlemen, you'll get your five minutes to talk about how the Bureau worked with us. But I've got to warn you, my captain hates feds stomping in after all the work is done."

Jace looked at Mara and mouthed, "What's up with this guy?"

"Okay, I'm signing off," Wycher said.

"I'm texting you my contacts," Jace said. "If I don't hear from you, I'll call you."

He didn't answer; he was already gone.

21

Later that same afternoon, my lower back was X-rayed at a facility across the street from Dr. Terry Yandovitch's office. I hand-delivered the new X-rays and originals taken after the bombing to Yandovitch's receptionist. Soon after, she led me to a small room where I waited for Dr. Yandovitch, who was tall enough that he had to duck at the doorway as he came in.

With him were both sets of X-rays. He clipped them up on a screen as he said, "Sorry I'm late. How's Jo?"

"She's good."

"Tell her hello for me. Now, talk to me about your pain. Be as accurate and detailed as you can. When it's bad, what's it like?"

"Knifelike. Very sharp."

"Sharp as in it feels like you can't move?"

"It can be."

"Show me where it's knifelike."

I touched that part of my lower back. He watched then turned to the X-rays taken after I was flown from Bagdad to Frankfurt, Germany.

"When they operated on you, they reconstructed muscle. Some of that has atrophied or torn in the years since. That's led to more scarring and pressure on the disc. You also have a degree of scoliosis, though that's not a significant concern. Lateral pressure on the disc is what worries me. Your biggest issues are degrading bone and nerve irritation that's likely to evolve into a much bigger problem. The atrophied muscle is a difficult aspect. Without surgery, you could end up in a wheelchair. With surgery, there are a lot of ifs and zero guarantees. All bomb surgeries are different."

"So, you're saying it's nothing to worry about."

He smiled for my benefit, but he'd heard all the jokes and false bravado before. He ran through a list of questions.

"How much of the day are you on your feet? Make a guess."

"On average, thirty percent, sometimes more."

"What was it yesterday?"

"Yesterday I made a long drive so probably less than ten percent standing."

"How's your posture when you sit in front of a computer?"

"I wouldn't call it good or bad. I try to sit straight."

"Exercise?"

"I have a lap pool and the FBI gym. The pool I haven't used in months."

"Due to pain?"

"Yes."

"At the gym, what exercises do you do?"

"The treadmill, and I lift weights. I've had to stop just about everything."

"Stopped when?"

"Six weeks ago."

"What kind of weights?"

"Resistance weights."

"Good. But use a lighter weight and be particularly careful. How long have you been off work?"

"I'm still on active duty."

Yandovitch glanced down at his notes as if contemplating something, then asked, "How do you control your pain?"

"With Aleve and Tylenol, and NORCO 5s at night. I take one, sometimes two NORCOs, and I have Percocet if needed."

"How often do you use the Percocet?"

"Not often. I try to avoid it."

"So how often?"

"With a flare-up like this, it could be every other night. In general, I don't like taking pills."

"I don't either, and I'm glad to hear you feel that way, although I'm not saying you should avoid them. They're to help you when needed. If we go forward with this, you'll need to commit to daily exercise for the rest of your life. That may sound like drama, but it's realistic. Primary is keeping your core strong. Nothing else you ever do will help as much. Do you have the discipline for that? If not, I wouldn't advise surgery."

That was more a statement that a question, so I passed on affirming my discipline and asked, "If I go ahead with surgery, how long before I'm active duty again?"

"What does active duty require?"

"That I can run and protect the agent I'm teamed with. I need to be in good shape."

"You won't run for months."

"Months?"

At that point he must have realized where I was coming from.

"You're not asking about pain after surgery or the other things I'm usually questioned about. Is your anxiety solely about how long you're off before you can return to work?"

"I worry about it."

"All right, well, let's talk that through. Am I correct in assuming you're often in significant pain at work?"

"I'm here because I'm in pain, and it's getting harder to deal with. Jo spoke highly of you, so I made this appointment." He took that in as I added, "It's a big deal to me to remain an active agent. I'm fighting to keep my badge and gun. For me to stay on active duty, my back has to get better."

"We can make that a goal to work toward, but we can't connect it to the surgery. In other words, don't expect surgery to be a guarantee."

"I understand."

"It's important for you to understand where you're at today, as well. The knifelike sharp pain is pressure on the nerve root as the disc is being pushed toward herniated. If it herniates, you could end up on constant painkillers, and surgery might no longer be viable. You're micromanaging a degrading condition."

He paused, and I got the feeling he was sizing me up. Fair enough, I was doing the same with him. The surgeons I've known all have some hero in them. They don't want to prescribe pills; they want to fix the problem themselves. But that doesn't always work.

"Do you see the white line on the floor?"

"Sure."

"I want you to walk across the room, landing your foot on the line with each step. Then turn and do the same thing walking back."

When I tried, I fell off to the left as I stepped forward. I just couldn't hold to the straight line. I tried several times and was surprised at how hard it was.

"Can you feel where it's tight?" he asked.

"Sure, there's a noticeable pull that's pretty constant."

"Those are locked muscles as your body tries to compensate. Landing each foot in rhythm on the line is natural balance. Our goal will be to get that back."

"I've had flare-ups that lasted as long as five or six weeks and then would go away."

"I believe you, but what you're experiencing now is different. What I see is a necessary surgery and increasing risk in waiting. That's something I almost never say. I won't do the surgery unless you commit to strengthening key muscles before surgery and what will be a lifelong discipline of careful exercise post-surgery."

He took me through what he would do, reworking muscle and removing a hardened mass of scar tissue, and then how over time the disc might be coaxed back into place, as well as his desire to avoid fusing. When he finished, I repeated my earlier question.

"If we go ahead with the surgery, what am I looking at in terms of time off work? A month, six weeks?"

"I see three, maybe four surgeries, although it's the first that's by far the largest and most complicated. You'll need a year for rehab. It could be less, but you should plan on a year."

"If I take that back to the office, they'll say disability, early retirement."

"All I can help you with is your back. We'll make a recommendation on meds to your doctor this morning so you get better-quality pain relief."

I couldn't get my head around a year off work. The ramifications sank in as I talked with Jo on the drive to the office. She was apologetic, as if by recommending Yandovitch she'd caused my new diagnosis.

"Did you know how long the recovery might be?" I asked her.

"I could have made a guess."

"Why didn't you?"

"He's the surgeon. Does he recommend surgery?"

"He advises it conditionally. Let's talk later. I missed several hours. I've got some catching up to do."

"I love you," Jo said and hung up. I called my primary care doctor's office to give them a heads-up that a call was coming from a Dr. Yandovitch's office with a prescription I'd want to fill right away.

That's when I learned their office hadn't received any faxes from Potello requesting approval for a refill in the last eighteen months.

"Are you certain?" I asked. "Because I've been getting prescription refills from him."

She checked again and said, "No, I'm sorry, we have no record of anyone asking for a refill. The doctor will have to call you later."

I was in the FBI garage when I called Potello and left a message to say call me. I'd just reached my desk when he returned the call. I could feel he was on edge, so I was careful with my words.

When he said, "I was meeting your needs," that told me all I needed to know. I'd need to brief Mara, who could alert the ASAC.

"Gary, when I asked, you've always said you'd sent the fax and had gotten my doctor's okay to refill."

"You asked for painkillers, and I got them."

"Did you get my prescriptions refilled through my doctor's office?"

"I got you what you wanted."

"You got me what I wanted?"

"That's right."

"You didn't refill them in the normal way through my doctor's office?"

"You knew where I was coming from."

"I don't know what you're talking about, but we're done doing business. We're done, but we're not done. You lied about the prescription refills, so you don't just walk away."

"Mess with me and see what happens."

"You're not walking away, Gary. I don't know what you've got going on, but I'm going to find out."

He hung up, and I started with the Nevada State Board of Pharmacy. I wrote a letter and sent it to the e-mail listed, then scheduled an appointment and called a lawyer I know. That was all to cover my rear. Whatever Potello had going on was going to take more. After I left the message for Brady, my lawyer, other things started fitting together, and I began to feel like a dupe and a fool. I walked down to Mara's office and told him, "I've got a personal problem I need to alert you to. It's not an FBI problem. It's mine, but I'd like to talk it through with you."

Mara, good guy that he is, loves bad news. He was on his feet right away.

"Let's find someplace quiet," he said. "Follow me."

22

DALZ

The delivery truck was an ordinary white commercial van Dalz asked to test drive before building a bomb inside. Sean allowed that, and Dalz drove a route that took him past the FBI building, then north to the street that passed by Agent Paul Grale's house.

After Croatia, it took less than a week to identify and locate Grale, the FBI agent who had traveled to Europe and almost trapped him. Those he worked for identified Grale as an American FBI bomb expert, but he should never have requested their help. He should have found Grale on his own. Grale was part of why he'd accepted this job, but, of course, those who'd long protected him couldn't really be trusted. Sean's leash-like hold was proof they'd been briefed.

As he passed Grale's house, he saw a woman get out of a blue four-door vehicle, a compact SUV. She turned and looked, perhaps sensing him or anticipating a delivery. A single glance at her and the house was enough. She lived there. He was certain from how watchful she was.

When he returned the van to the lot, Sean was waiting.

"The van will work well," Dalz said. "It handles the weight. The shocks are new enough, tires good. It is sturdy. I'm fine with it."

"Then build the bomb."

"Give me the driver so I can teach him, and he can also help pack the bomb into the van. The driver will arm the bomb as he parks. He'll flip two separate switches that will be marked with the color red. He'll turn both clockwise ninety degrees."

"That's stupidly complicated. Why not detonate with a cell phone?"

Exactly the question Dalz wanted to hear.

"Either way," Dalz said.

"Why wouldn't we use a cell phone?"

"They may interrupt cell signals in that area outside their office. You could send someone to check that."

"We already have. We know outside the building is fine, and I prefer a cell phone, and I'll detonate it, not you."

"The driver will need to park in the correct spot. He'll then have sixty seconds to get away. How will he get away?"

Rather than answer, Sean asked, "Where else did you drive today?"

"I drove north into residential streets to test the van on turns."

"What residential streets?"

"I cannot say, I don't know street names, but I was careful. I was testing the van more, that's all. I am here to destroy the artificial intelligence and for no other reason. I agreed not to go near the FBI agent. Isn't that what you're asking?"

"Your lies bore me. No more warnings, Dalz."

Sean stepped in so close his face was inches from Dalz's.

"Tell me that you understand," he said. "Tell me that I should kill you if you disobey again."

Dalz squinted at him but said nothing.

"I promise you that I will," Sean said. "I give you my absolute word. You can count on that. Do you understand?"

Dalz again said nothing. He stared back and waited until Sean turned away.

23

At the office I fielded a call from the head of DARPA, Kathy Tobias, who said, "I've heard FBI is concerned about a man who calls himself Bismarck and followers who think they're going to mind-meld with Indie. Is that crazy talk or real?"

"It's real. There's Bismarck and there are other groups gathering in the Las Vegas Valley. Bismarck, I know personally. I have a history with him. We also know he's getting help from a bot army repeating and amplifying his call to followers. Those bot swarms originate outside the US."

"I've heard something similar, which is part of why I'm calling. What should DoD do about Bismarck, his followers, and these disparate groups who are romanticizing the AI into some kind of all-knowing entity?"

"Beef up the borders and turn back those who still make it onto the base. I wouldn't charge them. It's a big base with porous borders. They can cut through chain-link. They go around it or over the mountains where there's nothing."

"Who's going to climb over that dry, steep range?"

"Somebody will. Even with constant patrols, some are going to get through, but it's scorching hot and it's a big base with no water. DoD will need to plan on rescues, although I think most will give up and go back, if they aren't arrested first. Another approach would be to lean on the local police and the governor to keep them from massing outside the base. But I wouldn't go that way."

"Why not?"

"Some of them have crossed the country to mind-meld with Indie. They're living a different reality. They won't give up easily. I'm repeating myself, but I'd turn them back or arrest and release. But that's me talking, not the FBI."

Mara and Esposito walked in on the last of the call.

"I'll call you back when I get a chance," I said.

"Please do."

ASAC Esposito I've known forever. I shook his hand.

"Good to see you," he said, without any inflection at all.

"Likewise."

Mara said, "We just got off a conference call with Metro police. Your pharmacist, Gary Potello, was apparently arrested and charged yesterday. He's named you as one of those he supplies illegal drugs to. Painkillers. The conversation you described to me may have been recorded. It sounds like he's trying to use you to trade for lesser charges."

"Aw, no . . ."

"I didn't know that when we talked. We just found this out and really shouldn't be telling you anything. His lawyer wants to cut a deal that the DA's office is receptive to. We can't talk about that here, but now you know. Talk with your lawyer, and you aren't obligated to talk anymore with us if you choose not to. You can leave this meeting without any repercussions."

"I'd like to know anything you're willing to tell me," I said.

"Potello claims he can name cartel middle managers operating in the Las Vegas area. He's also said through his lawyer that he can provide proof of illegal drug buys you've made. He's kept records and has you down for quite a lot of OxyContin in the last eighteen months. You'll need to work through your lawyer from here, but do you want to say anything to us now?"

"I've never bought illegal drugs from Potello. I've done business with him for eighteen months with the belief that he was getting prescriptions renewed through my primary care doctor. If an undercover officer has videotaped me buying, it *wasn't* illicit drugs. Potello has a pharmacy business and makes home deliveries and has—"

"We know he does deliveries. We know about his business," Mara said.

"Do you? He told me once he has seven hundred clients. Some are shut-ins, some are disabled, and some are like me, regulars who don't want to wait in line at a pharmacy. I have payment records that I'll turn over to my lawyer, but I could also bring a copy here. I haven't made any illegal drug deals I'm aware of. He doesn't have anything on me. He's just looking for an out, something he can trade."

"We're not going to suspend you today, Paul," Esposito said. "But neither do I have to explain how serious this is. And complicated. The reality is you've been in more obvious pain lately than any of us can remember. You may think you're handling it, but we see something else. In that light, the painkiller questions are fair to ask. You'll provide a urine sample after this meeting. Do you have an issue with that?"

"None."

"You keep your badge, creds, gun, and car. You're not suspended, you're still active duty but with restrictions we'll figure out. If the DA brings charges against you, you get suspended until it's resolved. If not, we'll still have to restrict what you investigate because we don't know yet whether you'll be around in a year to testify in court on cases you've worked. At this point it follows the usual path. Right now, we're telling headquarters a suspect who's admitted he's a Zetas cartel operative pushing counterfeit pills has accused you of buying substantial quantities of painkillers from him and is trying to trade on that."

"He's framing me."

"I believe you," Mara said. "We both do or wouldn't be having this conversation. Even so, we're walking a tightrope keeping you on active duty."

Esposito stepped back in, saying, "Wake up, Paul, this one is on you. You've been FBI as long as I have, and you made the decision to buy from this jackass. You know perfectly well what it looks like when you meet him on the street and exchange pills for money. Then add to that Potello's claims of large quantities. It couldn't come at a worse time. Right now, we need everybody. You used bad judgment with Potello and let the Bureau down. That's where we're at. You're angry at Potello, but I'd bet I'm angrier at you. You of all people should have known better—why didn't you? I want an answer next time I see you."

24

JACE

Jace wanted to reach out to Grale that night but didn't know what to say. He wasn't officially suspended, yet there was no pretending things were normal. Without giving her details, Mara had let her know Grale was headed for hard times. Probably gone.

She texted Grale, Want to meet for a drink and talk?

Twenty minutes passed without an answer, so she looked up his address and drove over. Grale said Jo had just bought a new four-door Toyota SUV, but the only car in the driveway was his Bu-car. That didn't mean Jo hadn't parked in the garage, and Jace didn't want to disturb them if they were home together. She debated several moments, then parked and rang the doorbell.

When no one answered, Jace started to leave then turned when she heard footsteps from around the side of the house. Grale came out of the shadows.

"What's up, Jace?"

"I came to see you. Did you get my text?"

"I didn't think going out for a drink was a great idea. Are you sure you should be here? Because I'm pretty sure you shouldn't."

"You're still active duty. We're still working together. No one has told me otherwise. Mara even stressed that you're still active duty."

"My problems are my own, Jace."

"Can we at least talk?"

He was in shorts and a loose T-shirt, a look she'd never seen on him. She showed him the bottle of red in her left hand.

"You don't have to patch up anything with me," Grale said. "I figured out they asked you to help determine if I was buying illicit drugs from Potello. I had to do something like that ten years ago. It's a lousy feeling, but there's not much you can do about it. You were doing your job. I'm also betting Mara told you to keep miles away from me until this is sorted out. Am I right?"

"If he'd said that, I wouldn't be here. He said we're still working together."

"Until tomorrow morning or afternoon or whatever it is."

"Until Metro brings charges, if there are charges. I just want to talk without getting into details."

Grale hesitated, then said, "Then you'd better keep this flyby to yourself."

"It's between you and me, no one else."

Grale led her around the side of the garage and through an open patio gate to the back where the view beyond the fence was desert and mountains. She got why he chilled out here. She saw the lap pool and the outdoor shower and the patio lounge chairs she remembered he said he sometimes slept on when his back hurt.

"I need to tell you I'm sorry," she said.

"You might need to make yourself feel better, but you were just doing your job. Don't fault yourself."

"I want to talk."

"All right, let's talk. Hang on while I get a couple of glasses and a corkscrew."

Grale opened the wine and poured two glasses. He handed Jace a glass as she said, "I'm sorry this has happened."

He was quiet, then said, "We're good, Jace. You and I are fine, and what I've told Mara is the truth."

"If I didn't think that, I honestly wouldn't be here," Jace said.

He nodded, and she got the feeling he believed that.

"Let's clear up a couple of things between us," Grale said. "When we talked about you and Mara asking the same drug questions, did you know Potello was going to get busted and charged, and that he would implicate me?"

"You mean when you took off for Pancake Lake without me?"

"Panguitch."

"I was looking at Potello's hole-in-the-wall pharmacy."

"Then you saw the pharmacy board license in the window."

"I saw it. They think it's fake."

"It's not. I've checked every so often that it's still valid. I've called the pharmacy board to find out how to file a written complaint." He paused then looked hard at her. "We're talking about what we can't talk about. You could get yourself in trouble."

"Well, supposedly we're still working together, so they must know we'll talk. What can you tell me about you and Potello?"

"Before we go there, when did you learn Potello was plea-bargaining?"

"After you did."

"Okay, that matters to me. Thank you. Potello's story as I knew it before all this was that he started off delivering prescriptions mostly to people who didn't have a way of leaving their houses. For me, like I said, it was about convenience, and in a sense, it was the same for people who were shut-ins with no relatives or friends to pick up their prescriptions. Plus, I knew him."

"You've told me."

"Right, but I'll say it again because it figured in. I knew Potello and had for a decade. He worked in a mall pharmacy near here for a long time. But . . . everything for me has some root in me not wanting to be seen buying painkillers. I was ashamed I needed them. I didn't want to be recognized buying them."

"But you knew buying from Potello on the street didn't look good. You had to know that."

"Sure, how could I not? But I've never kept it secret. He delivered to the FBI office before I was told to get him out of there. I used to meet him outside and pay him. I didn't see it as bad. Unorthodox, sure, but Amazon deliveries were unorthodox when they started out. Things change."

Jace said quietly, "Mara believes you."

"No, Mara likes it that I work investigations and get results. But he's a career climber, and I'm tainted no matter how this comes out. He's a good guy, but he's taken a step back from me and will never risk it again. It's about the Bureau's reputation. Everyone he supervises is a reflection on him. I'm in a very bad spot, but we're not talking about that tonight."

"I'm like you. Nothing is real until there's evidence."

For some reason, that made Grale smile.

"Okay, we're not talking. I get it, but just tell me what happens next," Jace said. "I've never been around something like this."

"Two things, if they haven't happened already. First, it goes to the Office of Professional Responsibility and the ASAC tells the SAC there's some bad press brewing that they have to get ahead of, a serious problem that could make the Las Vegas FBI look bad. The ASAC also cuts Mara loose from the investigative end and takes his statement. It becomes strictly OPR, which is a dark cave many never return from."

She mulled that over. Agents talked about getting OPR'ed like it was worse than hell, but Jace didn't know much about it. One agent had told her that radium has a shorter half-life than an OPR investigation.

"Could surgery fix your back?" she asked.

He was slow answering the change of subject.

"I don't know, I'm hoping so," he said. "The surgeon I'm talking to is very careful about predicting success. And it's not just one but three or four surgeries and no guarantees."

"Whatever you do, don't quit," she said.

She drank another glass but didn't feel any better when she left. She knew Grale understood she'd been asked by Mara to help, and she'd done what she'd had to do, yet Jace felt sad driving away.

Grale was up against it, and she was part of taking him down. No matter what, it was just as he'd said: he'd become the agent who bought pills on the street.

Grale was the one who'd once told her, if you have to explain yourself, you're doing something wrong. That had stuck with her, but here he was buying from Gary Potello, ex-pharmacist, new inmate. Maybe it was like he'd said, he was ashamed of his injuries. Or something that came from the struggle with his back. But either you can do the job, or you find something else. A basketball star doesn't blow out his knees then expect a higher salary and a starting role next season.

If it's murky in any way with Potello, they'll wash Grale out, she thought. Grale was right about that. If that happened, then it would be what Mara had told her. It'll leave Grale in his midfifties with a reduced pension and few prospects. That, and dealing with multiple surgeries. But if Grale was innocent, then she'd figure out how to help him. Were his buys legit or was the pain so bad he'd gone down the drug road?

Jace knew what she wanted to believe, but to learn the truth she needed Potello. And what if Potello has convinced the DA's office and Metro police of something that wasn't true? Then what happens? Does Grale get framed?

Potello was squirming around trying to please everybody. Someone has to stand up for Grale. It wasn't going to be Mara or the ASAC. Jace decided it would be her. Even as she thought about her next move, she knew it was a bad idea. But she couldn't just stand by and do nothing, so maybe she'd just have a quick conversation with Potello, nothing crazy. She pictured the scene in her mind and knew what she was going to do.

25

I was outside near the lap pool in the warm night air when Jo got home. She gave me a quick kiss, picked up the wineglasses, and asked, "Who did I miss?"

"Jace. She had a role in trying to figure out whether I was buying illicit drugs. It was tough on her."

"Don't ask me to feel sorry for her. How are you?"

"Not as good as I could be. It's strange to feel like an outsider at the office. Everybody seems to know what happened, and I'm sure they were told not to talk to me about it. I get the feeling Mara and Esposito expected a confession. Other than Jace, everybody has me at arm's length—"

"She feels guilty. That's why she came over. You've been a mentor to her, and now she has to decide whether to distance herself. She's unsure what to do and trying to play both sides. You need to get the drug questions answered definitively."

"There's not a lot more I can say. There's a process that'll take place. If we didn't have the heightened threat alert, I think they would have sent me home."

"What about other agents on the squad? Isn't anyone sticking up for you?"

"I'm sure they are, but it's out of their hands, and my supervisor will be very careful with what I work on. If I'm working an investigation where my testimony is critical later and a defense attorney can say I was suspended or under investigation for illegal drug buys, the whole case could get thrown out."

"Are they really going to suspend you because a discredited criminal pharmacist accused you?"

"I have to prove my innocence."

I didn't want to have this conversation with Jo. I'd sought advice and turned over my situation all day. I didn't want to continue it tonight, but I owed it to her.

"Do you blame yourself?" she asked.

"I do and I apologize. You've always warned me to verify my prescriptions were refilled by my doctor."

"But it's not just about that."

"No, it's not. It's connected to whether I'm fit enough to be an active agent and whether my judgment is up to Bureau standards. Metro police have evidence Potello has moved thousands of counterfeit pills for the Zetas cartel. I've been in association with him. That won't go away."

"I know who you are," Jo said. "Have you eaten?"

"Not yet."

She showered, and I made omelets and a salad. We sat outside under the stars near the pool and drank what was left of the bottle of red, then opened another.

"Do you really think they want you gone?" Jo asked.

"I'm asking myself that. I've got a very good solve rate, so if Potello admitted to lying, that could turn things around. Otherwise, there's nothing the FBI protects more than its reputation. I've hired a lawyer I like, but I'm not clear yet on the right moves."

"I am. Start by kissing me."

I leaned over and she leaned toward me, but it was an awkward kiss. I was in a bad way. I was very blue tonight. She moved closer. I smelled the shampoo in her damp hair. I love the feel of her.

When I leaned back, she kept hold of my hand and said, "Did you really think no one was noticing your limp?"

"Sure, they have. Everyone has, but I've had flare-ups before that have come and gone. I'm supposed to get back to Dr. Yandovitch soon. He called my situation a fragile balance where a few back muscles were overcompensating to hold it all together. What would you do? I'm asking, Jo."

"I'm not sure, but I know you. You wouldn't have gone to Yandovitch if you didn't believe this was different than previous flare-ups."

In bed she probed along my back with her light, cool fingers so I could tell her where the pain was sharpest. I don't have words for why her touch nearly always calms me.

"This may get into the media," I said. "It probably will. If it does, it'll burn hot and fast, in which case headquarters will step in and quarterback the response. If I'm charged with anything, I turn over my badge then try to save my reputation."

"You mean your sacred honor," she said in a quiet voice. "As long as I've known you, nothing has mattered more."

"You matter more."

"I don't think so, and I love you for it. You'll get cleared," she said and slid nearer and went quiet.

In the distance that night, I heard sirens. Very early in the morning as I left for Panguitch Lake, I learned that the Metro police lost an officer last night during a second Zetas bust. Four cartel members were killed in the firefight, three from bullet wounds and a fourth who drowned in a pool after being wounded.

A call came from a Metro detective as I neared the lake. He told me Metro believed the cartel was tipped off about the raid, and then he asked if I might have any leads for him. At first, I thought the call was genuine, and then realized what it was. I heard laughter in the background before they hung up.

26

AUGUST 8TH

Mara called and then texted me a letter Alan Eckstrom had allegedly handwritten, photographed with his phone, and then posted to an AI forum site late last night. "The media is all over it," Mara said. "Read it and let me know what you think."

I sat in a lot at Panguitch Lake and read. When I checked out media coverage there were claims independent handwriting experts had verified the signature. A well-known conservative radio show celebrity and, I believe, a Fox talk show host—I'm not certain it was, but it sounded like a Fox host I'd heard before—termed it "Eckstrom's Plan" and labeled both Eckstrom and Indonal "probable traitors."

Whether that was true or not, no TV or radio host would know, but in our FBI office there was new concern. I called Ralin after talking with Mara. Not only had Ralin read it, but it was sent to him at an e-mail address that only a few people would know about, meaning that it probably came from Eckstrom.

"What do you make of it?" I asked Ralin.

"That's not Alan talking."

"What do you mean?"

"That he wouldn't use those words. Those don't sound like sentences he'd write."

The news outlets turned to handwriting experts for analysis and comparison to other Eckstrom signatures. How they got the other Eckstrom signature samples that quickly, I don't know.

A handwriting expert we use at the FBI qualified her conclusion because there wasn't much of Eckstrom's handwriting to work with. Eckstrom's signature was on some DoD forms he'd once filled out, and not much else, and yet the expert still came back with a high probability that Alan Eckstrom had signed the letter or statement of philosophy, or whatever you want to label it.

Indonal's signature wasn't there. I didn't know yet what to make of that. The pair, according to Ralin, were inseparable, and at one point all three were philosophically on the same page. For Ralin, national defense trumped medical advancement hence their quarrel and divide. The letter read:

Dear America and to All People,

I have worked along the cutting edge of artificial intelligence. Recent breakthroughs and advances will greatly alter the world. These changes are so significant that I believe it is imperative that the decision be made by the many, not the few. I am not the traitor I will be labeled, but I believe the source code for the breakthrough we made should be shared with the world. I intend to share it.

Until eighteen months ago, I and two other computer scientists worked toward the common goal of bringing the breakthroughs in AI capability to medicine and the diagnosis and treatment of disease. AI will eventually allow all that is known about a disease and similar cases to be accessed within seconds no matter where a doctor is in the world.

Those breakthroughs have been co-opted for military purposes that will give the United States a unique advantage over all other countries. I believe this will lead to instability and war. The breakthroughs are now labeled "top secret." This will slow and impede many advances in more positive applications. I urge every American to protest and resist the sequestering of these breakthroughs. The world needs to advance together. We are, I believe, otherwise doomed to war.

Sincerely,
Alan Eckstrom

Eckstrom's message, if it was Eckstrom, was short. I read and reread it. We needed Indonal, Ralin, and other people who knew him to weigh in. I called Ralin back.

"Where's Indonal's signature if they both left for these reasons?"

"I don't know what to make of that either."

"Have you spoken with Indonal?"

"Do I have to answer that?"

"It would be a mistake to lie."

"I have, and the DoD is aware."

"Who else is talking to him?"

"The head of DARPA but you didn't hear it from me."

"Why are you talking?"

"I'm trying to get him back on a temporary basis. The project needs him."

"One of you needs to go public with that. What's going on in the media this morning puts him in danger."

If me going back to Panguitch had been a question in Mara's mind, it wasn't anymore. There was no pushback. He didn't say a word about my back either, and I made a fast drive that morning. An older gentleman living there had gotten my cell number from a card I left with a store owner at Panguitch. The message he left was, *Your drive would be "well worth it."*

When I say older, this guy was a lot older. I turned into a lot near the lake looking for a blue '89 Ford pickup, but didn't see any blue pickups or Fords. I saw trees swaying in gusty winds and a lake with whitecaps and no boats. But within ten minutes, I found Clint Maldon, the man who'd called me. He was parked a quarter mile down the road.

When we shook hands, his were cold and trembling, though firm.

"Follow me," he said.

"Follow you where?"

"My granddaughter's cabin. She knows you're coming."

Fifteen minutes later he coasted to a stop at a narrow dirt road and pointed at a driveway.

"I can't go down there with you. I'm not supposed to drive, and she'll be angry."

He smiled as if we were in on some practical joke together, and I thanked him again before following the narrow gravel road down to a small cabin. A late-model black Jeep Cherokee was parked out front. Maldon's granddaughter stepped out into the sun and introduced herself as Cindy Maldon. I showed her my badge and gave her a card. She was thirty-one and had met Indonal here at the lake when she was sixteen.

"Eric and I kept in touch on and off through social media, then reconnected when he moved to Vegas. That was before

I came here to take care of Grandpa. He's ninety-four, with a heart condition. His doctor told him to move to a lower elevation, but he refuses to. Did he call the FBI office in Las Vegas?"

"He did."

"Do you want to come inside?"

I followed her then asked her straight up as we got inside and I took another look at her square-shouldered posture. I'd seen enough in the video to ask.

"A woman picked up Indonal and Eckstrom the night they disappeared. Was it you?"

"Am I going to be arrested?"

"For picking up your friends? No, and I'm not here to arrest you. We need your help."

"It was me."

"Do you know where Eric is?" I asked. "I'm asking because he's in danger."

"He's not worried."

"He should be."

I let her absorb that for several seconds then sketched some of the FBI concerns before asking, "Do you also know where Alan Eckstrom is?"

"I don't. Eric is the only one I've seen, but they both left for the same reasons. They couldn't deal with the situation anymore. There were all these promises that got broken."

"What promises?"

"Eric will have to tell you."

"Then you need to get him to our office or tell me where to find him."

"I'm not sure where he is this morning."

"How about you call him, tell him the FBI is at your cabin, and hand the phone to me?"

I took a closer look at the cabin: a bedroom, a bath, and a small kitchen. Along the east wall, a stone fireplace. If he was staying here, then clothes, shoes, something was likely lying around.

She called Indonal, and I heard his voice as he answered, and then her voice lowered as she walked into the bedroom. I overheard her tell him an FBI agent was here. When she came out, she handed me her phone. Indonal sounded low key and level headed. He wasn't defensive, suspicious, or self-righteous.

"Is this about the letter Alan signed that's all over the news?" Indonal asked.

"Were you part of writing it?"

"No, it kinda shocked me."

"Did he mention a letter he was working on?"

"No."

"How about a statement you'd make together and possibly sign?"

"No, but I agree with what he wrote. We want to bring AI to medicine in a big way, but we never drafted a letter or even talked about it, and it doesn't sound like him at all, so maybe he figures we're done working together and has started talking with others. That looks like his signature, but somebody else wrote it. That isn't Alan talking."

Which was what Ralin had also said.

"You need to come to our office, and if you don't see what danger this letter puts you in, I'll spell it out for you."

"You don't have to, I get it. Our quitting in the stupid way we did all came from the screwed-up agreement we had with the DoD and Mark. We were supposed to be replaced in June, and that was going to be after we trained our replacements. It just kept getting delayed. And now they're making us into traitors for not staying on. That's total bullshit, and Mark knows better than anyone. Haven't you talked to him?"

"Have you since you left?"

"Several times and the DoD knows we're talking. We quit and we're totally fired, but Mark wants me to come back temporarily. He's trying to get DoD approval. I know Alan won't do it, but I might help Mark. I wouldn't be coming back for him. It would be for the project."

"You got burned out."

"Yeah, basically, that's it, and Indie isn't what we got into this for. This is a different AI than we wanted. But Alan and I did keep up our end of the deal. DoD must have thought we'd do what Mark told us to do indefinitely. We were like the assistants to him in DoD's eyes. But that wasn't close to true. We were okay with Mark being the Einstein of AI on TV, but not okay when he tried that crap on us. It was one thing too many. I'm sorry we disappeared like we did. I really am. I didn't realize it would be such a big deal."

"Who agreed to the end of June as the end of your contract?"

"It wasn't the end of June we agreed to. It was the start of June, and DoD agreed. The problem was, it was all verbal. Mark was supposed to start interviewing coders by March or early April at the latest. He blew it off. He was in London more than he was here in May. It was very unfair, and the disrespect ate at us. The three of us worked a long time together, so it was pretty personal what he did.

"It's like he started to believe he really was a genius. Not that I really care about stuff like that, but he'd be gone, then come back and question us about some little breakthrough that happened while he was gone, then talk about it like he owned it. That really got to Alan. And Mark knew we wanted to get back to where we started. When we got into this, it was about improving medicine, not war machines."

He started to say something more, then stopped himself. I had a sense of where he was headed and said, "You can talk to an FBI agent about anything. You were going to say something. If it was a test that went badly, I may already know about it."

"The observers?"

"I know about it."

"Okay, well, that was it for Alan and me. That was when we decided we'd just disappear some night."

He'd said it several ways and I didn't need to ask again, but I did.

"You and Eckstrom hadn't been recognized in a fair way."

"I don't care about that."

But anyone would.

"I just don't like pulling all-nighters then having Mark come in and tell us we should have written a different algorithm. I know that sounds petty, but it got to be a big deal. He'd tweak it, then claim it." I heard him clear his throat before he added, "I get that what we did was stupid."

"If you get that, why didn't you let us know?"

"Because the traitor talk on TV really pissed me off."

"And what about Alan?"

"I don't know. We've barely talked, and when we do it's about an offer we might get for a project in Switzerland that has to do with using AI to advance medicine. The people he's talking to told him they want to deal one on one for the moment. Then later, I'll be brought in."

"But, for now, you're willing to come back in and work on Indie?"

"For a defined period of time."

"And Eckstrom?"

"I don't think so, and doesn't the letter today kind of say it all?"

"You have to come in, and where do we look for Alan?"

"I don't know. I really don't. We split up that night and agreed to keep our locations secret. He might be with a woman we met up with the night we took off—Margaret Landis. He hasn't said he's with her, but before he and Laura broke up, he said he'd met somebody. I'm pretty sure that's who sat down with us at the Jaguar the night we left. She just kind of introduced herself to me, but he knew her. Alan is shy around women, but he wasn't with her. She came over and said you guys look like a lot more fun than my boyfriend, then asked if she could hang with us. DoD definitely drilled into us to watch out for stuff like that, but she got us laughing. When I came back from the restroom, she'd slid over next to Alan. Can I ask you a question?"

"Go ahead."

"Have we broken any laws by quitting?"

"As long as you didn't take anything, you're good to go. But you didn't just quit, you disappeared, and we've pulled manpower off other cases to try to find you. That's put other investigations on hold. You need to be in an office tomorrow morning. How far away are you?"

"I'll come in within two days."

"Make it tomorrow."

I called Mara as I drove back from Panguitch.

"You were right about the lake," he said. "But you won't be the one to interview him when he comes in, or if you do, I'll be in the room as well. Until your situation is resolved, your assignments will be very limited. Those are my orders as of today. That's where we're at, and it was a decision made above me and Esposito."

"And if I'm not okay with that, who do I talk to?"

"I wouldn't push it if I were you. Good work on finding Indonal. Now, let's find Eckstrom. I've got somebody on hold, Grale. Let's talk here later."

27

After returning from Panguitch Lake, I met for an hour that afternoon with Michelle Brady, the lawyer I'd hired and had always liked and respected. She jotted notes as we sat across from each other in her office.

"Give me everything," she said. "Give me texture. Tell me what I don't know, tell me what you've taken for pain and when and how. I want to know what it feels like to be you. And not so I can talk about your pain. I want to talk about how much you love your job and what you've endured to keep it. Things are heating up, Paul."

"What's happened?"

"I've talked to Metro. I have one or two friends there and one well up in the brass. They're never going to talk specifics about an investigation, but they did tell me Metro is looking at you very hard, and the FBI isn't resisting."

"Not resisting?"

"What they said is there's no pushback from the Bureau. The FBI is asking for proof, but that's all so far. Tell me your drug regimen. What do you take and why?"

I told her, and she started putting together her approach, verbalizing her thoughts as she did.

"You stayed on your dosage and avoided the heavier painkillers. You put the FBI and your duties first. When the pain became unbearable, you consulted with a top surgeon. You trusted your pharmacist, and it turns out he's a criminal and part of a cartel flooding the US with illegal drugs, so we hate him. There's no middle ground here." Brady verbalized her whole strategy, with me chipping in pieces to help, and then asked, "How well do you get along with the Metro police? My friend inside says an undercover officer named Wycher has it out for you. Is there something with you and him?"

"Not that I'm aware of. I've worked with Metro many times. We've always gotten along."

"Will your supervisor fight for you?"

"Yes and no. The Bureau doesn't do gray zones. He's a good guy, but I'm not sure where he'll land on this. He tried to investigate using one of our squad agents first, and that's a good sign, but it's out of his hands now. It's the Office of Professional Responsibility from here forward. He'll have to protect himself to protect his career. He'll probably distance himself from me."

"Do you get along with him?"

"I do. He's a good guy, good supervisor."

"But he'll distance himself?"

She watched me for several seconds as if I might have some further revelation about Mara and me, but it's about bureaucracy and career, and I'd given my opinion. She asked for my case clearance rate. I said it was the highest on the squad but that I didn't want it mentioned.

"Here's why we need to mention it," she said. "Could an agent strung out on painkillers solve cases? No. Absolutely not, and they can't challenge your solve rate, so we hammer that. We're artists, Paul, and we have to paint a vivid picture. It has to be vivid because we'll only get so much time to argue your situation. But I have to say something else as well.

"Even if we're successful, highly successful—and I expect to be—you can never get back to where you were. We'll clear your name, but still, some people who'd never heard of you before and don't know a single thing about the facts will always believe you got away with one. I know you know that, but I have to say it."

"If you help me save my career, I'll owe you forever," I said.

"The way I bill, you'll owe forever anyway."

***

Back in my car I made several calls, talking through my situation with an old friend at the DEA, and another on the New York office DT squad, and then a retired district attorney in Virginia I'd gotten to know on a case fifteen years ago. I got the most from him.

I wanted to hear what people thought, but even as I listened, my mind jumped around. I was in a bleak space when Mara phoned and said, "Metro wants to interview you today, but it's voluntary. They called here looking for you. Do you have a lawyer?"

"Yes."

"Bring him."

"Her."

"Okay, her."

I called Brady and met her outside the main Metro police station late in the afternoon. Inside, we crowded into a small interview room with two officers where I described my injuries and what I do to manage the stiffness and pain. We had a frank conversation after they said they had videotape of drug buys I made from Potello. They implied they had other evidence, insinuating that a confession would be best for all concerned.

"We respect the Bureau," Officer Wycher said. "We have to. We work together."

I shared my private drill for dealing with pain, what I've talked through with Jo and have shared with no one else other than Brady earlier today. "My girlfriend is a physician. She knows what I take and at what dosages. She has for a long time."

"How did she miss the prescription renewals?" Wycher asked.

"That was on me, not her. I trusted Potello to get the prescriptions renewed the way they're usually done."

"We don't doubt you once had prescriptions. You just don't have any right now."

"Actually, I do. They were all just renewed. You can check with my doctor on that."

"Potello says when you first called him you were looking for painkillers."

"That's not true."

That got a long pause out of Wycher, who was clearly the one taking the lead. The woman officer had largely gone silent, and I could feel Wycher debating. I knew from his face his tone was about to change.

Sure enough, he said, "Man up, Grale, own it. Your pain has gotten worse. I saw you make buys from Potello. I work undercover, and I know the look. I know you're going to say how you thought it was all legit, but guess what Potello is saying? He says he didn't have any prior relationship with you. He didn't know you, didn't know anything about you, until you came looking for drugs."

"Yeah, he did."

"Can you prove that?"

"I dug up an e-mail this morning that Potello sent out when he started his business. I can send it to you along with my e-mail telling him I'm going with him, and him thanking me in his response."

They gave me two e-mail addresses, and as Brady went back and forth with them, I forwarded the Potello e-mails from my phone. Maybe Potello forgot I was on his blast list when he started up Potello Pharmetrics or assumed I would have erased our back-and-forth.

What he'd sent was an electronic flyer to "customers who've known me a long time," "a select list as I start a new type of pharmacy. Very personal service delivered to you." His photo was there. So was a photo of the ticket-booth pharmacy office he'd leased.

"I liked Potello's idea," I said. "It seemed better suited to Vegas than other companies delivering. Those companies typically deliver to the front door or mailbox. But we live in the desert, so it sits and cooks on the porch or in the mailbox. With him, it was a handoff, which seemed safer all the way around."

"And he got you the drugs you wanted," Wycher said.

He didn't believe a word of anything I'd said.

"Potello floated that same idea when I told him we were done. That was before your bust. How do you explain that away?" I said.

"Junkie ESP. You felt it coming and covered," Wycher said.

The other officer followed with, "This e-mail flyer contradicts a number of things Potello told us but doesn't answer everything. His main business has been pushing painkillers. He's confessed to a cartel relationship and fingered suppliers that led to the two busts. He's not lying about that, so why would he lie about you?"

I started to answer but stopped. Brady had said something true before we walked in here: "They don't want it to be you, Paul, but they don't want it not to be you either. They don't want to be wrong. When they go there—and they will, they always do—you go quiet, and I'll take over."

I went quiet. In a noncombative, borderline-gentle voice, she said, "My client fought to return to active duty after multiple surgeries and a long rehab. That should tell you plenty about him."

"And that was how many years ago again?" Wycher asked without waiting for an answer. "A long, long time ago," he said, "and a lot of drug use between then and now. Look, the street is the street. Who are you fooling? You've got some good years back there, and that's worth something. You can make some sort of deal, but you're not walking away just because you're FBI. Or maybe you will, but it will be with a stain that never goes away."

He nailed my fear with that. I stared across the table but stayed quiet.

"You've made a big bust in Potello and the cartel distributors," Brady said, holding on to a calm tone as if Wycher hadn't said a word. "It's something to be proud of and great for the city, but you can't prove Potello sold illegal drugs to my client."

Wycher jumped on that. "Your client was videoed more than once buying from a Zetas front man. Get real."

"I couldn't be more serious," she said.

Wycher shot back, "And I know drug buys and users." He turned to me. "You've used for a very long time."

"You've got it wrong," I said, "and you need to know I'll never take a deal and I'll never stop fighting it. I'll run through my savings. What you're saying isn't what happened. We both know Potello will say whatever he has to." I looked to the other officer. "Are we done for now?"

We were.

28

JACE

Potello's financial situation stank. His house had a first and second mortgage, yet the $95,000 Mercedes inside the garage was owned free and clear, as was a quarter million in artwork. Against that he had high credit card debt and more cards than a blackjack dealer. The judge must have had a problem with it as well. She set bail at an impossible $1.5 million. Potello's new lawyer posted it. *If anyone had questions about the value of the drug trade, there you go,* Jace thought, *there's your proof.*

She tracked his release by making phone calls and drove up as Potello came out of the building. A chunky lawyer in a black suit led him toward a car, but Potello resisted getting in. It was a scene straight out of a bad movie.

She couldn't hear the words but watched as the lawyer ratcheted up the threats, the last as he was in his car and rolling slowly alongside Potello. The lawyer pointed a finger like a gun then drove away.

As he turned the corner, Jace eased up along the curb, keeping pace with the walking Potello.

"Can I talk with you for a minute?" she asked.

"Talk to my lawyer."

"I watched Grale buy pills from you. I don't want him to get away with it."

"Who the fuck are you?"

"Look at my car, what do I look like? You're about to get completely screwed," she said. "Do you know what's setting up?"

She slowed to a stop. He glanced in her rearview mirror before leaning toward the open passenger window.

"Grale's an asshole," she said.

She could almost see Potello thinking. Unsure. Confused. Woman in a fed car who looks like an FBI agent. *He's also thinking he'll recognize me easily,* Jace thought, *and he could.*

"No one told you that you'd be bailed out, did they? Of course not, and you saved your life by not getting in that car."

That hit home.

"How often does Grale buy from you?" Jace asked.

He hesitated but only for a moment. "Every week. Sometimes more."

"No pharmacy is going to refill a prescription that fast, right?"

"Monthly for most," he said.

"Right."

He looked into her car again. Jace's heart sank, but she kept her game face.

"What do you want from me?" he asked.

"Nothing from you. Just the opposite. I've got information for you. When he called you to order up some more relief, did he ever use his work phone?"

"He didn't, but sometimes I called it just to mess with him."

"Good. Smart." She looked over her shoulder again, then back at him. "I don't have much time," she said, "but here's the deal. Some of your delivery dates are wrong."

"Says who?"

"Grale's lawyer can prove Grale was out of state and even out of the country on days you wrote down as delivery days. They've compared it all and may drop all charges against him due to the discrepancies. Maybe you winged it a little when you put your dates together. I get that, but they're going to push hard for any possible way out."

That stopped him for a moment. He fumbled then recovered.

"My old computer crashed. I knew some of the dates were off, but I can fix that."

"Good. There's an explanation. Your computer went down, and some of the dates got transposed. Let the investigators know *you* caught the problem, not them. If they catch it, it'll throw your plea bargain into review."

"They can't change that! It's already agreed to."

"What world are you living in? They can change anything they want. If you're not credible on that, how can you be credible about anything else? You're either a liar or you're honest, and the deck is already stacked against you. Grale's a career FBI agent, and you're a pharmacist pushing counterfeit pills. You've got a new Mercedes in your garage and you live in a 4,500-square-foot house. They'll show the jury the car, the pool, your gardens, everything. Grale's attorney will blow you out of the water."

"It's not a big deal. I just messed up a few dates," Potello said.

"I know you did, and I get it. But I also know how the system works, so the question is what to do about it. I'm not telling you to do a thing. That would be your decision. I'm not on your side, but if Grale was doing opiates while backing up a partner, well, I can't live with that."

He nodded.

"You hear me?" she asked.

"Yeah."

"We never talked. Is the other deal with you finalized?"

"Almost."

"Push for it, and make noise about the bailout today. Hide. Get off the street. Get Metro to find you a safe place or a one-person cell, and not next to some guy talking to himself as he chews off his fingers. Where are you headed now? Do you want a lift?"

"Not a good idea to be seen together," he said.

"Then where's your ride? You shouldn't be walking out here alone after they bailed you out."

"I didn't know I was getting out, and my phone battery is dead."

She looked hard at him, but her own heart was pounding. She knew she was out of her mind doing this. "Have you got another lawyer you can call?"

"No."

"So what are you going to do?"

"I'm going to call the DA's office and tell them I messed up some dates."

"I mean what are you going to do to stay safe?"

"Not your problem."

"Okay, got it. Be careful."

She took a last look at him in her rearview. He was already across the street moving toward a drugstore that advertised throwaway phones. The boy was a survivor, and saving his own life was a whole lot more important than framing Grale. Nothing sharpens the mind like owing a million and a half in bail and angry business partners waiting out on some lonely desert road.

She thought to herself, *Agent Blujace, were you tampering with a case? Did you tamper with Potello's lies? I'm out of my mind, but Potello saying he could fix the dates was just as wrong.*

It was about not watching passively as the system got worked. It was about keeping someone good from getting framed. It was about what's fair. And yet, she'd just risked her career. It was insane. Like flicking a lit cigarette into dry grass, a crazy risk. Yeah, Potello bought in, but what had she risked? Everything she'd worked years to make happen. But never again, not for anybody, not Grale, not anyone.

What would he do now? The seed was planted. Potello would go to work on his new lie.

29

JACE

AUGUST 9TH

"Where's Eric," Jace asked as she walked Cindy Maldon to an interview room the next morning. Jace felt tense and was angry with herself over what she'd done with Potello.

"Eric is on his way," Maldon said.

"When did you last talk to him?"

"An hour ago. He was told to be here at nine."

"He'll get here, and I'm sorry I'm late. There was bad traffic."

Jace went first to the night Maldon and Indonal reconnected at Panguitch Lake. She moved forward from then to this morning, when Eric left her cabin very early and said he'd meet her here. When they'd covered that, she moved on to Eckstrom.

"What do you know about Alan Eckstrom's whereabouts? Eric must have said something to you."

"He doesn't know where Alan is and doesn't talk that much to me because he doesn't want me dragged in. Alan might be with a woman they met up with at a bar the night they quit. I don't know her name, you have to ask Eric. But she might also be the one Alan is staying with."

"You heard that from Eric?"

"Who else?"

"Yes or no?"

"Yes, and Eric thinks she knew Alan already, like before Eric first met her at the bar."

"The Blue Jaguar?"

"Yes."

"And now he's possibly staying with her?"

"I don't know if he's with her, but I think Eric believes he is. Eric doesn't know either."

"Did he say that?"

"Something like it."

"Come on, Cindy, you know her name."

"Eric needs to tell you."

"Do you know if Alan Eckstrom and Eric Indonal had some sort of disagreement after they quit?"

"I don't know, but I think Eric has gotten his feelings hurt. He's talked about the letter that got published that Alan signed and Eric didn't even know was going to happen. They were going to go forward together, but Eric says that's not happening anymore. He was surprised by the letter."

"What has Dr. Ralin said to Eric?"

"Eric is talking with him, but I don't know what about except that he might go back to work on the project for a little while. You should ask Eric."

Jace continued with more questions and doubled back to earlier ones. Her anger at herself hadn't diminished, but she eased up on Maldon whose answers were consistent. Maldon knew more than she was saying, but Indonal had promised to tell all, and as Grale had pointed out, they could lean harder on Ralin who undoubtedly knew more. Ralin she didn't trust. Maybe Grale was onto something there.

Maldon's gaze was straight ahead, hair parted down the middle and falling close to her shoulders. She wore jeans, a clean shirt, and sandals to this interview. She wasn't trying to impress. She sounded worried for Indonal but not for herself.

Eckstrom's letter had gone viral. *Half of everyone in the US, if not more, must be aware of it,* Jace thought.

"What else did Eric say about the letter?" Jace asked. "You said Eric got his feelings hurt over it. Why?"

"I don't know if it was the letter. I said I thought it was. He didn't understand why Alan did it without him. When they quit, the plan was to contact people in the medical field and make a proposal. They were supposed to get together soon and start working on the proposal. He thought what Alan did was weird since they both left for the same reasons and had a plan."

"Would Eric have signed it along with Eckstrom?"

"You'll have to ask him."

"Do you know if they worked on the letter together before they quit?"

"Eric said no."

Jace took another look at her then shuffled the papers and pretended to read for several seconds before switching subjects and asking, "Did Eric say anything about a test that went bad?"

"He told me about something, but... I promised I wouldn't say anything. He's going to get here very soon. You should ask him."

"I'm asking you."

"I wasn't there, so ask him."

"But you know about it."

"I know there was a test that went bad and that what happened with the high school kids in the jeep was the same thing, or that's what he said. It came from the same problem or flaw, whatever you call it."

"Two missiles hit the jeep," Jace said. "I saw it, and so did Agent Grale. The children were blown apart."

"That's awful."

"It was. What did Eric say about it?"

Maldon wanted to be forthright. Jace sensed that about her. She'd attempt to defer to Eric but would still answer, which she did, saying, "Eric told me Indie was specifically programmed against that kind of strike, but that it could also follow an alternate path where different decisions could be made. Depending on how it interpreted the data, it could change what it thinks it's seeing almost instantaneously. Like when the world was thought to be flat then changed to round, everything else had to change, all the assumptions. Eric said Indie can shift realities in less than a second depending on the data it's working with."

Jace had no idea what to do with that and moved on. "Had you met Alan Eckstrom before the night you picked them up?"

"No, that's the one and only time I've met him. He was a little drunk but very funny. I haven't seen him since. I told that to Agent Grale."

"You told Agent Grale the night they quit you called a number Eric gave you and the woman who owns the van told you where it was parked and how to find the keys."

"That's true, and I picked up Eric and Alan in a parking lot. They sat in back so their faces wouldn't show. I hugged Eric first. It was like a fun thing. Like a prank or something. They never thought the FBI would be looking for them. It was about them making a statement to Dr. Ralin. We dropped Alan on a street about a mile away—Eric will remember the name of the street. Then I dropped Eric off where he'd parked this pickup and trailer of his. I took the van back, got my car, and was almost to the lake before I caught up to Eric."

"Almost to Panguitch Lake?"

"Yes."

"And Eric Indonal has been staying with you at your cabin?"

"It has a bedroom and a couch that becomes a bed."

Not ready to say she's in bed with him, Jace thought. "And you personally never saw or talked to Alan again?"

"That's right."

"Let's return to medical uses for AI. Do you know how long they've had that goal?"

"Eric says it's why he got into AI. All three of them had that goal. He says AI is so fast it can give doctors instant information about similar cases and what was done to cure people. All of that in just a few seconds. He's very excited about starting work on it again."

Jace asked another list of questions but learned little more. Maldon's face reddened as she talked about how outrageous the news coverage was.

"I think all of the conspiracy websites on the Internet should be shut down and some of those people should go to jail."

Jace listened without commenting on that then stepped outside and talked with another agent monitoring the interview. That agent agreed that Maldon didn't have much more to offer.

"Okay, I'm going to tell her and wrap it up," Jace said and went back in. "I think you've been honest with me, Cindy. Thank you for that. We very much need your help with Eric and not tomorrow or a week from now, but *today*. We have concerns about the woman Eckstrom may have been staying with, so rack your brain for anything more you can remember. We're also going to take temporary measures to protect Eric, starting today. That could mean you're separated from him for several days as we get sorted out."

"Where will he be?"

"At a safe location. You'll be able to talk with him by phone. I'm sure you understand. I'm going to leave you here alone for ten to fifteen minutes now as I go check with my supervisor. Are you okay with that?"

Maldon nodded. Jace left the room and was surprised to find Grale and Mara already interviewing Indonal. She knew Grale had arrived but had thought this interview would wait until she finished with Maldon. She texted Mara as she listened and watched a video feed.

In the interview room, Grale said, "Last time we talked you mentioned a Margaret Landis. Describe again how you met her."

"It was at the Blue Jaguar the night we quit. Alan was kicking back on the couch, and I'm in a chair. We're talking about the usual stuff, and this woman walks over and sits down with us. I figured she was a little buzzed or bored with her date. Turned out she was fighting with the guy she'd come there with and wanted to sit with us for a few minutes. Or that's what she said. She was classy and super funny and quick. We'd worked the night before and worked through the day and were fried but wanted a drink before we did our disappearing thing. Margaret sat down and I just kind of rolled with it.

"We had a drink or two, and she keyed in on Alan in a flirty but not super aggressive way. I went to the restroom. When I got back, they were sitting close, like up against each other. That's when I figured out, they knew each other already. I asked him later, and he didn't really cop to it. He didn't deny it either, and that night there was a bunch of stuff that later didn't make sense."

"You were a little buzzed too?" Grale asked.

"I was. We were quitting Indie after all those years. I was freaking. She got us to tell her our full names and then said she knew who we were and asked, 'You're the ones who really built it, right?' We could have cut it off right then—it's not like we haven't been warned about who might approach us—but Alan and I knew we were quitting, so what's the diff if we weren't going back to Indie Base?"

"You were having fun," Grale said.

"Yeah, we had a secret and great drinks and were back to where we started. It was wrong, but things were crazy that night."

"What do you mean back where you started?"

"Wanting to take what we'd learned about AI to the medical world."

"What kinds of things did Landis want to know?"

"She didn't ask much and changed the subject, pointing out a dude across the room who she said was her date. They'd had a fight and she wanted to stay with us. So pretty weird, right? What I think now is it was all staged. He was with her but not her date. She targeted us, or they both did. She wanted to share contacts with us, and we both said great. Alan shared his. I didn't."

"Why not?"

"It felt funny. We didn't know her. After she got Alan's contacts, the dude at the bar started toward us. She saw him coming and asked me for my contact info really fast, like she had to have it before the guy got to us, but I said I'd send it later."

"And what happened with Landis and the boyfriend?"

"Not much."

There were questions about that and then they took a break. Grale left and Jace went in, introduced herself to Indonal, and the interview continued another two hours. When Jace came out, Grale was gone, and she learned he'd gotten a call and left for an abandoned silver mine in Lincoln County where a body had been found. He'd left a message for her. He'd text or call after meeting with a Lincoln County investigator. She relayed that to Mara and added, "He's not sure there's cell coverage where he's headed."

"Then text him now."

She did, and Grale wrote back, Lincoln County investigator thinks it's Eckstrom. Tell no one until I've seen the body. Will call when I do.

30

I called Bill Juarez-Smith, the Lincoln County investigator, as I got close, and he made sure I didn't miss the cutoff. The unpaved road there led to the abandoned mine. When I parked and got out, we shook hands and he asked, "Ever been here?"

"No, but isn't it on some tourist list?"

"It is. It's named for the guy who dug it, worked it, and lived and died here. It's on one of those lists the state puts out to get more people to visit Nevada. Long before that list, it was a draw for college kids. They party out here and explore the mine, but mostly party."

"Did they find the body?"

"Yes, two college kids found the body. If it turns out to be the guy you're looking for, how do you want to do this?"

"We'll come to wherever you've got the body and pick it up today."

"That's what I wanted to hear. We're budget strapped and shorthanded. The media would be all over us." He pointed at heavy-gauge wire covering the entrance with a hole cut in it big enough to walk through. "Every so often it gets blocked off again and six months later someone has cut through it. It's a misdemeanor to cut the wire, but that doesn't even slow them down."

Inside the mine Juarez-Smith and I walked with flashlights along rusted tracks laid a century ago. They sloped into darkness.

Juarez-Smith warned, "Watch your head. The ceiling gets lower the deeper we get in, and there's a small cave-in we've got to climb around. After that it's no more than another two hundred feet to where he was found. You okay in here?"

"Yeah, it's everything I'd hoped for today."

"What's your limp about?"

"Injuries from a Bagdad bomb. Remember when the FBI sent agents to help the Army defuse bombs?"

"I was in the service right about then. I do remember. That's a long while ago. You're still hurting?"

"On and off."

"Well, take it easy in here. I don't want to have to carry you out. I'm not even sure I could do it anymore."

Our voices echoed in the mine. The air felt cooler and smelled of wet rock deeper in. I heard water dripping as we scrambled over loose rock around a ceiling collapse. Not far from there he lifted his flashlight beam to an old iron hoop set in stone and a four-foot-wide half circle of rocks mortared together to form a well against the rock wall of the mine.

"There was water here back in the day," Juarez-Smith said. "Not so much anymore. When I was a kid, there was still enough water in here to get us soaking wet." He turned to face me as he said, "I hope the FBI takes over this investigation. We got the body out, but we don't have the resources in Lincoln County to fully investigate the hanging."

"You don't think it was suicide?"

"No."

I studied the crude well as he talked me through what they'd found. Either you climbed up on the semicircle of mortared stones forming the well and looped the rope through the iron hoop and hanged yourself, or it took two people to lift and hang you. Like Juarez-Smith, I didn't see a lone killer doing the moving and lifting required. But neither did I rule out suicide.

When I told him that, he said, "When you see the body, you'll get where we're coming from. We have the rope and that iron hoop up there was swabbed for DNA. If the FBI takes over, we'll turn that over to you today as well as contact information and notes on the interviews to date. I don't know how many people were in here before the kids reported it, so you'll have to do what you can with it."

"When did you get tipped there was a body in here?"

"Two days ago. The kids who found him say they didn't touch the rope or anything down here."

"Do you believe them?"

"With the body and the rope, yes, but I don't know about the chairs and the car batteries."

"Car batteries?"

"I just spoiled my surprise. I was going to show you when we looked at the body. There are some bad electrical burns; third-degree burns in places. They tied him to a chair. We have the chairs, rope, batteries, everything we could find. From blood spatter, he may have tipped over backward and spent most of his time on his back. This is conjecture, but I saw something like this once before where they hooked electrical cable up and fried parts of an informant until he gave it all up. He didn't die but lost his ears, nose, and genitals. It was awful. Similar kind of burns here but not as bad and they didn't touch his face."

I called Mara from my car after we left the mine and before I followed Juarez-Smith up the highway to town to see the body.

"I'll call you when I get there," I told him.

It was an hour drive, and then I was inside looking at the body, including the burn injuries, which were disturbing.

"It's Eckstrom," I told Mara. "It looks as if he was tortured. How do you want to handle it?"

"Make the calls to get the body picked up today and say nothing about it until we've officially verified it's him. Don't talk to anyone, and ask the investigator to stay quiet. It'll find its way out anyway, but that'll buy us some time to get a team out to the mine. They'll want to meet the county investigator. Write up your walk through the mine and include any photos you have. Any evidence they collected goes to the lab first. It can get sorted there. We'll need to call a press conference. How bad was it?"

"He was tortured. It's bad."

In fact, I was left with a vivid image that raised questions about the morality of the human race. After Mara hung up, I drove forty miles before calling Jace.

"Eckstrom is dead. If you're babysitting Indonal tonight, you'll need a plan for that."

"I am babysitting him."

"Well, you know how these things go, it's going to leak out this afternoon. It'll be a body found that may be one of the missing coders . . ."

"It'll rock his world," Jace said.

"Where are they putting Indonal?"

"In a casino hotel room on a secure floor. I'll be in the room next to him. Mara says we're here because the rest of our local witness protection sites are full. Are you coming back to the office this afternoon?"

"I doubt it. Mara is sending agents. I've got to go back to the mine and later meet the crew that picks up the body and evidence bags."

"Mara let you go out there?"

"Yeah, it surprised me too. It really surprised me. I almost didn't tell him I was going, but he was okay with it as long as I understood I wouldn't be working the investigation. Hey, let's talk later. I've got to get going."

"Okay," she said, and I ended the call.

31

DALZ

Dalz followed Sean southeast of Las Vegas to a small business park on the outskirts of Boulder City, and with a spotting scope watched him park. For several minutes Sean sat in his pickup. Then he was out and squinting in bright sunlight and heat looking for or waiting for somebody. It turned out to be a man standing in shade near a building talking on a cell phone. The man signaled with his hand for Sean to approach then held his palm up for Sean to stop when he got within ten meters. Sean waited like a trained dog for twenty minutes while the older man finished his conversation.

Then he waved Sean over and looked displeased. He pointed a finger and appeared angry. The interaction said Sean had exaggerated his control of the operation.

He was more likely a puppet reporting back, and from his body language must have sensed his vulnerability, so not a complete fool. *If they were successful, the hero would become a liability,* Dalz thought, and realized Sean was expendable same as he was. What he watched changed his view of Sean somewhat.

This isolated business park explained how the more delicate components were protected and stored. Only an experienced nation could pull off a sophisticated operation of this kind. Not that he ever had any doubts. They'd bought the business park and probably the land surrounding it years ago. Within it they had full control but had to know the Americans would uncover this later and were gambling the US would choose retaliation over war.

With that realization everything made more sense: the misfit team, the low-level leader, the enticements. *They'd baited me too,* Dalz thought. They knew he'd go after the FBI agent. They knew he'd lie and intended to deal with him later. That led to other realizations. First, he would continue to carry through with the operation and obey. The second was to terminate all connections and disappear when it was over.

He stowed the scope, drove back to the ranch, then worked through the night assembling the bomb for the van. Tomorrow they'd begin on the missiles. Assembly would progress quickly; the countdown would start soon after.

32

JACE

Jace listened quietly as Mara described the electrical burns Grale saw on Alan Eckstrom's body. Burns from torture Eckstrom endured before dying. He coached her on how to talk to Indonal.

"At some point, probably tonight, if not sooner, Indonal is going to hear about it, or you can tell him. It could get rough."

"Where is he now?"

"He's there at the hotel."

"Why didn't we let his girlfriend stay with him?"

"Bureau policy."

"Somebody could bend that rule."

Jace checked into the hotel and rode the elevator to the secure floor where casino security monitored the corridors all night. She knocked and quickly looked in on Indonal. He was sipping a beer and on the phone to Cindy Maldon. He'd eaten two small bags of potato chips at seven bucks a bag, and the smell was strong. He looked at her blankly as she pointed next door to let him know she was there.

Unpacking in her room, she realized she'd forgotten her toiletries bag as well as missed her planned stop at the apartment for clothes for tomorrow. That got lost in Mara's speech. No clean clothes, not even a toothbrush. It left her moody. Indonal knocked on her door half an hour later. He wore socks with no shoes as if he were on a business-class flight and had just gotten up from his seat.

"I was wondering if I could get a few things from your minibar."

"What's wrong with yours?"

"I ran out of some stuff."

"So, you want to pilfer mine?"

"It's okay."

He started to back away, and she swung the door open.

"Come on in, take whatever you want. How are you doing?"

"I just heard there's some rumor Eric is dead. I don't really believe what they said. It's someone else. Would it be okay if I had a beer?"

"Go ahead, and I'll have one too."

"I drank the ones in my room. There were two, and I don't really know why I'm here."

"It's to keep you safe. Come on in. Let's have a beer together and talk."

Jace changed her mind about beer and unscrewed one of the little bottles of red wine that cost way more than it should. But she figured she was due for something for babysitting the coder. She didn't feel as harsh as that, and looking at him, she worried about him.

She handed a beer to him and a bottle opener. When she did, she saw grief rise in him. Jace watched but didn't go there yet.

"What's it like to have two million in public money spent searching for you?" she asked as a way of setting a different tone and calling him out on something that had annoyed her, though didn't matter to her or him, right now.

"It was nice at the lake."

So back at her—not quite what she'd expected, but she was down with a little attitude from Indonal. It made him more interesting and tougher than she would have guessed.

"You don't feel any guilt hiding there while people worked long hours thinking you were in danger?"

"You must not watch much TV," he said. "On TV we were traitors, trying to sell the source code for Indie."

So back at her again. Jace was starting to like him. He took a pull of beer and added, "No one from DARPA or DoD contradicted those news reports. But they knew why we left. Mark definitely knew."

"You can't put your disappearing act on Ralin. You could have gotten a message to us to say you were safe. You could have let us know it was a family fight with Ralin."

"We thought Mark would do that."

"Yeah, well, like I said, you can't put it on him. You're the ones who took off."

"We're also the ones who did what we promised to do, building Indie, then staying on months longer than we'd agreed to."

"I heard that from Agent Grale. You still took off without telling anyone."

"Mark had months to find our replacements. He didn't even try, or maybe he did and I never heard about it. He was supposed to interview and we'd train our replacements as Indie went live. We took it up in stages, and it's pretty much debugged."

"What about the two military observers and the four high school kids?"

"That's on DoD, but I'm not allowed to explain why."

"Did you communicate with Ralin after you vanished?"

"Sure, I knew within a day or two we'd screwed up by just disappearing. I talked to Mark. Mark was all apologies and 'let's work it out.' He was going to make sure the police and FBI and anyone looking for us would know we were safe."

"He didn't do that."

"I didn't really think he would, and I was fine with Cindy. Agent Grale found my trailer and pickup."

"Yeah, Grale," she said. "Honestly, if you and Eckstrom had sat in jail six months, I wouldn't have minded. What you did was bullshit."

"I know you think that. It's why I'm wolfing through your minibar."

She smiled, but they were right on the edge of acknowledging the truth.

"We made the country safer," he said. "It's going to be a fight, but we helped get the early lead, which is going to matter."

In a softer voice, she said, "Agent Grale identified Alan's body early this afternoon. The body was brought to our lab here in Las Vegas. I'm very sorry, Eric. I really am."

He started to say something but was unable to for several minutes, and then talked as if he hadn't heard her. "Alan is hoping to meet with people funding a huge medical AI project in Zurich. But I don't know if it's happening."

"Did you tell that to Agent Grale or Supervisor Mara?"

"I told Agent Grale, but it's not like I know much about it. I think Alan got the Zurich connection from Margaret. He said we'd fly to Zurich and interview."

"Was Alan staying with Margaret?"

"I think he was, but I don't know that for certain. I never got her phone number. I don't know whether she's a spy or whatever."

Jace watched him fight a wave of emotion.

"I have all these weird thoughts. How would she know we were quitting that night, and how far before did she meet Alan? She knew him when she sat down with us. I can't tell what's true. Alan believed her, so maybe it was somebody else."

"But something about her worried you."

"That night was weird in how she sat down."

"Could you ID her from a photo?"

"Probably."

"How tall? And make a guess at her weight."

"Five foot eight but in really good shape. I'll guess 140 pounds. She's strong."

"We think it took two people to hang Eckstrom."

As soon as Jace said that, she regretted it. It was unnecessary and had no place here. Indonal looked like he'd been slapped.

Indonal went quiet until she moved the conversation back to Ralin and when that went nowhere asked, "How are you feeling?"

"I feel terrible."

"I know, and I didn't know whether to tell you."

"I'm glad you did."

Jace poured more wine, then said, "We can't find a Margaret Landis. She doesn't seem to exist. Do you know anything more that could help us?"

She saw grief flooding his face again. How could it not? She wanted to keep him talking, saying, "Look at you: no big payday, no twenty million, but you're in love. If you had to choose between the two, which would you take?"

Without answering he lifted his beer in a quasi-toast then opened another bag of chips. He was trying to hang in and keep talking, but the grief was overwhelming him. He was a good guy, she thought. He seemed like a normal enough guy and yet Ralin admitted he had trouble following written equations for some of the math Indonal did in his head.

It tripped her out to think that. Ralin said it was a spatial gift in geometry that only a few in the world have. She didn't have anything vaguely like that. Strong intuition maybe, could tell when she was being lied to, but mostly that was learned the hard way. She was a good athlete with quick reflexes, but so were millions of other people. Ralin, the Einstein of AI, couldn't keep up with the guy sitting across from her on the couch who'd just beer belched again and had tears running from the corners of his eyes.

"I am in love," he said. "I've never really been in love, but I'm in love with her."

She reached over with her glass and clinked it against his near-empty beer bottle.

"Wish I had that," Jace said, then, "Don't be too hard on Ralin. He made all the connections. He made the money happen and talks a good game. He looks the part and, in his way, he's helping America come to terms with the whole idea of artificial intelligence without thinking it's going to take over the world."

"It may take over the world," Indonal said.

"Uh . . . ?"

"It won't be in a *bad* way if we're smart about it. It'll just mean people don't have to work in factories and medicine, and many other things will take some huge steps forward and be more affordable. We'll have to figure out new jobs, but it'll be cool to have the freedom to rethink a lot of stuff. The military apps are scarier. Everything 'war' will speed way up and become autonomous. There's no way humans will be fast enough, and when fighting starts everything will happen very fast."

"You built the thing, but you talk like a bystander," she said.

"We built one aspect. It was going to happen anyway and better it happened here." He stopped, maybe waiting for her to respond, then asked, "Who does the FBI think killed Alan?"

"We don't speculate if we don't know."

"Spies for another government?"

"They're in the mix."

"Is that why I'm in the hotel here?"

Without answering that directly she said, "It's assumed that whoever killed Alan knows about you." She watched his face. "When this is over, get out on a lake in a boat with your girlfriend like the first time."

He smiled and asked, "She told you about back then?"

Jace nodded.

"We're talking about getting married," he said. "It's not like we haven't known each other long enough."

"Have you asked her?"

"Not yet."

"Tell me after you've asked her. It's all talk until then."

He lifted his beer to that, and Jace felt something change inside her about him. Advanced geometry in his head, but he was still human. She knew he sensed something terrible in Alan's murder and his grief was genuine, but he was still trying to be here. She started to say something more, then stopped and reached across and laid her hand over his and kept it there as silent tears ran down his face.

33

AUGUST 10TH

It was a beautiful morning, cooler, with a clear blue sky that made me remember how much I love the desert. No heat advisory warnings today, no late-season monsoon talk or flash flood warnings. I hurt as usual and felt burdened over stupid decisions I'd made with Potello, but not the criminal ones I was suspected of.

Jo was right. My honor was everything to me. I'd sell my house and use that money to fight if I needed to. I bought coffee, took a call from Jace, and then one from Sylvie Ralin, Matt's estranged wife.

"I have to tell you something," Sylvie said. "It's not your problem, and I'm sorry to bother you with it, but I can't take this anymore. I can't handle the way it makes me feel. I just can't do it any longer. I wanted to save my marriage and it's very hard to say I'm giving up. I made a mistake eight years ago that Mark has never forgiven. He never will, and I'm done trying. I'm filing for divorce today."

I heard sadness in her voice. I heard defeat.

"I'm sorry I have to bring it up, and I know I shouldn't be calling you."

"It's fine to call me."

"I don't want to burden you with personal problems."

"That's okay, you can talk to me."

"This doesn't have anything to do with the project. The idea that Mark has to be watched is ridiculous. After we moved here from Palo Alto, I was ready to leave the marriage. The head of DARPA convinced me to wait. She talked to me about her own marriage and the mistake she made splitting up with her husband during a difficult time.

"She said give it eighteen months. Make sure he agrees. If it doesn't work after that, leave him and never look back. That advice made a real impression on me. Maybe she was just protecting the Indie project, but I think she meant it. It rang true then and still does, but for us it's over. I'm done."

"Has it been eighteen months?"

"More," she said. "It's been too long."

I heard her stifle a sob. She was quiet, then took me through her move to Vegas with the kids, loading the car, finding a house, getting the kids into schools and settled while keeping her business going. Then she told me something that happened yesterday that she called the last and final straw.

"I got a call from a young woman, a grad student at Stanford," she said slowly. "I don't even know how she got my phone number. She said Mark isn't returning her calls, and she wanted to know if Mark's visits to my house were more than just to see the kids."

She stopped there a moment.

"We aren't even divorced yet. We're separated and supposedly trying to salvage our marriage, and here's this young woman in tears asking me if Mark is cheating on her. She asked if he was at the house and if she could talk to him. I said he's not here and that he's in London *with his girlfriend there*, and she hung up. Was that mean of me? I don't even know anymore.

"I'm sorry, Agent Grale. I'm sorry to trap you with my problems and waste your time, but I just can't do this any longer. I've been fooling myself. But if I file for divorce, will the FBI agents watching the house stop protecting the kids?"

"The threat doesn't change, so no, I don't think they'll pull the agents. Although I also know they're reassessing how to best protect the families and those commuting to Indie to work."

"What, like on base? That would mean pulling the kids out of their school."

"I'll see what I can learn."

"I won't stop him from seeing his children, but don't drop him here anymore, no matter what he says. I'll work it out with him so he gets to see the kids as much as possible. But I am so done with it."

"Hang in there, Sylvie."

I was barely off the phone with her when Mara called. "Metro wants to reinterview you this morning."

"Yeah, my lawyer told me yesterday. I'm heading there soon."

"Good luck."

***

I found myself in a Metro police interview room sitting across from officer Wycher again and an undercover officer named Mary Fallon. I'd never met Fallon but recognized her name. She'd taken significant personal risk to bring down a drug ring a few years back. My lawyer, Brady, seemed to know her personally. They exchanged hellos and chatted before we got going.

Lighting in the room threw shadows in the hollows of Wycher's cheeks and made him look gaunt. He looked smaller and more compact than last time, but he was just as certain about himself and hostile. He gave me a tight-lipped smile and leaned back, watching me as Fallon launched into questions.

"Some of these will be very direct," she said and tucked her hair behind her left ear and straightened. "Please don't take offense that we're the ones to deliver the news. Guess what? You're not going to be charged with anything. You're probably more shocked than we are." She smiled at her next thought. "You could have blown off this meeting." She nodded toward Brady. "It would have saved you money on your lawyer."

"No has told me that," I said and to my right, Brady said, "Nor me. Why wasn't I called?"

"Because you would have skipped this meeting," Wycher said. "So the captain said we couldn't tell you. Like I told you before, he's not a big fan of the FBI."

"Tell your captain I'm going to bill him for this meeting," Brady said.

Wycher smiled big. He loved that he'd gotten under her skin.

"Good luck with that," Wycher said.

"And I'll copy the chief," she said. "I've known him a long time."

"Who says I'm not getting charged?" I asked.

"The DA's office," Wycher said. "They wussed out on us."

I put it together now. "Your captain asked that I not be told yet so you could ask more questions and hopefully get enough to change the DA's mind."

"You're too canny, Grale. Is that the right word? We didn't expect to get anything but more of the same. You're going to get to keep your pension, but how you wriggled out of this I can't figure."

"I can. It's easy, Wycher. You talk a lot, but you didn't come up with any evidence. You didn't build a case."

I watched his face harden, and it made me happy.

"We're not thrilled," Fallon said.

"I've told you the truth, but I have no faith in you either. All you want is to take me down. You've been driving hard for it, and now someone higher up undercut you. Your captain backed you, but the DA's office called bullshit on the lack of evidence. Is that right? You're champions of truth, and you got robbed. That's assuming what you've said about the charges getting dropped is true. Have they really been dropped?"

"Oh, they've been dropped," Wycher said. "Call the DA's office if you want and then get up and walk away or"—he pointed a finger at me—"we can watch some video of you and Poco."

"Play the video," I said, and he did, a clip that was roughly two minutes long.

"That's you looking around as you walk up alongside his car," Fallon narrated. "Just the two of you, and oh, look, let me freeze this. Isn't that you paying with cash? Yeah, there we go, those are twenties. Didn't you say all your buys were with a credit card? Didn't you tell us that? Oh, and then you're leaning against his car door as if you didn't want him to get out. You want to do the deal and get gone, right?"

"I'm leaning because my back hurts."

"And here he is handing over the pills, and that's you ripping the top off the prescription bottle as he drives away." She backed up, froze on me with my hand reaching out, and asked, "Do you agree this transaction was in cash?"

"Yes."

"Do you always carry bottled water when you do a buy?"

"Not always."

"Do you always scan the street like you're being watched?"

"I scan the street when I take out the garbage. That's just the way I am."

That got an unexpected smile from Wycher. Fallon followed with, "You reach in your car for bottled water to wash down the pill even though you live no more than half a mile away. Is that because you crave the pill so bad?"

"I'd run out of pills and was hurting."

"You run out a lot. How does it happen you're running out and needing more pills so often?"

"I have a degrading condition due to a bomb injury. The pain has gotten worse, but I try to take the minimum number of pills. I count every one and keep track."

"Your girlfriend or wife or whatever, she's a doctor, right?"

"Yes."

"Has she ever seen your injury?"

I sat on that comment several seconds, and Brady whispered, "Let's go, this is spite."

"Forget that last question," Fallon said, "but let's replay the video again, if you're up for it."

"Why replay?" I asked.

"Because you've got a look and a way that we associate with junkies, and leaving your neighborhood is a textbook move for a high-performing drug addict."

"I'm not the user you think I am. I've been telling you the truth. I made a bad mistake with Potello, and a lot of that was my pride. That's about all I have to say about it."

Wycher reacted. "Like Officer Fallon, I have a real hard time with your *injury* story but whatever. You get to skate, but at least we made sure it'll follow you. And I gotta tell you, your supervisor asked me my opinion. I told him you're a pill popper if I've ever seen one. He called and was worried, but I don't think it was about you. He's got ambition, your super. He wants to go to Washington and work at headquarters."

"Are you ever wrong?" I asked.

"It's happened, but I'm not seeing that here. By the way, I was in Afghanistan four tours."

"I heard that from a good old friend at Metro. He said you were stand-up."

"You checked into me?"

"Why wouldn't I, what with you trying to frame me and all?"

Wycher shifted so he was more face to face with me. He was about to say something much harder but Fallon beat him to it. She asked, "Would you mind if we got a look at your injury? I'm asking because we've got an office pool going, and Wycher and I have a lot riding on no injury. If there's nothing there, we win big, and I've got some things I'm looking forward to buying."

"And if you lose?"

Neither answered, and Brady stepped in saying, "Paul, please don't do it. At the FBI they know who you are. So do the people of Las Vegas. You don't have to do any of this crap."

I stood and untucked my shirt, unbuttoned it, and took it off as I faced them.

"Which side should we concentrate on when you turn around?" Wycher asked, "So we don't miss it."

"You'll figure it out," I said.

My scars are ugly scars. Jo said one is like a red spider as big as my hand with legs that reach around to my abdomen. Even Jo isn't really used to the scars, especially that hard lump of scar tissue the surgeon wants to cut out.

I turned around. Fallon made a sound, then they were both very quiet.

Wycher asked, "Where did that happen?"

"Bagdad. In a market."

He nodded but didn't say anything. Fallon looked down.

I said, "Look, I know I screwed up buying from Potello, but I'd known him for a decade before he started the business."

"I'm an asshole," Wycher said.

Brady said, "That's the only thing you've gotten right since this started."

I put my shirt back on, and Wycher, Fallon, and I made a point of shaking hands. It didn't mean we liked each other or ever would, but it was a way of saying good-bye.

34

When I got back to the office, Jace wasn't there but Mara was waiting for me. Jace had signed out on something personal and was due back midafternoon. Mara was in his office on a conference call. He held a finger up to keep me there and wrote on a piece of paper he slid toward me, *Give me ten minutes. Want to meet with you.*

I read that as a sign he'd already heard the DA wasn't going to charge me. We met in a conference room fifteen minutes later. Mara had heard. The DA's office called him earlier that morning.

"What time?" I asked.

"Between nine-thirty and ten. I didn't call you because I knew Metro wanted that final interview."

"And you thought it was important they get it?"

"I heard it went well."

"That's not what I asked."

There are times when you look at the face of someone you've known forever and see someone different. He looked back at me then shifted his eyes to the table and back to me. I put it together that he'd anticipated this meeting and was once again ahead of me.

"You've known they were unlikely to bring charges. Something got said to you before today," I said.

"I'd heard something. I didn't want to give you false hope, and there's no betrayal here, Paul. I never believed the charges, I've always been in your camp, but there are some hard realities."

"We'll get to them. I've got a few more questions for you."

"Go ahead."

"Who did you call this morning after the DA's office called you with the news they were dropping all charges?"

"ASAC Esposito."

"And who else?"

"No one."

"Did you tell anyone on our squad?"

"No."

"Did you talk to either of the Metro undercover officers before they interviewed me today?"

"Officer Wycher called me."

"Before or after the DA called you?"

"After. They knew charges had been dropped but wanted to proceed with the interview."

"And what did you say?"

There was a long quiet in the room before he answered. We've known each other a long time; we've worked a lot of cases together.

"I didn't think it would do any harm. Wycher wanted the interview, and I thought about the bigger picture, our ongoing relationship with the Metro police, and thought it might be for the best. I regret that decision. It put you in an unfair position."

"That's why you didn't call me. Did you tell Esposito that's what you were going to do?"

"I'm not sure."

"You're not sure?"

"I may have told him."

"And he agreed?"

"He said it was my decision, and by then you were probably in the interview."

"The two undercover officers, Wycher and Fallon, told me right away."

"They did?"

"Then we went forward with the interview."

"I'm sorry."

"I'm just putting pieces together, Ted."

"I'm very, very glad charges got dropped, but there are big issues that haven't gone away. The investigation by the Office of Professional Responsibility will take months. You know that as well as I do. It limits what I can assign you to because there's no guarantee you'll be here a year from now to testify on cases. Or you'll get suspended and I have to assign another agent and the chain of evidence gets weakened. We could get left apologizing that we don't have the agent who started the initial investigation because he got suspended and decided to resign. But I don't have to explain this. You know it as well as I do."

"So why are you explaining it, especially after you, Esposito, and I talked?"

"Then there's the question of whether you're fit for active duty, a question that would have come up whether or not the Potello fiasco happened."

"What would you do if you were me, Ted?"

"I'd look hard at my situation."

Mara had clean features, what people would call an honest face, even handsome, with a chiseled look and an easy smile. He was a popular supervisor, and as Wycher pointed out, he was ambitious. The FBI hadn't yet reached the level of the incessant Internet question that would sooner or later infiltrate even the

FBI: "On a scale of one to ten, how would you rate your experience with Supervisor Ted Mara this morning?"

We weren't there yet, and agents would laugh at the idea, but we might get there. Mara will do well if we do. He's made for that new world. I'm not.

"We need everybody right now," I said.

"We do, and you're right at the top for solve rate. I'd hate to lose you."

But you've been planning for it and you were surprised charges got dropped. So was Esposito.

"Did you think I'd bought street drugs, painkillers?"

"I never thought that."

"I want to believe that."

"It's true. Grale, you're the best investigator in the office. I've done everything I can to protect you. You've been a supervisor; you know the realities. I'm very glad charges got dropped. I wish I'd been there to hear the interview. Did your attorney ask for a copy of the interview video?"

"She did."

"Can you get a copy to me?"

"If and when we get it."

We both knew I'd never see a copy, but what went down in the interview room would get around. Brady, my lawyer, was very angry about it. She called it "demeaning and humiliating," but I felt something closer to relief showing them my scars. What Wycher said was true—cops need to see things. I'm the same way. It's why I had to drive to Panguitch Lake. It's what I was trying to show Jace: you can't do it all with a computer.

"Tell you what," I said, as we stood to leave the conference room, "I'll call my attorney. She wants to talk to you anyway. Her last name is Brady. I'll see if I can get her to call this morning."

"Good. I'd like to hear what happened."

"I'm betting she'll call you."

When I called Brady and gave her Mara's direct number, I also told her that Mara had gotten a call prior to the interview that charges were dropped.

"You've got to be kidding," she said. "Why would he do that? I'll call him right now."

35

JACE

Jace's father left on her sixth birthday. Went to work one morning and never came home. For years she blamed herself.

He left because . . . she had all kinds of reasons that had to do with her. She'd hunted for him and finally located him three years ago, but she still hadn't contacted him. Eddie Blujace was sixty-two and working for a firm that repaired heavy equipment. She'd driven by the business, a warehouse with a metal roof and rows of vehicles and machines outside. Funny that it could still affect her the way it did. The hurt was still there.

After her father left, her mother had boyfriends who stayed at the house. Mama didn't like to drink alone, and to be with her you had to be fun. To be fun you had to smoke dope and drink, but still be a man later in the night. Some of the boyfriends lasted months, most only weeks, if that. They couldn't handle the pace, but one, a tall, skinny guy with a made-up name, Jimmy Strings, made it almost two years.

The summer Jace turned sixteen the skinny man raped her while her mother was passed out drunk on the couch with the TV turned up loud. He came into her room quietly, got in bed with her, and put a big bony hand over her mouth. She woke and fought him, his thumb holding her jaw shut. He squeezed her nostrils shut, and as she struggled and forced her head back, he kept whispering, "You gonna quit fighting?"

She didn't tell her mother. She hadn't gone to the police. Where they lived, no one went to the police. What Jace did was leave.

At the FBI, as she'd gotten to know other agents in the San Francisco office where she'd worked four years, she made a kind of painting in her head so they would understand what the streets looked like where she grew up. The painting included the type of people living there and why the streets were safest near dawn. She put the agents in her old neighborhood, but she never took them inside the house.

But they're FBI, they're investigators, so they kept digging and asking, and now she was in a new office and the questions were there all over again. Same as when she and Grale went back to Ralin today, agents on the DT squad came back to her with new questions. Her current version was more heavily themed on an alcoholic parent. There were plenty of those to go around, so the agents absorbed that more easily. The full thing was, *My mom was an alcoholic and messed up. My father left. I owe my aunt, my mom's sister, everything.*

The night she was raped she went out her bedroom window and called her aunt Lilly, who took her in over the phone right there. That had been and still was the single biggest act of kindness anyone had done for her in her lifetime. Driving now through the summer dusk heat in Las Vegas, she could still easily feel what it was like when her aunt had said, "You're going to come live with me."

Her aunt Lilly worked long hours and saw sixteen as more than old enough to be independent and responsible. That's how Lilly had shaped her, independent and responsible.

Jace took the next exit and went left at the underpass, not more than a mile from her father's house.

Way back when, but years after her father left, a local wannabe drug gang loomed large. She was bright and tough, but tough doesn't protect you from gangs. Neither does bright. There was a twenty-three year old, Teddy Duluth, who called himself TD. He came up behind her, wrapped an arm around her shoulders, and said, "I want you to come work for me."

"Doing what? What do you do besides sell drugs?"

"We'll find something for you."

He never let up. He gave her presents, rides home, even tried to give her a car. He bought books he was told were things she'd want to read. He'd reach for her, touch her, put his arm around her, walk her halfway down the sidewalk with one of his dudes carrying her pack. He wanted to own her and pressed her to leave her mother's house and stay with him. He'd give her money.

That all ended when she moved in with Aunt Lilly. At nineteen, Jace had a high school diploma with midrange grades and a year and a half at junior college where she felt like she was fighting all the time to catch up. She'd known she wasn't making it in a way that mattered.

She quit junior college and walked into an Army recruiting station. She'd traded with the Army, figuring they'd keep their word mostly. A year in the Army for a year of college later. They taught her discipline comes from inside. You make yourself something. Dreams don't make things happen. You do.

Then college, and a conversation at an FBI recruiting station one afternoon changed her direction and her life. It wasn't overnight, but when it finally happened, it gave her identity. It gave her purpose. She was working hard now to get better at investigating, but she was still messed up in some ways inside. Things she hadn't dealt with, things that needed to be dealt with.

In San Francisco her boyfriend became her fiancé. His wealthy liberal mother didn't like him being with someone of mixed race, but they didn't care. He had motorcycles and taught her to ride. They were riding in Marin on a beautiful morning when he got hit by a car and was now brain-dead. Still numb with shock, she'd visited him once a week until his mother said, "Never come here again. If he'd never met you, this never would have happened."

Why was all this coming up now? She knew why. She'd taken a career risk messing with Potello. How and where Grale took what drugs he needed was his to deal with, not hers. His goofball arrangement with Potello was nothing she could solve. So why had she done it?

She'd thought about that a lot. In a way she was trying to protect Grale. She'd learned so much from him. Grale knew how to press and when to hold back in interviews. He had a natural feel for people. She knew she had it too but she was still learning things from him, how to move with the right question, how to be quiet and let people come to it their own way. Grale gave her confidence. He'd helped her. He wasn't trying to make her respect him. He was trying to make her respect herself. There, that was the true thing. That's why she liked him so much. That's why she'd done that crazy thing with Potello. She thought about that with her heart pounding as she knocked on her dad's door.

36

JACE

When she approached the house, Jace saw a man in the backyard and in an instant knew it was her father. She leaned over a short wooden fence to call out to him.

"That you, Eddie Blujace?"

Maybe he didn't hear, maybe it wasn't him. She moved to the porch and rang the doorbell and tried it again before knocking. Her mother always said her father was a drug user, but her aunt Lilly said, "That's your mother lying."

Jace was close to leaving when she heard firm footsteps. The door swung open, and she didn't need the photo. It was her father.

"If you're selling something, no thank you," he said.

"I'm not."

"Okay, then?"

"Don't you recognize me?"

He looked. She saw his eyes change, his disbelief. She said, "Invite me in."

He stepped back to do that and said, "Kristen? Kristen, oh my God, child," and she stepped in.

He smiled but looked puzzled, as if he didn't know what to do with her. He didn't reach out and hug her. "This is a big surprise. How did you find me?"

"I just moved to Las Vegas," she said. "I live here now."

"You do? You work in Vegas? Doing what?"

"FBI."

"FBI? My daughter is FBI?"

She took him in as he looked her over. His face was smooth, his skin good, hair black and gray. She got the feeling he lived alone and liked it that way. He had the same cheekbones Aunt Lilly used to say were from Cherokee blood.

"I recognize you, daughter."

He opened his arms, and it was an awkward hug but she needed it, and stronger emotions welled in her as he led her into his kitchen.

"I'm sorry, Kristen, sorry for everything. I've thought about you so many times."

"Did you ever look for me?"

"For a long time, I knew where you were. But . . . but I thought you were better off without me."

"Why?"

"Because what was done was done."

"I don't understand. Did you know I moved in with Aunt Lilly?"

"I knew."

"Then why didn't you reach out? She was your sister."

"Because I'd left, and time had gone by. I didn't think you'd respect me, and I understood that. But I thought about you all the time, Kristen. I still think about you every day. You're my big regret."

"They call me Jace."

He smiled. "They do that with me too. Are you married?"

"No."

"You're an FBI agent?"

"That scare you?"

"No, but I never met one before."

She showed him her ID.

"Look at that," he said, then stalled and fumbled around with *so good to see you* and apologies without looking at her. Her heart was sinking, but then he said, "FBI, how about that? I'm proud of you and sorry for what I've never done. I'd apologize if I could."

"What's that mean?"

"That I wish I hadn't lost you."

"I'm standing right here."

"I just can't believe it, but it sure enough is you. It's you, Kristen. I see that."

They talked in his kitchen and made a plan for her to come to dinner. It was all over in less than half an hour. When she drove away, she felt a hollowed-out sadness and knew why. She'd just sat and talked to an older man still working hard and getting on toward retirement. He was her father. And he didn't know her.

Maybe they'd get to know each other, or maybe the truth just got driven home. She'd thrown out a few names she remembered from where they'd lived. He hadn't remembered any of them. He even had trouble remembering the name of the street. That one really got her. *Didn't remember the street.* It was all gone for him. *We're strangers,* she thought. Tears ran down her cheeks. She drove and wept, and her phone rang. Mara. She pulled over and took a few deep breaths before taking his call.

37

DALZ

When he walked in, Dalz saw well-cared-for tools and a pickup that was older but clean. Sean nodded toward the pair of Hispanic carpenters there to build the missile assembly tables. Preassembly was complete. They were on to the next steps. Dalz drove the boom lift out of the way, and the carpenters moved their pickup inside. Without explanation Sean had them turn their truck around so it faced out toward the big folding doors of a former bowling alley and restaurant.

Dalz then showed the carpenters his drawing and explained how to build the four twelve-foot-long by four-foot-wide tables and secure them to the floor so they wouldn't wobble. He'd marked where the wooden table legs would attach with metal clips to the flooring. Cross bracing would reinforce the legs and join them so the tables became sturdy platforms.

He spoke Spanish and answered questions as they built the first table, and then he picked apart small imperfections to drive home the point that they needed to be exact and would have to build a replacement for this one. The next three tables they finished in three and a half hours and were perfect.

The carpenters dripped sweat but smiled. They were good men, modest and efficient, and Sean paid each a hundred-dollar bonus after they'd swept up and put their tools away. When they were ready to leave but not yet in their truck, Sean pulled a gun and explained to the carpenters that they needed to get into the back seat of their pickup and lie on their sides with their knees pulled up.

"I know what you're thinking," he said, and Dalz translated. "Nothing will happen to you if you do as I say. Lie down and stay quiet and you won't get hurt. We'll drive ten miles then give you back your truck. No worries. *No problemo.* This is not cartel. Don't worry."

Sean handed the carpenters another two hundred dollars each while apologizing and telling them to pull the tarp not just over them but tight around them. He leaned over as they covered their bodies and drew the tarp tight. The larger one trembled and prayed.

"Perfecto," Sean said and started the engine as he handed the gun to Dalz, who gauged where their heads were and held the barrel no more than eight inches away. He shot both twice quickly then shot the one who'd spasmed a third time. The bowels of one released, but Sean didn't seem to mind and turned on the radio as Dalz handed the gun back.

Dalz followed in his car south twenty miles then five and a half more along a desert road. Sean left the radio on after they stopped. He swung his door open and sliced through a bag of cocaine then spilled it across the passenger seat and into the footwell before dropping it there. He locked the doors with the windows up tight and the engine off and said nothing as he got into Dalz's car.

Several miles later he threw the truck keys into mesquite and said, "You'll install the cradles tonight. Missile housings will be delivered. After that, assembly of all remaining parts begins." He turned and asked, "Do you have a problem that the carpenters are dead?"

"None."

"But there's something. I can feel it. You're tense. Is this worry, or is it that you're used to working alone? If you're uncomfortable, you can still leave. You can walk away. I'll let you do that now that the preassembly is done."

There was no walking away, and Dalz was careful with his answer.

"I am a . . . I don't remember the correct English word. But things made exact. I like things exact. I focus until that's done. I understood what you said before, and I'm fine. We don't need to keep having this conversation. If you need to kill me, let me build the missiles first. It's why I am here."

Dalz didn't know why, but that got through to Sean.

"I want to stay," Dalz added.

"Then we're good."

38

Mara scheduled a squad meeting for late afternoon. I knew Jace had finally gone to see or confront her father—I wasn't sure which—but she made it back in time for us to do another Starbucks coffee walk and talk ahead of the meeting.

"Sure, let's do it," I said. We walked slowly and I figured Jace would talk about her father, but that wasn't what she had in mind.

"I did something I'm angry at myself about," she said. "I may need counseling or a new career," Jace said. "I'm not kidding. I really screwed up and in a way that makes me wonder if somewhere inside I want to get kicked out of the FBI because I don't think I'm worthy."

"I know the feeling. In my first few years as an FBI agent I'd rush investigations. I'd get to ninety percent of the evidence and think I'd get the rest in a confession, but it didn't always work that way. But are you sure you want to tell me?"

"I should. It involves you."

In the bright sunlight outside, she squinted sideways at me and said, "Supervisor Mara recruited me to help investigate you the day I drove down from the Bay Area. I was still in

California when he called. He wanted someone from outside so rumors didn't spread. I pulled off at the next exit, almost turned around and went back to the Bay Area."

"Good you didn't."

"It was out of the blue," she said. "I didn't see it coming or know how to deal with it."

Some of this she'd already said, and I'd put a certain amount together on my own. We cut off our conversation as we went into Starbucks and ordered. I waited outside with a black coffee as Jace's latte got made. When she came out, I was standing in the shade along the building where we were out of earshot of anybody.

"I grew up around drugs. I know how the system deals. Courts get manipulated," Jace said then took a deep breath. "I waited for Potello after he got released. He didn't know what was going on. He was out on surprise bail and blinking in sunlight with a slicked-up cartel lawyer yelling at him to get in a car. He looked like a kid whose parents forgot him at a gas station on a family trip, but he was smart enough to avoid the cartel goon screaming at him."

"You saw all that?"

"Yes. I'd driven there thinking I might catch him coming out then talk to him."

"About what?"

"You."

"Why, Jace? Why take that kind of risk?"

"I don't know. But I didn't threaten him or anything. I just fed him some bullshit I sort of made up on the spot."

"Don't tell me what you said to him."

"I have to tell you, at least a little. I won't tell you much, and you don't have to tell me how bad a call I made." Jace paused, then said, "I tried to convince him he got his dates wrong about when he sold to you. I said you were out of town on a couple of the dates he had down for sales. He said he'd fix those and some mumbled crap about it being a computer problem."

Hearing that swept aside the buoyant feeling I had walking out of the Metro police station. What Jace was saying disappointed me.

"That could easily be a career-ending move," I said. "He goes back and tells somebody you threatened him, then they go back through the video and find you talking with him . . . What were you thinking?"

"That you cleared Metro undercover but could still get framed! I've seen drugs planted, people framed. Careers get built on top of other people. Once the momentum starts, it's hard to stop."

"How can you have as much talent as you have and do something that stupid?"

"I don't know."

"I don't believe that. You know yourself better than that."

I said that but didn't know if she'd answer. After a minute or more, she did.

"At times I don't think I'm good enough. I don't deserve to be here. That's it, that's really the truth. There are mornings when I think I don't belong in the FBI. I'm a fake somehow."

I faced her and said, "I've worked with a lot of FBI agents and I promise you, you're more than good enough. If you take yourself out by not believing in yourself, it'll be the mistake of a lifetime. You one hundred percent belong here. Not only that, but if you keep getting better, you'll rise right up. Whatever's going on, you need to figure it out or find a therapist or someone to talk to. Don't blow up your career, you are way too good. And you're needed."

She took that in. "I have a crazy streak. Mara's taken a liking to me, I think, and I want to tell him he's wrong. And I should tell him what I did. Shouldn't I?"

"What's the crazy streak?"

"I see something and know it's going down a certain way that's wrong but I can't just stand by and watch. I can't deal."

"You have to learn to. I had something of that streak until it got to a place where I scared myself enough. You need a code you follow and to make peace with your doubts about yourself."

"I don't understand why I confronted Potello. No, I know *why*, but I just don't know why I let it happen."

I wasn't sure if she was hearing me.

"I'm going to say it again, Jace. You need a personal code you never violate. A way you do things and a way you don't. You don't hesitate and debate. It's a no-hesitation thing."

"I get that."

"So put it to yourself and either turn the badge in or change."

***

Half an hour later, we were in a conference room with a lot of the DT squad, and Mara talking about Dalz and some other new leads. I gave a rundown on Dalz.

"He's known to most intelligence agencies you've worked with or heard of," I said. "The Russians have tracked him, and Mossad, Interpol, MI6, CIA, NSA, you name it, but the French know him best. They believe Frederic Dalz is his true name. I've tried to trace it back but got nowhere. The French call him the Numbers Man, a moniker that goes to something they found in a hotel room after he fled ahead of a raid.

"He left behind a drawing of people sitting around a long table. Each person at the table was numbered, but there was no obvious correlation between them. Number three sat next to number seventeen who was next to thirteen and so forth.

"The French have the most complete file. They think the reason his background is so hard to trace is that he was chosen at a young age for aptitude in math, physics, and chemistry, then tutored in near seclusion for most of his childhood and adolescence."

Mara shook his head and said, "Our psychological profiles have him as withdrawn, unable to communicate well, and stunted socially."

"He's more nuanced," I said, "and from the little we know, often the opposite of what they concluded. He can be a talker and gregarious. He likes people. If you want it firsthand, call the border patrol agents at Metaline Falls and ask if Dalz was a quiet guy. Two witnesses may give widely different descriptions. It's not unusual with him. It mystified the French. It could be he's that good of a character actor. Sometimes witnesses sound as if they weren't looking at the same guy. If you find him, check with your partner before you write your report."

That got a chuckle and a couple of smiles. Everyone was tired, and in truth I wasn't one hundred percent on board with the conviction Dalz was here to attack a heavily guarded DoD project. An airliner, a high-speed train, a televised soccer final, that's Dalz, but a US government military base? That's a lot to take on. I threw out another idea.

"It's possible Dalz had no choice but to accept a role on a paramilitary team put together by an adversary of ours, someone who has sheltered Dalz from other intelligence agencies and is now funding mercenaries who can't be directly traced if caught or killed. Could be they protected him for years and he owed them. But, as far as we know, he's avoided the US, so why now? That's the big question."

"A big payout, maybe?" an agent said. "Isn't there something like a billion dollars in the AI and that new base? So, say he gets five million and a paid vacation in America. He gets headlines and big money."

"But he's always avoided the States," I said. "Or that's what Interpol and the CIA think. It's always been a part of the puzzle, so maybe that was wrong or has changed or maybe he owes whoever has protected him all these years. That's what I think is going on."

"You think he was coerced into this operation, Grale?"

"I'd guess he's been involved with one of our enemies a long time. I don't know about coerced, but maybe he owes, and the payoff is large, so it's a combination. Attacking Indie, a top-secret AI machine of the United States, is something only a rival nation could contemplate. That could be what we're seeing. They field a strictly mercenary team sent to make a statement or, if really lucky, damage or destroy Indie. Either way, a message gets sent about what they're willing to risk.

"Dalz is a sophisticated infiltrator and a survivor," I added. "He has the kind of skills that would make him useful assembling missiles. That fits, but we may be focusing too much on him. Others on this alleged team might be easier to find."

"That's what I've been saying," a burly agent named Hidalgo said. "Why aren't we targeting the rest and letting them lead us to him?"

"No one is really getting anywhere," Mara said and he turned to me. "We're no closer. Everybody, let's put our heads together and come up with a new approach."

Jace jumped in saying, "We've reached out to commercial property owners, managers, and real estate firms leasing in the Las Vegas Valley. We're asking for their help searching all commercial leased spaces and other private buildings big enough to assemble missiles in. We're trying to cover all of Vegas in the next four days."

"Good," Mara said. "And why haven't I heard about this?"

"Because you stopped talking to me after that pound of heroin was found in my locker," I said. This time I got genuine laughter plus a smile from Mara.

But it wasn't as though I was back on the squad. I wasn't.

"We'll add agents to the commercial property searches," Mara said. "Let's go, everybody, there's still daylight. Whatever it takes. Let's break this wide open."

39

"That pale-green building off to the right at the next exit up ahead is the next stop," Jace said. "She said she'd be waiting for us on the south end of the building. Look for a white Mercedes. Her name is Tory Binelle. Before we get there, let me tell you a couple of things I just learned from Mara. One you already know. The body found is officially Alan Eckstrom's. What's new is there are traces of obscure drugs in Eckstrom's blood, and Mara's fine with you touring me through the mine where his body was found."

"You don't want to do that with me. I'll give you the cell number of the Lincoln County investigator, or get with the other agents working the murder. At least a half dozen of them have been in the mine. Where do you fit in?"

"That's not clear yet."

"If you're moved to that, we're done working together for now."

"I know, I get it, but let's see what happens. I really don't think Mara will move me onto the murder investigation. He just wants me to be up to speed."

We pulled into a large parking lot and I pointed out a white Mercedes. With Tory Binelle we walked the long green building and looked at forty-nine leased and empty spaces. Binelle told us she'd gotten her start as a real estate agent and saved and bought and worked her way into ownership of 60,000 square feet of commercial space in the Las Vegas Valley. She knew several other developers and was more than willing to make calls. She was a godsend for us.

She left her car behind and rode with us. She knew every inch of her buildings and knew who owned what buildings and who the tenants were in many others. We drove until after sunset with her, until we couldn't see well enough. Nothing we saw or walked through looked suspicious, but the two hours with her and her thirty-two years of knowledge about commercial buildings in the Las Vegas area was very helpful. That included her sense of where to look for the empty, begging-to-be-rented square footage where owners wouldn't be asking many questions.

The next morning at dawn, Jace and I drove more of Binelle's list of commercial spaces. We were close to done with that list when Ralin texted me. I handed my phone to Jace and she read aloud, "On board British Airways 946 London to San Francisco. Made an emergency landing after the passenger cabin filled with smoke. White smoke. Chemical smell. FBI bomb unit flying in from NYC."

I turned to Jace. "Call him. If he answers, put him on speakerphone."

She did and I asked Ralin, "What happened? I just got your message. Are you okay?"

"We made it down, but it was scary. I looked up from my laptop when I smelled something acrid, and suddenly the cabin filled with smoke. There was a bitter taste to it. I'm disturbed enough to consider quitting the project."

"Quit Indie over smoke on your flight home?" I asked.

"People are saying it's very likely a bomb attempt."

"That doesn't mean it was for you."

"A woman spit on me yesterday. A man jostled me in a restaurant. They recognize me and don't like me because they're afraid of AI. That bomb was in the luggage of someone on the plane. I'm not being protected the way I should be. I was followed again in London. I can't deal with things as they are. I'm going to step back and think it over. I just can't take it anymore. I'm on the edge of saying it's not worth it for me to continue."

"Where are you now?"

"About to board a flight to JFK and then San Francisco. I go from there to Las Vegas, but I may not go to the base. I may quit Indie. I don't know what I'm going to do yet."

"What can we do to help you?" I asked as Jace whispered, "Why is he telling us?"

"You can't do anything. Alan's death haunts me. I'm responsible somehow. I'm very down, and now this attempt to kill me . . . I have to go now to catch my flight."

He ended the call a moment later and I said, "We should relay that on to Mara."

Before we called Mara, he called us, and that was several hours later. We figured with Ralin in the air we had plenty of time, so we stayed focused on our search.

"MI6 reached out," Mara said. "They told us that yesterday Ralin staged—as in faked—waiting at a bridge for an hour in London for Claire Henley."

"How did they know it was staged?" I asked.

"It's a bridge where they routinely meet each other. Henley wasn't *in* London yesterday. Five days ago, she flew to Paris then Barcelona and on to Africa before flying to Rio. No one knows, but the suspicion is she's meeting Ralin somewhere. But there's a twist: Ralin's plane made an emergency landing. The plane had filled with smoke—"

"We called him. He seems to think it was a failed bomb attack on him. He talked about stress and possibly quitting the project. He said Eckstrom's death haunts him."

"Why tell you?"

"My guess is the bomb scare shook him up."

"All right, that's probably it. How is it going with the buildings? Any luck?"

"Not yet."

We put Ralin out of mind and worked a western section of Vegas. Our search ate up hours and then we were on the phone with Mara again.

"An update," he said. "Ralin has landed at SFO and is on his way across the bay to Oakland. He's going to catch an earlier Southwest flight to Vegas. As you said, he's shaken up and believed the British Airways flight fire in the luggage compartment was a bomb attempt to kill him. We're hearing that a laptop battery caught fire. Ralin called several reporters and a TV station before getting on a flight to San Francisco and told them he'd had a close call with a bomber targeting him. He went on a rant about being suspected but not protected and that his family is in danger. Agent Blujace, you there?"

"I'm right here and listening," Jace said. "What's his Southwest flight number?"

"I'll get it to you and when he lands in Vegas, I want you two there to meet him. He knows you and seems to trust you, Grale, though I wouldn't call that a compliment."

I smiled at that. That was more like the old Mara.

When Mara signed off, Jace and I picked it apart. We couldn't make much sense of diverting us to babysit an exhausted, paranoid Ralin. We kicked it around as we drove, walked buildings, and then headed to the airport. I called Kathy Tobias before we got there.

"I was just thinking about you," she said. "What's on your mind?"

"I'm thinking about Indie Base and Bismarck, who despite our warning is still encouraging his followers to go to the base and mind-meld with the AI."

"DoD is also worried. They're regrading old desert roads and augmenting the defenses and intercept plans. No one wants any injuries or more fatalities. I know you had a run-in with a DoD officer, but internally there's a lot of concern about the four teenagers killed. As you pointed out, Indie had all the information needed to identify them and did identify them as Las Vegas–area high school students. There's a new deflecting defense they're trying out with high numbers of small drones."

"How many *large* armed drones are there to defend the building?" I asked. "We're looking for ballpark numbers to get a sense of what the AI defends versus what those at the base will man in an active attack."

"There are twenty-six armed drones, and all but two are controlled by the AI."

"What about the surface-to-air missiles?"

"AI."

"Long guns?"

"AI."

"What doesn't it control?"

"Man-operated mobile fighting platforms. Anything mobile with an HE—human element—required to operate is under base security command, hence the roadwork. That includes several helicopters."

"Any attack helicopters?"

"You're thinking if they come at the building with all-terrain vehicles on graded roads and have a way to jam Indie's communications, they might reach the building."

"I'm wondering what we should be watching for outside the base."

"Call Bob Wharton at DoD. He's war-gamed a number of scenarios. He'll know who can help coordinate with the FBI.

I'll let him know you might call. How would *you* attack the building, Grale?"

"By cutting the DoD budget in half."

We both laughed, and I saw Jace smile.

"DoD has something they call 'express vulnerabilities,'" she said, "vulnerabilities that are difficult to protect in multiple ways. One of those is that we don't know how the AI will react in a simultaneous attack situation. It has war-gamed all of this internally millions of times, but it'll be an actual attack that determines whether this truly is a new generation of AI. Speaking of which, there's a high-level rumor that Indie has encountered something like itself in the Internet ether."

"That's spooky."

"I don't know if it's that, but it's worrisome. Let me ask the same question of you again: How would you attack Indie?"

"Asymmetrically. I'd try to cut off its ability to communicate with weapon systems."

"You and me both," she said, and we talked more, and then had a longer, quieter conversation about whether a known adversary would risk a sabotage operation to destroy Indie.

"I go back to the atomic bomb comparison," she said. "Indie is game-changing technology on a large scale. If I were an adversary, I'd be doing everything I could to stop the United States from getting there first."

"At the risk of starting a war?"

"They will have thought that through so that doesn't happen."

Our call ended just before Jace and I reached our next search site. We walked twenty-two more buildings with no more success that the prior walks. But we did cross this group off our list and were back on the road when Mara called and said, "Ralin's Uber failed to arrive at Oakland Airport."

"No one was tailing the Uber?"

"I don't know what happened, but the Uber driver was redirected by Ralin to San Jose Airport. In San Jose he didn't enter the terminal and we don't know yet where he went from there. You two get on a flight to the Bay Area. Our best guess is that Ralin is with a former Stanford colleague or someone else he knew when he lived there."

"What's the point of both of us going if the San Francisco office is engaged in the search?" Jace asked. "Grale knows him best, and we're shorthanded here."

"You both go."

The way Mara said that didn't leave any room. The message was clear: I don't go anywhere alone. Mara didn't want to say it, but for me it was an easy read.

"Get your gear and head to McCarran Airport," he said. "I'll text you as I learn more."

40

I called Indonal as Jace and I headed to the airport. After all the years at Stanford with Ralin and Eckstrom, Indonal should know the names of Ralin's friends. It turned out that he had more names than phone numbers. He offered to make a couple of calls, thinking that he'd have a better chance of getting an answer, so we took him up on that. He called back before we flew to Oakland with a tip he'd gotten from an unnamed professor of computer science who got it from a friend.

"Complicated," I said.

"I know. But it fits. Anytime Mark feels screwed up or is trying to work through a problem with something we're working on, he heads for water, a lake, ocean, whatever. It works for him. The professor I talked with knows someone who owns a house in Stinson Beach. Mark has borrowed it before. I think I've even been there."

"But you're not sure?"

"Not a hundred percent sure."

"Could you find it?"

"I doubt it. It was a long time ago and a kind of barbecue thing at sunset, so it got dark pretty soon after I got there. I remember going through a security gate to get into the area with houses. It was toward the end of the beach and it wasn't a big house, but it was a great spot, and the door from the main room opened onto kind of a patio and then it was just beach and ocean."

"How sure are you about the security gate?"

"There was definitely a gate."

"The professor didn't give you an address?"

"He wouldn't even say Mark was there."

"But you think he communicated that?"

"Yes."

"And you trust the tip?"

"Yes."

"Keep your phone close."

"Okay."

Jace and I waited to call Mara until after we'd ridden the BART airport connector and had caught a train from Oakland to San Francisco and borrowed a car from the FBI office there. That kept us out of the East Bay commute traffic, and since Jace was known in the SF FBI office, getting a car was easy. Mara was harder. Mara was angry.

"You should have called me after you got off the phone with Indonal."

"We didn't need to talk it through," I said. "And then we were in the air for an hour. It's summer. We'll still have daylight when we get there, but to maximize that we got on a BART train as soon as we were off the plane and made a beeline for the FBI office. Two SF agents are following us out to Stinson. They'll be about a half hour behind us. The SF office was able to get us the code to get through the gate."

"Where are you now?"

"Crossing the Golden Gate."

"Once you're through that gate at Stinson Beach, call me."

"We'll call you when we can or when we know something. But we'll call you," I said.

I ended the call and Jace asked, "Was it worth saying that last part? It's going to light him up."

"It will, but if you're in the field you've got to push back. Otherwise, a supervisor will tell you how to investigate. You're the investigator, not your supervisor. You've got to remember that. I've learned that the hard way."

We crossed into Marin and took the Stinson exit and went partway up Mount Tam, and then down to Stinson Beach. We were lucky to have the San Francisco agents and an additional pair that followed them—we needed all the help we could get going house to house. We had Indonal's description of a house right on the beach, although we couldn't count on Ralin to answer the door.

And he didn't. We were at a house with no car or cars parked out front and were down to a few houses left that fronted ocean. I walked around the side for a look. I was checking for a patio or deck facing the beach. Someone outside wouldn't necessarily hear a door knock with the heavy surf.

Ralin was there when I came around the corner, facing the ocean with one foot up on a low rock wall. He didn't see me, and I didn't want to startle him. I looked for Henley, didn't see her, and then waited for Jace.

"Dr. Ralin," I said and he turned and looked at me as if he didn't recognize me. When he did, his face fell. Jace called the SF agents to give them an address. Before they arrived, we confirmed Ralin was there alone. He'd picked up a rental car at SJC. That car was in the garage. He said he planned to stay here four or five days.

"I need the break," he said. "I have to have it and it's none of your business. Thank you for your interest, but leave me alone."

"Is anyone joining you?"

When I asked that, he just stared and I glanced at Jace, who then repeated the question.

"Is that why you're here?" he asked.

"You were due into Las Vegas on a flight you didn't show up for. That led to a search for you."

"Well, you found me. Congratulations, now leave me alone."

"Is anyone else staying here with you?"

"No."

It was hours before he told us. When he did, it was in a faltering voice as if he was piecing together fragments.

"Claire was going to join me at the airport in San Francisco. Her flight got in earlier. I had my carry-on bag and was going to call her as I got outside. Then we'd go get a car and come here."

I pretty well knew from his face what happened but asked anyway.

"She called," he said, "to say good-bye. She didn't get on her plane to the States and said she would never see or talk to me again and not to look for her. She wouldn't say why. She said, 'Forget about me. Forget you ever knew me.' I don't know what to do with that. We've talked about the future so much, I just don't understand."

We listened, we questioned, and then Jace stepped away and called Mara. I heard the back-and-forth. It struck me as one of those situations where you could overthink it. The simplest answer was that Henley was the spy the intelligence services claimed she was and had gotten all the information she was likely to get or was extracted for other reasons. My guess was, extracted for other reasons.

Ralin was head over heels in love with her and had just told us they'd made plans for their future together, but he wasn't a fool. If Henley was a spy and her organization had extracted her to avoid an espionage arrest, he'd get it. Right now, he was just shocked. He didn't know what to make of it.

The next morning, we flew home with a heartbroken Ralin. His last words as we dropped him off were "I've been a fool."

"Maybe you caught a lucky break," I answered.

Every human being is a contradiction, but my thoughts weren't on Ralin. I did keep turning over the timing of Henley's extraction. Was there a message in that timing? I kept circling that. Maybe it was as simple as she'd done all she could and the risks outweighed any future benefits. Or there was a darker answer—that they knew an operation was coming that would lead to her arrest. Could it mean an attack on Indie Base was about to happen?

41

AUGUST 12TH

We sat with Mara for an hour summarizing what we'd learned from interviewing Ralin. Mara listened but looked distracted as it didn't matter anymore.

"You did great work on short notice," he said. "DoD called to thank you both. Let's move on to what's happened since you left here."

"We saw a news clip this morning of chain-link fencing being pulled down," I said. "And aerial shots of the vehicles parked along the shoulder of 95 North."

"All kinds of people have made it onto the base and gotten arrested. It's a mess. The perimeter of that base is so big and so much of it is so remote . . . well, you know all this. What you don't know is Bismarck may be there. The AI is using drones to get clear images of the faces of the trespassers. Something north of eighty-five percent have been identified. One of them may be Bismarck. I'll show you what they sent us. They know the general area that the individual believed to be Bismarck is in. I'm debating sending you out there to help look for him. If he's arrested, we do the handoff with DoD and you take charge of him."

"Yeah, we'll go," Jace said and Mara held up a hand.

"Hold on, let's talk this through. It's 111 degrees out there. Soldiers are doing rescues as well as arrests. Some people walked onto the base in flip flops, shorts, and T-shirts, no water. It's nuts. What you two know, or Grale does, is that the AI is going to locate them all and probably identify ninety-five percent of them. The problem is the half-mile inviolable line. They're using bullhorns and loudspeakers to warn the trespassers, and no one has gotten close yet, but they're worried. Some of these trespassers made it up and over the ridge to the east and are working their way down, which takes us back to Bismarck."

"I'm not following," Jace said, but I could see where this was going.

"They want Bismarck to call his followers off by warning them they can't cross that half-mile line. Grale, will he do that? Do you have an opinion? At the base, they're asking and hoping you can help convince him. They want to avoid any more fatalities. You two would be going out there with that mission, but you'd be driving into complete chaos. They say they're getting it under control but we've got one of our spotter planes up this morning. They see trespassers everywhere."

"What's their estimate?" I asked.

"Four hundred plus people, including a handful of children and people without water walking in flip flops. There will be heatstroke deaths."

"And they know the general area Bismarck is in?"

"So they say. They think he came from the north end. There's an unpaved road that runs the perimeter and then around the back of the mountains. You probably know it. He got as far as he did because so many people trespassed at more or less the same time. It seems there was some coordination with that and when they cut the chain-link fence posts with battery-powered tools along the south side. Police were outnumbered."

"Who do we contact?" I asked.

"They'll meet you at the guard gate. Take one of the four-wheel or all-wheel vehicles and good luck. Take radios. Take water and beef up your first-aid gear, but you're not out there on a rescue mission. You're out there to get that bastard. Call me after you've met with DoD at the guard gate, or text me you've connected with them and it's a go."

Jace and I drove out in the blistering heat and brightness. It was that hot already. We passed through a police cordon and met up with the two DoD agents we used to meet with monthly. They'd been ordered to wear bulletproof vests and were streaming in sweat. The heat was too much with the vests on, so we didn't dawdle in the sun. We followed their vehicle on the flat road across the desert plain toward the Indie building.

We saw people walking and passed arrests in progress, and then realized what the DoD had done. The circumference of the mile-wide-diameter surrounding the base was just over three miles. To prevent deaths, they'd focused on intercepting trespassers before they reached that line. There wasn't a road that circled the three miles, and some of it reached up the spine of mountains behind.

"Why can't they just disarm the AI or shut it down for twenty-four hours?" Jace asked.

"They aren't going to, and I agree. We know bots originating in Eastern Europe helped drive people to Bismarck's dark web site. He's been preaching for six months how he's going to mind-meld with Indie and urging followers to do the same. They've given Indie control of almost all surveillance and a lot of the defensive weapons; shut it down and the base becomes more vulnerable to attack."

"With Nellis Air Force Base sitting in Las Vegas, you've got to be kidding. They can bring in all kinds of defenses."

"They're probably doing that, but the problem right now is I doubt they're comfortable shutting Indie down."

Dust devils swirled to the north and south as we followed the DoD agents across the desert plain toward the half-subterranean Indie building. Something glittering along the mountains caught my eye. A shifting, changing shape toward the northeast reflected shifting bright flickers of light. It was large and flowing like something draped in the sky.

"Look left along the mountains, Jace."

"I'm already looking. What is that and the dark thing inside?"

"I think we're looking at a helicopter surrounded by small drones."

"There must be hundreds of them," Jace said. "Have you ever seen this?"

"Never."

"They're coming our way."

Jace brought up binoculars. "I can see the helicopter. It's headed toward that airfield, and the things, the drones, are surrounding it. It looks like they're trying to block him."

As we got closer, we talked with the DoD agents just ahead of us who were watching the same thing. The pilot's movements looked erratic and dangerous. I could almost feel the fear in the helicopter as the drones enveloped it from above and flowed like water beneath. When they blocked the pilot from landing on the airstrip, it looked like he aimed for the road we were on. Behind the helicopter, a glittering wall of drones broke like a cresting wave.

"They're spooky fast," Jace said. "I didn't know a drone could move that fast. The way the cloud moves . . . I remember it from somewhere." A moment later, she said, "YouTube. I've seen that formation on YouTube. Birds. Starlings. Starlings do all that folding and unfolding. The murmurations of starlings. Did the AI get that from them?"

Before I could answer, the pilot executed an emergency landing maneuver, spinning down from several hundred feet up. They hit hard not far from the airstrip. With the DoD agents, we raced to the rescue. Dust billowed as the main helicopter rotor blade snapped. A piece cartwheeled through mesquite. I hit the accelerator, and we got as close as we could then ran out there carrying first-aid gear with the DoD agents alongside us.

The male pilot and two female passengers were injured, two of them badly. The woman in front had severe facial cuts and was bleeding heavily. Jace went to work on her as blood spattered onto the cockpit floor. The pilot's left hand was broken. The woman in the back seat was terrified. She was having trouble breathing and said she couldn't feel her legs. I coaxed her to draw deeper breaths as more vehicles responded and soldiers ran toward us.

"My back," she whispered.

"We're going to get you to a hospital. Hang in there. What's your name?"

"Sarah."

"Sarah, we're right here with you."

The woman in the passenger seat spit blood and gagged, and I heard a different voice of Jace's, a quiet gentleness, reassuring. The woman's upper lip was in shreds and upper front teeth were broken off. She tried to pick up piece of her lip off a pant leg until Jace reached down and wrapped it with gauze.

It was the pilot who told us why they were there. The woman in back was a videographer. I'd guessed that. I'd seen the gear. The one in front was a journalist with a successful news website she'd started. Her name was Trudy Dossin. I knew of her. She did in-depth pieces "exposing truth" and had an admirable reputation for fearlessness and taking risks. She took a large one today.

Soldiers lifted the woman out of the back seat and Jace walked the one in the front through the sandy soil to the ambulance along the main road. We continued on with the DoD agents. Ten minutes later, as we worked toward the mountains to the left of the Indie building, the DoD agents radioed, "The AI thinks it's found him. A line of four people is coming down the side of a mountain behind Indie. We're going to haul ass there."

"Let's go."

42

A paved road ran around the back of the Indie building. Behind that was sparse vegetation, dry gray sandy soil with mineral streaks of red and, higher, brown to black at the ridge. With binoculars we watched them picking their way down, heads shrouded and hooded. That raised the question of how Indie had identified Bismarck among them, but maybe they'd rested and sat with their hoods pulled back.

Their progress was slow. They were likely aware of us. A helicopter patrolling the mountain ridge dropped and was close to them. We heard fragments of a bullhorn warning and saw a red flare fired. The helicopter hovered then pulled back. It swooped back and dropped down closer when they still continued down.

Bismarck must know he won't get inside the building, I thought. He won't get that face to face with Indie so it must be theater, a convincing show he's planning. I watched their progress in a detached state. The half-mile radius from the building and up the mountain slope put them closer than they might realize to that *inviolable line.*

I had little respect for the inviolable claim. The murder of the four high school kids—and I think that's the right word—left me with severe doubts about Indie. I'd learned enough from Ralin to believe Indie had quickly ID'ed the kids. It followed a possible path to where they became threats, an efficient path. But not a rational one.

The helicopter returned and we could hear the bullhorn better. I glanced at Jace and turned and looked at the concrete building. It had walls and a roof three feet thick and heavily reinforced. It had piped-in utility power as well as a solar farm. The only vandalism reported so far was damage to solar panels and their connections. Standing where we were, I could see heat exhaust rising from several spots behind the building. That said they'd turned on the backup power system, diesel generators behind the Indie building and dug into the mountains.

Up the slope, the helicopter pulled away, and my cell rang. I answered, and a man identified himself as Major Collins.

"I got your phone number from your supervisor. I can see you. I'm in the helicopter off to your left. We've pulled back because they're nearing the line. They're having some sort of meeting now. The DoD agents with you have a laptop we can connect to. Let me talk to one of them, and we'll get a close-up using one of the drones."

I didn't need any more explanation than that. I handed my cell to the DoD agent nearest me and he leaned into their vehicle then brought out a laptop and opened it on the hood. I watched as an image of four men who were specks up on the mountain suddenly appeared as if they were standing right next to us. One had his hood off, his face exposed.

"Is that him?" Major Collins asked me.

"No, it's not."

"Okay, let's stay with them, they're starting down again."

The one who'd lowered his hood left it down and Collins gave a readout in yards as the foursome picked their way through rocks.

"Two hundred twenty-one yards to boundary," Collins said.

"I'm going to put you on speakerphone," I said.

"Go ahead."

We all watched as a second man pulled back his hood and exposed his face.

"That's not him either," I said as they came out of the rock field and zigzagged down a steeper slope of dried gray soil that crumbled with their steps.

"One hundred thirty-nine yards," Collins said and added, "Two raised their right arms to acknowledge they'd heard our warning. They are too close to the line now for us to go back in."

A few minutes later the other two pulled back their hoods and the one who'd been following moved to the front.

"That's him, that's Bismarck who just took the lead. They must know where the line is. It's not likely coincidence."

"Twenty-five yards," Collins said.

The slope flattened slightly and Bismarck opened his arms in the last ten yards. He looked upward toward the sun as two of the men shot video. Bismarck had something near a beatific smile on his face. I looked from the screen to the sky and saw a thin exhaust trail and the explosion that followed. I watched the second and third missile strikes before looking at the laptop.

All that showed there was smoke, and when it cleared there was bright-red blood and fragments and little left of any of the men. One of the DoD agents coughed and turned away as if close to vomiting. Intestines were strung out, a head torn open and hard to look at. None of us said anything for long seconds and then Jace said, "Only Bismarck was across the line."

The DoD agents nodded, and one said, "That's how it looked to me too. That's what'll go in our report, but drones will give an accurate read down to the millimeter."

He looked at me as he folded the laptop. "We'll figure out how to deal with the remains before the vultures do. We don't have a plan, we didn't see this coming, and we didn't know that thing would take out all of them."

Neither Jace nor I had much to say to that, so we exchanged contact info and Jace and I headed inside the Indie building because one of the officers had told her Ralin was there. That didn't jibe with what Ralin had said to us, but we decided to check it out.

43

Indonal and Ralin were both there. Indonal's face lit up when he saw Jace and they hugged like they were old friends. He left, and Ralin looked at us with a mix of sadness and exasperation.

"Don't ask me about Indie's role in anything today. I won't know the answer. If you have other questions, let's hear them, but I can't answer anything related to the strike that killed the mind-melder."

"We witnessed it," Jace said.

"Then you know more than me."

He went from there to a riff on his struggle to keep up with Indie and what it has taken to hold the project together. He didn't say anything at all about Stinson Beach or how he'd returned to work here. He pointed through the glass wall in the direction of the AI.

"I've been interviewed endlessly over Eric and Alan. DoD acknowledges how much they need him but still treat Eric like a suspect. Alan and Eric left to find a way to do what we started out to do—to create something that will be of great benefit to all humanity. If all goes well, Eric and I will still do that as we leave this project. For a very long time we worked with that as a goal. We didn't have the funding to go any further, so we turned to DARPA."

"You created the AI," Jace said. "People think you're another Einstein."

"Which is embarrassing and a complete joke, but if it got us the money to build this, then who cares? And for that matter, you're right, *Eric* is the only one close to genius. I've told Eric that many times."

That surprised me. I'm sure it surprised Jace, but she was already locked in on where she was going. I doubted it was worth it. I didn't see the reason to do it, but she was going there.

"I'm going to jump subjects on you," she said, "because the personal interactions between the three of you may help explain Eckstrom's actions. I have a question about Trent and Eckstrom's relationship."

"Can't help you there."

"I think you can," Jace said. "When I was there, she threw the flowers you brought down the hallway and appeared very angry at you. Then the two of you asked for some privacy to talk in the rock garden downstairs. Ten full minutes. I have notes. I'm a big notetaker."

"What are you getting at?" Ralin asked.

"Why was Trent so angry? We have to go there," Jace said, "because if Eckstrom confronted you over your affair with Trent before an unknown assailant killed him, then you're a possible suspect. What did you say to Eckstrom when he confronted you?"

"That's very offensive."

"We have to consider all possibilities."

"Please leave," Ralin said.

"We are going to leave, but you need to answer."

"He didn't confront me, but yes, Laura and I were seeing each other. Alan and Laura's relationship died years ago, and Laura and I saw each other only briefly. We both were lonely and needed someone to hold. It didn't mean anything beyond that."

"Did Laura tell Alan about your affair with her?" Jace asked.

"I don't know, but she was angry at me for wanting to end it."

"Even though it was just a fling?"

"She was angry at everything and everyone."

"Did she also tell you that she'd told Alan she was pregnant?"

"She didn't."

"She told Alan she was pregnant and that it wasn't his child. It couldn't be. She also said you were afraid she'd gotten too serious about you, so you made a point of telling her about other women you've been with or are still with. One is a young grad student at Stanford. Another was the woman in London who everybody we talk to seems to know about. Laura thought there might be more but hoped not for your wife's sake." Then Jace asked, "Did you view Laura as a temporary affair?"

"Yes."

"Did she?"

"That's how we talked about it, but now I don't know."

Jace softened her tone and fed him a couple of lines. "Women get attached more easily," she said. "And it's clear women are drawn to you. Is it possible she hoped for a much longer relationship?"

"What does that have to do with Alan's murder? You know very well I didn't kill Alan, so I don't understand this."

In a much harder voice Jace said, "You understand every bit of it. You're saying you broke off the affair with Laura. Why did you end it?"

"She was getting too attached. This will make you gag, Agent Blujace. She said she felt swept away and as if she could believe in herself again. She talked about a life we could build together, but that was never going to happen."

"Why not?"

"It was strictly a physical attraction."

"Really?"

"You're a caustic human being."

"Maybe so, but I have notes," Jace said. "Do you want to hear what Laura said about you?"

"Will it make any difference?"

"It might."

Jace fumbled with her phone and put on reading glasses, a nice touch, and the first I'd seen of them.

"Okay, here are my notes." Jace pulled out her notebook and flipped a couple of pages. "I'll read what I wrote when I asked her if she hoped to be with you. She said, 'Mark sleeps with anyone he can because he can't forgive his wife for something she did eight or nine years ago.' And, 'He's in love with himself. He'll never love anyone else as much as himself. I could never be with someone like that.' I tried to write it down word for word," Jace said. "I recorded it as well. So. What does she want from you now?"

"Money."

"How much money did she ask for?"

"A ridiculous amount."

"How ridiculous?"

"It's none of your business."

"Why would she ask for a ridiculous amount, to find a place to live and get a job?"

"Ask her."

"I did," Jace said, "and she told me she didn't sleep with anyone other than you. And that you'd had unprotected sex. Do you know where I'm going with this?"

He didn't answer, though Jace gave him thirty or forty seconds. Then she asked it a different way.

"Is Laura Trent pregnant with your child?"

Ralin gave her a hard, bitter look, then said, "Get out of here. Take your anger somewhere else. I'm done talking to you."

Jace didn't have an answer for that and was very quiet in the car. She tended to verbalize her summary of an interview but was silent on the long, straight road across the base. I didn't say anything either and thought of the two women injured in the helicopter crash. We were back in North Las Vegas before Jace said anything. When she did, she caught me by surprise.

"I didn't get anything from him. I argued with him. We didn't learn anything. I don't even know if he has anything for us. I think we should focus elsewhere. What do you think? Do you agree?"

I did.

44

That night was the worst in a dozen years. My life had changed irreparably in 2004 after an insurgent in a cobbled-together bomb factory near Bagdad modified a Senao cell phone, replacing the power cord with a battery and reworking the phone, adding an external relay switch that allowed triggering the bomb from a distance. Installing a battery, rewiring the page button became standard steps in the process of making IEDs.

The pain tonight took me back to the flight home from Frankfurt in 2005 that started with elation and finished in agony. I was more than ready to go home and excited. I'd convinced the doctors I'd be fine, that I could sit long hours on a military transport plane.

I was wrong. As wrong as I've ever been about so many things where my enthusiasm and a natural toughness were a good start but not enough. What my investigative career taught me is follow-through. You build a case, then you take it all the way home. You do that with tenacity and discipline. I've approached my bomb injuries with a belief that the two are somewhat similar: never give up and keep working on it. If I worked hard enough, I'd get back to how I used to be physically. It took me years to get to this point, to acknowledge I never would get back to how I was before.

Tonight, I saw white light behind my eyes and the sweat-soaked sheets were undeniable. Earlier, Jo urged me to take some painkillers, and finally, late in the night, I reached for the pills. They brought shallow sleep and haunted dreams.

I woke early, scrambled two eggs with pepper, salt, and olive oil, and toasted bread as the coffee brewed. Ralin had sent me an e-mail at 3:13 a.m. That seems to be a time of day he likes. I read his message as I ate. He wanted to talk about Eckstrom's murder. I referred him to Mara.

The final e-mail I read was from a missile expert in DC who'd concluded it was plausible that a terror group with the right team could field-assemble surface-to-surface missiles in a remote setting. He signed off with Call me. What you wrote worries me.

At the office, Jace and I learned 214 people were apprehended trespassing onto Independence Base. A dozen were charged with resisting arrest. Others had yet to be apprehended. I called Indonal to get his take on the situation at the base.

What Indonal said didn't surprise me.

"They took Mark out of the Indie building in an ambulance this morning. He was shaking and having trouble talking. A couple of hard-assed interrogator types flew out from Washington yesterday and questioned him for hours and hours after you and Agent Blujace left. He was pretty messed up afterward."

"Did you hear any of the questioning?"

"Are you kidding? They don't let me go to a bathroom alone here."

"How are you doing?"

"I'm working with the new coders. They're pretty into it and catching up fast. I talked with Mark this morning, before he freaked out, about the timing of me leaving. I may stay a little longer or until he's doing better. At this point, what's the difference if I stay a few more days?"

He was quiet before adding, "The head of security for the Indie building told me he wants to be there when we're both booted out. He thinks Alan got what he deserved and we got paid to give Indie's source code to an enemy. I'm only back because Mark said he had to have my help. Mark and the head of DARPA talked them into bringing me back temporarily."

"What did you say to the head of security after he said that?"

"That I can't wait to leave."

"Let me ask you something else," I said, "and I'm going to jump around with some of my questions. Did you ever meet Claire Henley?"

"No, but Alan did. He was in London with Mark a couple of times. He liked her, but the situation made him uncomfortable. We both liked Mark's wife, Sylvie, so it was awkward. If Alan hadn't met her, I wouldn't even know about her, and Mark has never said a word to me about his and Sylvie's problems."

"How are you doing with Alan's murder?"

"I can't stop thinking about it. After we split up, he said he was staying with a *new friend* who might be a great connection for us. That had to be her." He paused. "The interrogators who talked to Mark yesterday want to question me later today. I get the feeling they know something about her. I wish I'd said something earlier."

I sat on that a moment then realized he felt guilty he hadn't said more sooner. I sat on that a moment then said, "Eric, I have to tell you, you wouldn't have saved his life."

"Are you certain? Because we were texting."

Red flags started to go off for me.

"You were texting, but you may not have actually been texting with Alan. It might have been someone with his phone, someone trying to get you to tell them where you were. You didn't get Alan killed. And you just might have saved both your life and Cindy's by not communicating more."

"I . . . I want to believe that."

"From what you've told me, you shouldn't fault yourself for Alan's death."

"Everything I've done since signing on to build Indie is screwed up. Indie isn't just about defense. It's like a hawk flying into flocks of doves when it rips into other computer systems. Once Indie goes through one, it's wasted. Big bucks are going down. Someone is going to fight back. Something is going to happen. Cyber used to be like quiet warfare, but we ended that."

To keep him from going down that rabbit hole, I asked, "What do you want to work on next?"

"I want to be working on the AI machine that can follow every cell in your body. I want to help build the AI machine that can track all cells in real time so if cancer cells start to multiply, we can catch them. That's possible with the next generation of Indie."

"That's where your head is at, the next generation?"

"I want to leave here as soon as possible and go to work on that. I'm ready. I know it's possible. I know it can be done."

"Make it happen, Eric, and call if you ever need anything from me. When the interrogators question you today, tell them the absolute truth. Filter nothing. You don't have to speculate on what you don't know, but be very accurate about what you do know. If they want to talk to me, give them my phone number."

"Thank you," he said.

After he hung up and Jace left to meet with Laura Trent at her apartment, I sorted tip calls and talked with commercial real estate owners. I was in a melancholy mood when I left the office to go meet a real estate developer.

I have FBI friends who put in thirty years then retired with vested pensions and found new jobs. One is working for the police department in the hometown he'd abandoned thirty-five years ago. The town loves that he's returned. He's their one and only detective and says he gets paid next to nothing but up every morning happy. He told me his pension is more than enough where he's living now, and he can't remember when he's been as happy.

If I go ahead with back surgery, that may lead to forced early retirement and a pension not fully vested. Both Jo and I love our work, but there's a day out there we've counted on when we'll have more time together. A sudden loss of income would jeopardize the timing of that, and my back problem could curtail my chances at a second career. To me, that means I will have failed us.

That's where my thoughts were shortly before it happened. Not only that but on my way out I'd stopped to talk to the guards. Both were in upbeat, good moods. It all went down a half hour after I left.

45

DALZ

"It's ready to go," Dalz said and looked from Sean to the young man who would be driving the van. He showed the driver a photo as he explained. "When you park you need to be positioned over this spot. Do you see that No Parking sign?" Dalz touched the image of the sign in the photo. "Line up the front of the van with this sign."

"Front wheels?"

"No, the front of the van." Dalz searched for the American word. "The bumper," he said.

"What if the guard orders me to stop?"

"The guard *will* order that, but you roll to a stop in the correct position before you answer. If he's right there, make it seem like you couldn't hear him. That means you have your window up. He might be right there yelling at you to move on as you're stopping, so pretend you don't hear him and do not lower your window. You open your door instead and get out with the package you're there to deliver."

Dalz looked hard at the kid. He was unsure everything was getting through.

Dalz continued. "You've got the package, and he's not taking it from you. So, what do you do?"

"I say I'm new and try to get him to take it. When I hear the horn honk, I run for the car."

"You run, you dive into the back of the car, and the driver will shoot the guard if he chases you."

"If he pulls his gun as soon as I get there, what should I do?"

"You still run when you hear the car honk."

"What if he shoots me?"

He might and all the better, Dalz thought, but said, "All you need to do is get the truck there and into the correct position."

Sean, still standing nearby listening, stepped in. When he did, Dalz backed away picturing Sean's reaction after the bomb exploded. The young man seemed to be somehow related to him, maybe extended family. Perhaps that's why he was trusted.

After the young driver left, Sean came to Dalz and wanted to go through the detonation timing again, to reassure himself there was plenty of time for the driver to escape in the car that would follow him.

"The bomb detonates sixty seconds after you've made the detonation call. That's after I've called you and confirmed he's parked in the right spot."

"It doesn't just detonate when I call?"

"No, sixty seconds later. If the gap is too long, they'll see the getaway car and react. Remember, the guards will be on him already; he's out of the delivery truck and talking. I call you then leave, so everything is up to him at that point. Everything."

Dalz knew he'd be racing away when Sean called the detonation signal. Dalz had a place to get to. He'd built a smaller bomb to deal with Agent Grale. It was small but big enough for Grale to remember for the rest of his life.

46

At 2:08 p.m. a white commercial van turned off West Lake Mead Boulevard and slowed to a stop just past the guardhouse and adjacent to the painted metal fencing and a parking area that fronts our office. A white sedan rounded the corner eleven seconds later, right after one of the guards called out to the van driver, "No!" He waved him on. "No parking there, keep rolling. Move it!"

The driver lowered his window, leaned out and said, "It'll take five seconds. It's just one package."

The window went up again and the driver pushed his door open with his foot and hopped out holding the package with his arm extended as he hurried toward the guard, a guy I'd known for fifteen years.

"Freeze! Do not approach! Get back in your vehicle. You cannot park there. Do not take another step toward me!"

"Okay, Jesus, sorry, relax. No problem, okay? I'll move it."

This was all recorded. I listened with other agents as I arrived and suited up and watched video recording from before the blast. The guard's name was Enrique Jimenez. A good guy, observant, bright. In the video he looked aware of the danger.

He'd had time to radio the other guard, and I read in the way he lunged forward that he knew. All those drills, then it comes down to a few seconds.

He made it to the left front corner of the delivery van as he pursued the driver, who was running for a car that had slowed to a stop. Jimenez yelled something in the moment before an explosion enveloped both the van and the car and everything in close proximity. The blast blew out the steel fencing and shattered car windows and reinforced glass along the entry lobby. The face of the FBI building was pitted and scarred, and windows were broken across the street as wood fencing was hurled sideways. Most of the blast wave was directed downward.

The bomb design was different than initial reports. The asphalt road surface lay over a one-foot concrete cap that covered a gravel and sand joint trench carrying communication and power lines. Those lines were four feet below the underside of the concrete cap yet were still twisted and severed by the blast. The gravel covering the lines was blown out like buckshot.

Backup power had kicked in, and like Indie, we use JWICS communication for many things, but the hardwired Internet lines were compromised and enough other damage was done to provoke a temporary move of our office into three separate locations. For our squad, the DT, it was the fusion center out near the airport.

Agents came and went from the building in the hours after it was declared secure. I wasn't among them. I helped retrieve pieces of Jimenez's torn body and that of the other guard, Landers, and worked the bombing. I stopped hearing the sirens when I turned to the crater and twisted remains of the van and getaway car.

My reactions were about training. You do what you've learned. You react as you've been taught and draw from similar investigations. Later in the day, as I walked the street looking for pieces of the detonator, I thought more about Jimenez and Landers. Jimenez had two kids he adored, and Landers had survived multiple tours in the Middle East only to be killed here at home.

In humanity we have among us people with no empathy for others. Maybe it's the way they were born. Maybe it's chemical. Some of them are very successful. It's been argued that some of history's greatest leaders were narcissists with no real connection or feeling for other human beings.

It's the man acting alone and the glad-handing politician who remember the names that are temporarily useful. For the rest of us, a clap on the back, a warm handshake, a "good to see you again" is more than enough. Dalz had joked with the border patrol after they'd thanked him for his cooperation and patience and returned his false passport. They smiled from behind him at his offer to send photos from the parks, but what did Dalz feel?

Dalz had long favored three types of detonators. I walked and rewalked the street looking for fragments. Hour by hour, we recovered pieces of the bomb. I was able to visualize the bomb construction and the design's intent. I found detonator fragments that said it could be Dalz, but I puzzled over how the disruption of our office would work as an advantage. Sure, at first perhaps, but then what?

On some level it struck me as ignorant because the Bureau would react quickly. Surrounding offices would send more agents, and we'd ramp up hard. The FBI is America's investigative agency. Period. There's no one else. ATF is good at a lot of things, bombs in particular, and DHS has grown in ability and strengths, but it's the FBI when it really comes down to it.

To me, it meant we had to pull out all the stops to find whoever did this. We had to find who would dare do this as a prelude to whatever was intended next. Everything changed with the bombing. Intensity heightened without anything being said. The speeches would come, but it was already understood among all of us.

I heard from Jace late in the afternoon that Mara gave a good speech at the fusion center as the DT squad moved in. Headlines flashed, "Vegas FBI Office Bombed." Toward twilight our SAC, the special agent in charge and head of our office, stood in front of TV cameras and said we'd move back to the FBI office within three days.

"Nothing will stop us," he said as cable TV fixated on Bismarck's followers as possible bombers. For my part, I focused on the piece of a detonator similar to the type Dalz favored. It was swabbed that afternoon for DNA, but Dalz knew better. I didn't expect anything there. Something else was at the back of my mind, something Jo had told me.

47

DALZ

Dalz turned the images over in his head: the white van rounding the corner, brake lights, the van positioned just beyond the FBI guard station. Before it came to a stop, he was calling Sean, who then made the call that detonated the bomb.

Dalz felt the blast wave and he was already a half mile away. He didn't doubt Sean knew the bomb exploded prematurely. The bombing of the FBI was successful, but Sean would demand to know why the bomb exploded too soon. He would be the only one who cared, and it wouldn't matter. It was too late for Sean to replace him.

When Dalz arrived at the hospital parking garage, he'd found Dr. Segovia's blue SUV. It took less than a minute to magnetically attach the bomb to the undercarriage and tighten tie wire to help hold it in place.

He returned to the ranch and was in the main house well before Sean raced the unpaved road in from the highway. When Sean walked in, Dalz was sipping a just-brewed espresso.

"Success? Everybody back?" Dalz asked.

"Two are dead, but you know that."

"I am very sorry. What happened?"

"You're not sorry at all."

"Yes, that's true. The bomb detonated. It was successful."

"I should kill you," Sean said.

"You can, of course, if you can explain to your superiors why you killed me before the operation was complete. But before you do, I have to tell you that someone has tampered with the missiles. Every time I have checked them, I've had to reset them. If I had trusted you even a little, I would have told you sooner."

Sean pulled a handgun from his waistband, slowly brought it level to Dalz's head, then pulled the trigger. Dalz heard a bullet hum past him. Sean moved the gun slightly, and the next bullet nicked his right ear. Dalz felt a sharp sting then blood running down his neck as Sean gripped the gun with two hands and aimed at Dalz's chest.

"It will be the end of your career," Dalz said quietly.

Sean stepped close and swung his arm with the gun.

When Dalz regained consciousness, he was lying on his side on the floor. There was pooled blood and a wrinkled tear in his scalp. He rose slowly to his feet then moved to a chair.

His head ached but not terribly. He looked out and saw Sean's car was gone. Everything would be fine, and later, much later, even if it was five or ten years from then, he would find Sean. It would take time, but someday. Dalz touched his ear and looked at the blood on his fingers and knew he would wait as long as it took.

48

AUGUST 14TH

The next day Jace and I stood in the lobby of the Las Vegas fusion center, a nondescript building near the airport where multiple federal, state, and local law enforcement agents and staff work together to keep the city safe. "Better to work from our cars," I said to Jace. "The fusion center will become the Confusion Center with everyone scrambling for a space to work from."

"Well, we at least need a desk here. Come on, let's look around," Jace said.

"Yeah, let's do it, and let's find food and coffee. There's also a tip I want to check out, some defunct bowling alley on the southern edge of Vegas. The owner called it in. I listened to his message, mostly a vandalism report, but he also described three tables with plywood tops screwed down to the bowling alley floor."

"Sounds like pop-up drug manufacturing."

"It does, and most likely is, but I'll stop by. The owner's meeting me there. It's just off I-15 and won't take long."

"That place with the big rusted sign?"

"Hey, you're learning your way around. I'll check it out then call you."

Not long ago, Jo and I had driven past that same bowling alley. She'd looked over at the sun-scorched building and suggested the alley be reborn as a beer garden. Seemed like a good idea; I could see it working. I remembered the bowling alley having a restaurant with tall doors that folded open and a long bar with bad wine and cheap beer.

When I arrived, I walked in through a door left ajar for me. It had three sturdy locks on it. Inside, the owner, Ed Ducatti, was waiting. The air was stifling, and Ducatti looked agitated. He was midseventies and wiry, all sinew and tendons, and wearing lime-colored sneakers with neatly pressed khaki slacks.

"My wife and I are retired," he said. "Rental property is the cornerstone of our retirement. I manage our properties."

They owned five, and he told me about all of them. He'd flown in from Phoenix but lived in Scottsdale. Once a month he checked on their properties and collected rent. He walked through the metrics of investing in Las Vegas while I studied the long four-foot-wide plywood tables.

"They built those contraptions and screwed and nailed them down into old-growth maple," Ducatti said with gruff sadness. "Wood of this quality can't be had anymore. It's like defiling a church."

The contraptions, as he called them, were why he'd called the FBI hotline, responding to our outreach trolling for viable tips on any changes noticed, anything deviating from the expected use of a leased or rented property. Ducatti called over the damage done, but I wasn't sure he really understood the purpose of the tip line. He suggested wording for me to use in a report that could bolster the insurance claim he intended to make.

I studied what looked like wooden cradles of different sizes spaced every two feet and screwed down into each of the three plywood platforms. The cradles were shaped to hold something that was of a generally cylindrical shape. The platforms had wooden legs cross-braced with metal clips.

"They rented the building to make a documentary film on the revival of bowling. Bowling is catching fire. It's making a huge comeback all across the country."

"Is that right?"

"Absolutely. Do you bowl? My wife and I bowl twice a week."

"I don't get much time to bowl."

"But you would if you could, am I right?"

I didn't answer that but asked if the film crew had promised to protect the alley while shooting the movie.

"They did, and it's in the lease."

The platforms were waist high. The alley gutters and lane dividers were covered with plywood so the boom lift parked in a corner could drive across them without bouncing. I saw various shoeprints and could visualize the shape of what had rested in the wooden cradles. That they left it all here and walked away made me question my conclusions, but the more I looked, the more I saw that these were very likely assembly tables, possibly missile assembly.

A long shot, but it was possible. Beneath the tables and on the floor surrounding them were metal filings. I knelt and picked up several shavings. Final adjustments for tighter fits? Tire tracks marked the plywood pathway with dust from outside, so whatever was built in here got carried out by the boom lift. I studied a sling attached to the boom then turned to Ducatti.

"Ed, I need everything you've got on the people you rented to. Who did you call when you needed to get ahold of them?"

"The movie producer, but the number he gave me is an out-of-service recording. He's the only one I've had contact with. That's another reason I contacted the FBI."

"Wait here," I said. "I've got to call this in. Then I want to talk more with you. The people you leased to may not be who you thought they were. After I call to my office, we need to go over every interaction you had with them."

"Him."

"Okay, got it, the producer."

I took photos of the assembly tables and sent them to Jace and Mara then called and asked Mara for two evidence recovery teams.

"I think we've found them," I told Mara. "I just sent you photos. It's a maybe, but they sure look like assembly tables for portable missiles."

"Just left there intact?"

"Yeah, as if they were done and simply walked away."

"You think they're gone?"

"They're definitely gone, along with whatever got built here. They're not coming back."

When I got off the phone, I explained to Ducatti what the FBI interest was and retrieved booties and latex gloves from my car for us. Ducatti toured me through the rest of the building and showed me how the big folding doors worked.

"These doors are one of a kind because of the low humidity here. You couldn't do this back east. The maple would move around on you."

I listened to more talk about bowling and insurance, and when I couldn't stand it anymore, I stepped away and called Mara again.

"We need an expert on missiles. Do you know of anyone?"

"No, but someone here will. Let's take it a step at a time and confirm what we're looking at first," Mara said. Me, I was thinking, *No, we need everything and everybody thrown at this.*

When my phone rang again it was Steve Akaya, a missile expert, calling. He was staying in Vegas but working at Nellis Air Force Base.

"I can come out your way," he said. "Give me an address. What can you tell me?"

"That they must have assembled with component parts light enough to carry. When you walk around the tables you'll see metal filings, wire clippings, other debris on the floor that, to me, looks like they were assembled here then lifted in a soft sling and carried outside by a boom lift and loaded onto or into whatever they used to move them."

"Liquid or solid fuel?" he asked.

"How would I be able to tell?"

"Do you smell kerosene?"

I sniffed a table. "It's more of a sulfurous smell."

"Then probably solid fuel. That's what I would expect anyway. I'm walking to my car. See you soon."

Jace arrived, and Mara wasn't far behind, bringing eight agents with him. For the next few hours the building interior would belong to the evidence recovery teams. Steve Akaya arrived and worked around the agents. Jace and I stayed for an hour before leaving to do a quick check on another tip that came in two days ago, this one from a casino hotel not far from the bowling alley. It was close enough to check out then return before the evidence recovery teams finished. As it turned out, it was a lucky thing we did.

49

Both men had checked into the hotel August sixth. The older one, Samuel Stetts, was in a second-floor junior suite. The younger man, Richard Wu, was in a smaller room on the fourth floor. Both were due to check out the next morning, but Wu had just moved his checkout to tonight.

According to hotel staff, Wu was gone every day, all day, and spent nights in his room. He ordered meals from room service and kept to himself. He was polite, friendly, and likable. Nothing about him raised flags until casino security picked up on Wu's interactions with Stetts. Every morning he and Stetts pulled up alongside each other's car and talked just outside the range of casino security cameras.

A former Clark County detective, Don Schist, headed casino security. He wasn't there that night but came in when he heard we were investigating. Jace and I sat with him. I've known him for years, and it was good to see him again. He could tell we were serious and didn't waste time.

"You know how it is, Grale. We have to worry about all kinds of scams and whether they're working some angle. I doubt they realized, but they stuck out with their meet-up every morning. They might be a pair of salesmen talking over territories or just having a coffee before heading out. But to us, it looked like they were careful to get outside our camera range."

"Are you sure it was intentional?"

"I don't know, but it sure feels that way or I wouldn't have left the message for you. We've tracked both inside the casino, and they don't interact at all. The kid never comes out of his room, not even to eat. He orders from room service and the older guy, Stetts, got an escort service to provide him a temporary girlfriend. Uh, I'd appreciate you going at this as discreetly as possible." Jace and I both nodded.

"We're definitely seeing something unusual with these two guys," Schist said. "Sometimes I think my guys have watched *Ocean's Eleven* too many times, but with this I agree with them. Something is off with this pair. One of my guys actually followed them one morning. They both exited at the same off-ramp near that wreck of an old bowling alley."

"Interesting," I said. "We're inside that building tonight with two evidence recovery teams."

Fourth-floor Wu was tall and thin and told staff he missed his wife. He'd never been away from her this long. Second-floor Stetts contacted the escort service the day he arrived. The same young woman, Gina, had been his companion since the first night. It turned out Gina was in the hotel tonight and had yet to go up to Stetts's room, so we got a chance to talk to her first.

"I hear a lot of stories from men," she said. "This one says he's working a high-stress secret government project, but I doubt it. I've been around government types. They're more knotted up. He's different."

"How so?" Jace asked.

"Hard to describe, but it's like there's someone else in there watching me all the time."

"In the room?"

"No, in *him*, and that other person scares me."

"Scares you how?" Jace asked.

"So, Mr. Stetts is a chemist, okay. I mean, big deal, who cares about a chemist, right, but a couple of nights ago I'm showering, and he's on the phone. I left the bathroom door open, thinking maybe he could come in and have some fun. I got tired of waiting for him, left the shower running, and took a look. His back was turned, he didn't know I was there, and he's still on the phone. I overheard the word 'fuel' and the phrase 'intense burn' before going back to the shower. He finally came in, but then he got intense, asking why there were wet footprints on the carpet and what I'd heard."

"Is he expecting you tonight?" Jace asked.

"Yeah. Like right now. He's waiting for my call that I'm at the elevator ready to come up."

She made the call, and we rode up the elevator with her. When she texted she was at his door, Stetts opened it wearing a robe and slippers. He'd let his robe fall to give Gina a preview. Only it was Jace and me waiting to see him. We introduced ourselves while he got dressed. Then he got indignant when it sank in: we really were taking him to our office.

"Not without telling me what this is about."

"It's about a terrorism investigation, and if everything goes well, we bring you back in a few hours," I said.

Stetts turned to Gina. "You called the FBI?"

She shook her head, and I let him know she wasn't how we found him. More agents arrived, and we knocked on Wu's door. Wu was easy and seemed relieved when we said if everything went well, we'd have him back soon.

"I have a late flight tonight," Wu said.

"We'll do everything we can to help you make it in time," I answered.

Thankfully the fusion center's interview rooms were ready to go.

With Wu we went slow and easy. We let each question weigh on him.

"Talk to us but don't lie," I said. "The laws are different with a terror investigation. If you mislead us, you could end up with a life sentence. Do you understand me?"

"Terrorism? That's crazy."

"Are you certain you don't want a lawyer?"

That provoked pushback. "I don't need one."

Jace took the lead with him. He told her he was working in Spain until recently and described where he'd lived in Barcelona. He gave an apartment address and street names nearby but stumbled on restaurant names or shops or any other places he frequented.

He said, "I just worked."

His passport showed trips in and out of Spain, and he gave us a phone number for the Spanish aeronautics corporation that was getting into rockets.

"I do design work."

Wu pivoted to his wife and two young children in Florida and teared up talking about them. He said he would be ashamed to have to tell his wife the FBI interviewed him.

After he'd dried his eyes, I took the lead and asked, "Have you met anybody or talked to anyone else staying at the hotel?"

"No, I stay in my room."

"How long have you been staying at the casino hotel?"

"A week or so."

"You don't know exactly?"

"Does it matter? Aren't you going to check with the hotel anyway?"

"Who's the man you talk to every morning?"

"I don't talk to anyone."

"Where are you working?"

"I don't want to get the employers involved. I haven't done anything wrong."

The back-and-forth went on awhile before we showed Wu photos a plainclothes security guard had taken of him talking with Stetts. At that point he owned up to it. After he did, I walked back to the interview room with Stetts in it.

Stetts's earlier derision and outrage at being detained had passed, and he was calm and quiet as another agent and I sat down. From his chair Stetts could see through the empty glass-walled interview room next to us and into the one beyond it. The back of Wu's head was visible, and across the table sat Jace and another agent.

Steve Akaya had finished at the bowling alley and was on his way. Twice, Stetts shrugged off his right to a lawyer, and his impatience returned. He went out of his way to communicate to us that he was dealing with idiots.

"Okay, let's go through this once more and get you out of here," I said.

We went through everything again, that he was a chemist laid off by Dow fifteen years ago, now doing contract work. Then we went over the debts he was paying down and how he made it all work. Needed money, same as Wu, so another tie between the two. Or another storyline shared and rehearsed ahead of time.

"Is this your house?" I asked as I slid a photo of it across to him to make the point we were in his life.

"It is."

"When was the last time you were home?"

"What do you care? And why is it any of your business? I have debts, and I work all the time and don't get home often. That's it!"

"You're that busy?"

"I told you, I need the money."

I paused then said, "We have two evidence recovery teams at the bowling alley where you've been working. They've gathered DNA and samples of chemical residue. We're going to test clothing in your room. I also have to tell you that Gina overheard a conversation about fuel burn."

"She didn't hear anything! Look, I *am* working on rocket fuels, consulting for a Chinese billionaire who wants to seed clouds in Africa with silver iodide."

"What's his name?"

"I've never met him."

"You're working for him but don't know his name?"

"One of his representatives hired me. He lives halfway across the world! How would I know him? They transferred a deposit into my bank account, and I went to work. If money is landing in my bank account, who cares what his name is?

"I signed a stack of nondisclosure papers this tall." Stetts lifted his hand off the table in a dramatic gesture to illustrate the pile. "I was hired to rework existing chemical formulas with slightly different mixes to achieve the same altitude for the rockets used. They seed clouds all the time in China. He wants to do the same thing in the drought-ravaged areas of Africa where global warming is messing with their rainfall. If there's a new patent involved, I'll get royalties."

"How many launches have you worked on?"

"If I answer, I could get sued."

"Are you working with anyone else who's staying at the hotel?"

"No."

"Have you ever met with anyone who's staying at the hotel?"

"Not unless you count Gina."

"Do you know a Richard Wu?"

"Richard Wu?"

"A young man of Chinese descent, and before you answer I need to warn you to be very careful about lying."

"I might know who you mean. There's a young guy who may be working with the same employer."

"But you're not sure he is?"

"I think he is, but I don't know what he does. I don't have any contact with him other than giving him driving directions every morning. And I mean *every* morning. For some reason he can't get the route down, though it couldn't be simpler."

"He's working for the Chinese billionaire who wants to seed clouds in Africa too?"

"The billionaire is already seeding clouds. He just wants to do it cheaper. Look, I give the guy directions and we talk some, but that's it."

"Let's forget about the Chinese billionaire," I said. "It was a good story, but we're way beyond it. You can stick with it if you want, but I strongly advise you to start cooperating."

"I am cooperating."

"No, you really aren't."

"I don't know where you're coming from, Agent Whoever-You-Are. It's like I told you: silver iodide, cloud seeding in Africa, a Chinese billionaire, my screwed-up life, my debts, everything. Put me in a cell. I'll get a lawyer tomorrow morning."

"Sit on it a little longer and think about this: casino security followed both of you to the bowling alley, and now we're in there. We got there a different way. We've gathered DNA, and if yours is there, that's a problem. I'll be back after I see how they're doing with Wu."

50

Wu jabbed the air as Steve Akaya, who'd joined us in the interrogation room, shook his head. We were into night now. I closed my eyes and listened while he told his version of the silver iodide cloud-seeding story and the work he was doing programming the missiles. Many of the words he used were the same as Stetts's, though otherwise they spoke in dissimilar ways. That grabbed my attention when I first started talking to them, and here it was again.

When I opened my eyes, I could see Stetts watching through the glass two rooms away with a bored expression, as if to send a message that he was interested but not worried. In here, the missile expert continued to contradict and correct Wu, who became more animated then agitated as he described a cloud-seeding test flight in Mexico that Akaya doubted ever took place.

I stepped outside with Jace and tested an idea on her. "Wu and Stetts memorized the same story. Their speech patterns are nothing alike *except* for when they talk about cloud seeding in Africa."

"What do you make of that?" she asked.

"This is going to sound off the wall..."

"Nothing is off the wall tonight."

"Well, we're not coming up with much background on either of them, and no one can find record of Wu's wife or marriage or the schools where his kids are registered. These two guys have got the same story down pat but claim they didn't know each other before this project. Add to that, Akaya is punching holes in everything Wu says." I paused. "I think they're working for a US government agency."

"Whoa, Grale. Seriously?"

"Yeah."

"And do you have one in mind? It can't be CIA because they can't work inside the US."

"Unless an exception was made for a particular crisis. Let's go back in, and I'll question Wu. He's already on edge. Akaya is taking him apart, and he knows he's in over his head."

We went back in and took our seats. I looked Wu in the eyes and asked, "What if I told you we've already figured out who you work for?"

"I *told* you who I work for."

"I'm guessing you were promised that if anything went wrong, they'd be here for you. But I promise you it won't work like that. Especially after you're moved to a supermax prison, and we investigate you as a terrorist. It could be months, even years, before your cell is quietly unlocked. I say this because your employer would likely wait until no one is watching."

"My employer is a Chinese billionaire!"

"We're past that. We're way past it; it's time to get real."

Wu turned to Jace with a puzzled look. "What does he mean?"

"Agent Blujace isn't going to help you, or for that matter, play along any further," I said. "Look at me."

He turned back to face me.

"You aren't credible in the role you're selling," I said. "The man at the end of the table is one of the top missile experts in the US, and he's having difficulty following your explanations of what you've worked on. That much even I can understand. I'm guessing you believe you've accomplished your mission and now you go home a quiet hero. But in reality, you've screwed up. Your cover story is goofy. Why would you lie to hotel employees about your occupation? Is cloud seeding illegal? Not as far as I know."

I pointed at Akaya and continued. "It sounds like he believes your missile guidance settings will revert to default flight trajectory settings. The missiles won't be able to 'fly into the clouds.' That software can't be altered."

"I don't know what you're talking about."

"Tell us what you think will happen if a top US missile expert is correct and you're wrong. What if the changes you made are overridden by a default setting intended to thwart sabotage?"

"I have no idea what you're talking about!"

"Oh, I think you do. You believe the missiles will miss their targets, a phone call will be made, and you'll be released. Maybe we even shake your hand and thank you for your service. No. We're going to move you *first*, and if the missiles launch and hit their targets, you're going to face the same terrorism charges as the rest of them. I bet your employer will keep a very, *very* quiet background presence if that happens. The promises they made you? They'll deny them. Not only that, they may well deny even knowing you, if we let them know you and Stetts thwarted our efforts to stop an attack."

I leaned in then pointed once again at Akaya, now working at a laptop at the end of the table.

"I've listened to the back-and-forth between you and him, and he says they could hit their targets despite what you've done to reprogram. You say you helped build these rockets.

We have you on record saying that. What are you going to do when you can't come up with your fictional Chinese billionaire? And the president who gave your agency the go-ahead doesn't acknowledge it for political and security reasons? At that point, you'll get hung out to dry."

He tossed me an indulgent smile.

"You're smiling?"

"I'm listening."

"Keep listening, and let's take it another step, and this is an important one. You're with us, or as I've said several times now, you're impeding us. We're in a race to find these missiles, and if your employer is who I think they are, they'll ask, Why you didn't contact them when the problem arose? Why didn't you cooperate? If people get killed due to your bad judgment, there's no scenario that has a happy ending for you."

At that he went quiet. Jace and I went out with Akaya, and the three of us talked outside the interview room. We went back in and let Akaya try to reach Wu by showing him the exact mistakes he'd made reprogramming the missiles. Akaya turned his laptop around, and we saw the Indie building as a glowing dot at the center of what looked like an illuminated radar sweep with a seventy-mile radius. The sweep was shown in a lighter color, so it was easy to make out the edge.

I asked for a copy before Akaya started dots moving, white lights representing missile launches at the seventy-mile mark, to show how the simulated missiles quickly closed on Independence Base. Akaya explained again to Wu how the onboard computer self-corrects any changes made without the correct series of passwords.

"In this simulation I can alter their flight paths, but watch what happens when I do," Akaya said. "Here, I'm altering the target location and guidance."

He typed for several minutes, and we all watched the screen.

"Keep your eyes on the uppermost missile in this simulation," Akaya said.

We watched it veer off course to the north then turn back three seconds later. Wu's face changed. He'd watched closely as Akaya typed and sat frozen now. That was enough for me.

I got up and went to Stetts's interview room.

"The missile expert just got through to Wu. That's the bald guy in the room. Wu thinks it's okay not to come clean with us because he's too stubborn to accept that his alterations to make the missiles fly straight up were overridden by a preprogrammed default code. In simpler words, there's one expert in there, and it's not Wu, or whatever his real name is. We've got a screen up, and it looks like Wu is finally getting it, but is it too late?"

When Stetts didn't respond, I asked, "Why are you two impeding the FBI? Do you see the guy touching the screen?"

Stetts nodded.

"Do you want to look him up? We can do that together. Then we can Google Wu and see what pops up. Not much, right? And you, heck, you barely exist. What's that feel like? Yeah, you're an 'independent chemical expert.' I read that. Who are you really?"

"Who's the missile expert in there?" Stetts asked.

"Steve Akaya."

"That's Akaya?"

So he did know something.

"It is. You're looking at Steve Akaya. He's out here on some tweak they're making at Nellis Air Force Base, and we're trying to thwart an attack on Independence Base. When we found the tables where the missiles' components were assembled in the shells, we went looking for an expert and got very lucky."

The wall fell. "Okay, Grale, I can't say much about us, but we're on the same side. But I've got to talk with Wu. Akaya really said they'll self-correct?"

"Yeah. They added passwords after some screw-up somewhere else. I know about it but can't talk about it here. Akaya took Wu through the steps to determine whether he'd actually overridden the prior programming. Wu missed a critical password step. You can question Akaya."

"I need to talk with Wu."

"Before we go in there, how do we find the others who worked in the bowling alley?"

"They kept us all separate and watched everything very closely. They had one guy per table watching, and no talking. There's a little guy who came by twice who was running the overall. He drives a black GMC 2018 pickup, but I was never in position to get license plates. You're going to ask about Dalz, right? Wu saw him. Wu's the only one. I saw him but not close enough to be certain. Right height. Right look. That was less than twenty-four hours ago."

"You're probably lucky we found you."

"I've had that thought."

"How many missiles?"

"Twelve. They're 9 feet 3 inches long, 281.94 centimeters, payloads of 113 kilos, 250 pounds of explosives."

"What type of explosives?"

"You need Dalz for that. He fitted the warheads with a helper at night. Some Pakistani. Missile range is about seventy miles, but they'll want to be in closer if they can so they get a secondary blast from the remaining fuel. And these things will click along. It's kickass fuel."

"How fast?"

"Four hundred and fifty miles an hour plus. You don't want to be home when the doorbell rings."

"How sure are you?"

"I'm certain."

"How were they shipped?"

"Three at a time in plywood boxes that looked like long coffins. We used four-by-ten-foot sheets of plywood to build boxes to hold them. They were lifted onto a flatbed truck. Two missiles were side by side, five feet back from the truck cab, and the third was centered behind them. Four loads total, two of the four went north, two others went south on the freeway. The truck cab is green and white, and the driver was Hispanic. He's big with black hair. He's got a belly. The green paint is an olive color and the truck cab is in decent shape."

"Stenciling, a name, anything."

"If anything was there, I didn't see it. But there was some sort of curlicue in white paint to give it a little flair."

"Air foils?"

"No, this truck is back a couple of decades, no flash. It's older but cared for. The cab is a Ford."

"There you go. A Ford. That'll help," I said and asked if he thought the driver knew what he was hauling.

"No, and all the loads rolled in the early morning."

"What time in the morning?"

"Right around dawn. As we finished three missiles they shipped."

I walked him to the other interview room, and he talked to Wu with all of us listening. Then I left to call Ralin. I knew drones patrolled out to the highway and Indie stored the video. When my call went to voice mail, I hung up and called again. I did that three times before Ralin picked up and said, "I can't talk right now."

"You have to. We need Indie. We need your help."

51

AUGUST 15TH

Ralin asked for an image, a graphic, anything depicting long plywood boxes strapped down on a flatbed truck.

"I'll get something to work with," I said, though I didn't have any idea how to do that yet. "Six missiles were shipped north, but we don't know that they shipped up 95 North so you may come up with nothing."

"And your understanding is they were shipped in wooden boxes resembling long coffins strapped down on a flatbed truck?"

"Yes, two side by side and one by itself with straps holding them down. The boxes are raw plywood, no paint. The driver is a middle-aged Hispanic male at or around six feet tall. The cab is older and more rounded than current models. No wind foils or spoilers."

"I can work with what you've given me. We'll generate an image for Indie."

"Thank you for that. Call my cell if you find anything."

He hung up, and I walked back into the room where Jace and Wu were saying good-bye. Wu was on his way but wanted to apologize. I wasn't having it but did my best to be neutral.

"You take care," I said because there was nothing else to say. I walked him out, and a car slowed to a stop on the other side of the street. Stetts hadn't bothered with good-byes and was already gone. Now, I watched Wu disappear. Half an hour later the Director of the FBI called our SAC and reconfirmed both Stetts and Wu were legitimate and that their actions inside the US were approved at the highest level.

"Highest levels or level?" I asked.

"Highest," the SAC said. "You did well. Now it's down to what we do with what we know."

He left, and I found a spot in the fusion center to lie down for a few minutes. Stabbing nerve pain was making it difficult to concentrate. I could hear people walking by in the corridor. At one point I heard someone say, "What's up with him? He can't do that right now."

I kept my eyes closed and didn't move. Every pulse brought pain as I waited for the Tylenol and Aleve to kick in and knock it down enough for me to move again. I drifted to a less-aware state and heard more voices in the hallway then opened my eyes to someone much closer. Jace was standing there.

"Hey," she said, "Mara wants a squad meeting in about half an hour. Let's get coffee. Have you eaten anything?"

"I'm okay on food but, yeah, let's go find coffee."

We found the kitchen, and while we waited for a fresh pot to brew, Jace said, "Mara is moving us around again."

"When?"

"In this meeting so that's a heads-up."

"Do you know what's coming?"

"He told me I'll be jumping around and so will others."

***

The meeting went down and got noisy as Mara announced that SWAT was already back in the FBI office so the DT squad wouldn't be far behind. He bounced from there to a list of agent assignments.

"Grale, you're still on Dalz. He's your primary and anything else is temporary. Don't carry the ball with anything other than Dalz, and you don't do anything alone. If you find him, you do not engage. You call in, and we'll respond with maximum force. Blujace will rotate between squad teams. She'll move around and be on and off with you. We're going to absorb some DT agents coming in from Salt Lake, LA, and Phoenix, and they don't know the area, so there'll be more rotation. With the missiles, the consensus is if they're viable they'll get launched sooner rather than later. Every resource possible is looking for them. It's that simple, people. Blujace, why don't you summarize last night?"

"Grale should. He's the one who figured out Stetts and Wu."

"All right, Grale, what do you know?"

"I know if I'm working only Dalz and come across him after looking for him for twenty years, I'm not going to blow him a kiss and wait."

That got laughs, but I didn't understand Mara reinforcing in a squad meeting that my role was to be limited. It stung. I talked as video from the bowling alley showed on a screen.

"Both suspects gave us information that led us to believe twelve missiles were built and shipped. Their identities turned out to be a surprise, as I'm sure you've heard. They had attempted to sabotage the missiles but failed. We're looking for missiles that are in boxes about ten feet long and four feet wide." I spread my arms to show the approximate width. "Six went north from the bowling alley and six south. Ninety-five North runs past Independence Base, so we're asking for video from the surveillance drones there."

"It'll take four people to lift them into a launcher, and even with four it'll be awkward. Watch for a converted truck with a launcher welded on the back or something like that. They're heavy, so there may be a hoist to assist in moving them. Maybe something used in construction that could be rented.

"We've talked with a couple of experts at the Pentagon who've suggested they may spread the missiles out. We may be looking for several sites with three to four missiles at each or as few as two missiles each. Look for extraneous vehicles, four-wheel desert-type vehicles, but they could as easily be in a warehouse and wheeled out onto a parking lot, or a mix of both. We know the fuel and general design, and missile experts put their range at seventy miles. The AI at Independence Base puts it at seventy-five miles, so I'd go with that."

"We're sticking with a seventy-mile radius," Mara said. "That AI doesn't run this office."

"But it's killer at math," I said. "So don't rule out the seventy-five-mile range."

Mara nodded but said, "Okay, people, that's the end of the meeting. Let's get to it."

After we broke up Mara wanted to talk alone with me.

He said, "The ASAC wants to meet with you."

"Okay, but let's not do it today."

"That's not yours to decide."

"It's not, but you know where we're at today. What's the meeting about? If it's just so he can go on record with me and cover the list of infractions, let's do it later."

"I'm just delivering a message. If it's a meeting you don't have time for, you can tell him yourself. But between you and me, you're making it worse."

"I don't see it that way."

"I know you don't, and I know you're feeling isolated when you should be in the thick of things. I saw your face in the meeting, but you need to man up to the realities."

"Man up?"

"All right, I'll put it another way. Get over yourself. Esposito has a job to do same as you and me. He's always been your advocate, and so have I. But today I'm going to be blunt. I don't want to endanger another agent by assigning them to work with you. Your physical issues are significant and limiting. If that's hard to hear, too bad, it's the truth and we're through dancing around it."

"Who's we? You and Esposito?"

"Grale, I was told that you were in a room sleeping on a bench an hour ago. I know you were up all night questioning Stetts and Wu, but you've questioned suspects all night many times before and then worked the day after and longer. It's not good for squad morale to have agents see you sleeping."

I hadn't been sleeping, but that was beside the point. I said, "I get it. I'll work alone. I'll stay on Dalz, but in doing that I'm part of the search for missile sites. I can search alone."

"We need everybody searching so we'll figure that out, but knock off the martyr crap. You've worked alone plenty. That was the best idea we could come up with to keep you on the squad. If you come up with a viable Dalz lead, I may put two able-bodied agents on checking it out. That's the new reality, and I don't want any static from you about it. We just cleared this drug mess and you're limping, so I don't want to hear a single word about who I team you with or don't. I can fill an auditorium with agents who like and respect you, but I can't fill a small closet with agents who want to go out on a dangerous assignment with you as a partner."

"How sure are you of that?"

"Don't ask."

52

"Do you have a TV screen or something?" Ralin asked. "Indie may have found the truck by reviewing older video."

"Yeah, we can run it on a screen. We need just a few minutes then send it."

Ralin had called with a lead, and I was trying to figure out the AV console in the conference room.

"Run what?" a voice asked, and I turned and saw Esposito.

Before I could answer, Ralin said, "It's what you described. From two thousand feet up, they still look like coffins. A truck ran right past the base. I'm ready when you are."

"Keep talking," I said as I plugged in the screen. It lit up right away. "We're watching," I told Ralin, "and so far, it's just cars and other trucks."

"Give it fifty seconds, it's coming."

"What about other vehicles near the truck?" I asked. "Can we pull license plates from them?"

"We can do that. No one wants you to stop this attack more than me."

"I don't know about that," Esposito said.

Ralin came back with, "Whoever just said that doesn't know me and how long we've worked on Indie."

We watched from above a spread-out flow of traffic passing in both north- and southbound directions. I focused on the northbound lanes as Esposito asked, "What are we watching for?"

"A flatbed semitrailer carrying three missiles in plywood boxes that look like long coffins," Jace said from the doorway.

She softly shut the door behind her and stood watching with her hands on her hips as the drone's cameras zoomed in on a truck approaching from south of Independence Base. The image changed in an instant from fuzzy to perfectly sharp.

"How is the AI getting it this clean with drone video?" Esposito asked. He kept on with questions we didn't have time for, but who could blame him? We were like people from an earlier time marveling over the invention of color TV. We were so used to black-and-white, and often fuzzy, video, the clarity and depth of Indie's imaging was stunning.

"It's rerunning the video and simultaneously cleaning it up," Ralin said and answered more of Esposito's questions until we all went quiet when a truck with plywood coffins passed underneath the drone. We watched it disappear from sight then replayed it as Ralin sent us a string of vehicle license plates that included the make and model of the vehicles ahead and behind.

A search for the truck began before we left the room, and we turned to other agents on the DT squad to help chase down the owners of the vehicles the border drones videoed near the truck as it passed by. I watched the full clip once more then picked up my phone.

"Who are you calling?" Esposito asked, and I hadn't put it together that he was here to talk to me.

"Kathy Tobias, head of DARPA. It'll be a quick call."

When Tobias answered her phone, I said, "Kathy, it's Agent Grale. We know what's coming. They'll be surface-to-surface missiles, a total of twelve with modern guidance systems. I'm sending you a video of what the Independence Base border drones along 95 picked up on. It's a flatbed truck with three boxes strapped down. From the point you start the video, it's one minute thirteen seconds before you see the truck coming from the south. The drone video is two days old, so they may have already arrived at wherever they're going. We believe there were four shipments, two that went north, two south. Most likely looking for mobile missile launchers. Are Ralin and Indonal still in the building?"

"Yes, both are."

"If they launch missiles from multiple directions simultaneously, what's the level of confidence Indie can handle that?"

"I don't think anyone can truly say."

"I'd get Ralin and Indonal out of there."

"You think it's imminent?"

"We don't know but it could be, so why wait? You said Indonal was a one-, maybe two-in-a-generation mind. Is it worth the risk to let him and Ralin help manage the defenses?"

"I'll get on the phone, but it's a DoD call."

"Convince them, Kathy."

When my call with her ended, I put my phone in my jacket pocket. As I did, I moved my arm too fast and was hit by a wave of pain. Esposito saw.

"Come find me as soon as you have a chance," he said. "And I mean soon."

I didn't get a chance in the next few hours. Or I didn't make the time. I didn't want to hear bad news from him with everything else going on. Whatever was on his mind was urgent but also private, or he would have said it in the room instead of waiting. I had yet to come to terms with what Mara had said to me earlier. I didn't want a closed-door meeting in Esposito's office, at least not yet.

I didn't dodge the meeting out of disrespect for the ASAC. Esposito took it personally, but we had much higher priorities that afternoon. Why would my issues jump to the front? Maybe I didn't want that answer either.

53

JACE

"How long until you're ready to hit the road?" Jace asked Grale an hour later at an ad-hoc desk he'd set up.

"Soon."

"Did you meet with the ASAC?"

"No, I'll sit down with him after the missiles are found."

"What are you thinking?"

"That whatever he's going to tell me can wait."

"That's going to light him up."

"I know."

Jace knew Grale was recharging and liked being among other agents as everyone geared up. He fed on the energy. They were all headed out for long hours checking desert roads and possible missile sites that overhead surveillance had identified. Mara had cleared her to go with Grale but he'd also said, "This is the last time until he's healthier."

She knew Grale was aware of that and thinking it over. They could talk on the road. Grale was asking for trouble dodging the ASAC after Esposito made such a point of wanting to talk to him, but he knew that. Grale looked over at her now and smiled.

"Stetts and Wu," he said.

"I know, totally crazy. I'm not even sure I believe it yet."

"It happened."

Jace was tired. So was Grale, and he was hurting.

"Let's get something to eat before we go," she said. "It can be out of a machine or fast food on the way out."

"You're right, it's time to roll."

She watched Grale rise awkwardly then heard ASAC Esposito call Grale's name loud enough to quiet the room. Grale stopped and turned.

"There you are," Esposito said. "You're eating up way too much of my time, Agent Grale. Let's go talk."

"Let's talk here."

"I don't think you'd like that."

"Try me."

"All right, if you want to, we'll do it that way. Here's my problem to solve. How can the FBI get the benefit of your investigative skills without endangering another agent? Agent Blujace will go with you today, but here's my requirement for you. Within seventy-two hours after we find the missiles and shut these terrorists down, you take the active duty physical. You run. You do the whole thing. Are you prepared for the run?"

"If you run ahead of me."

Agents laughed, some hard. *Grale had to know what he was doing,* Jace thought. He was just that proud, he wasn't going to take it alone in an office when he got told things weren't looking good for him. Grale probably knew Esposito had been told to schedule some gym time himself. But Esposito didn't like the laughter. His face tightened and got hard.

"I'll do the physical, or let you know that I can't," Grale said.

"Are you putting Agent Blujace in danger?"

"I don't think so," Grale said, "but why don't I go alone?"

"I'm good riding with Grale," Jace said.

Esposito turned and pointed a finger at her. "Stay out of this."

Jace raised her hands in mock surrender and went to get food and coffee for herself and Grale. She brought it back to the desk, but Grale was gone. She was told that he and the ASAC went to the ASAC's office, or what passed for his office here. She ate a leathery protein bar and drank lukewarm coffee as she waited.

When Grale and Esposito finally came back out, Esposito looked calmer. Grale was quiet as they carried their gear and headed out. It struck her as they hit the highway north that Esposito and Mara had never really acknowledged that it was Grale who kept talking to Ralin and found Indonal and got him to safety. Or that Grale had connected with the head of DARPA, had uncovered Stetts and Wu, and all in the long hunt for Frederic Dalz. Wasn't it Grale they originally asked to look at the Metaline Falls video and photos?

Yes, his back was a big problem and he was hurting, but who'd done more with this investigation? Even hurting, Grale pulled a big oar. She broke the silence. "What are you thinking?"

"I'm thinking that leaving everything behind in the bowling alley including their DNA was a statement. A big fuck-you to us."

Grale's phone rang before Jace could answer. It was Mara. Grale put him on speakerphone.

"The CIA gave us some information I want to pass on to you and Agent Blujace."

"I'm listening," Jace said.

"This is from a redacted report. I'll send it to you, but there are some things to bear in mind when talking to Ralin."

"Go ahead," Grale said.

"In 2001 a fifteen-year-old English girl in Bedford named Claire Henley died of a rare form of pneumonia that killed her inside of seventy-two hours. A year later a similar-looking young woman with the same name, Claire Henley, enrolled in an English-speaking school in Warsaw. Seven years later, the new Henley met an up-and-coming computer scientist named Mark Ralin at Stanford.

"At that point she was on her way to becoming a skilled coder. Her aptitude in computer design was how they connected. She also has unusual gifts with languages. The CIA believes her skills and aptitude were identified early, and she was pulled from public school and trained.

"The next part is very heavily redacted, but it compares—or at least it appears to compare—the very early identification of her gifts as similar to theories on Dalz. Big gifts. Genius level. Identified young, sequestered, mentored, et cetera. That's all. I doubt it's going to matter while you're out there looking, but I wanted you to know it if you end up talking to Ralin."

As Mara hung up, Grale's niece called him.

Grale smiled but let the call go to voice mail. "My niece. You remember her?"

Jace looked over and smiled at the happiness in his voice. "Yeah, I do." Her phone rang. "It's Indonal."

"Hi, Agent Blujace. Is now a good time? I remembered a little more about when we met Margaret Landis," Indonal said. "It's along the same lines as I said before but with more detail."

"We want to hear it," Jace said. "I'm putting you on speakerphone."

"Okay. Do you remember I told you I thought something happened between Alan and her when I went to the restroom?

Well, what's coming back is me seeing Alan's goofy look and her right up against him. Until she saw me."

"She pulled away when she saw you?"

"Yeah."

"And that's bubbling up as even more weird?"

"Kind of, yeah, but she also had Alan's phone and was doing something with it."

"Did he know?"

"It looked like it."

"So maybe no big deal?"

"The guy who was supposedly her boyfriend got to his feet right after."

Jace glanced at Grale. This was more about anxiety and grief over Eckstrom's murder.

"It's haunting you," Jace said.

"It's doing a number on me for sure. She sits down on the night we're quitting Indie. That's not coincidence is it? She knew somehow."

"How do you think she could have known?" Jace asked.

"She couldn't. Right? I'm just thinking aloud. Maybe she could have already been there and watched us come in and order drinks? But I think they came in a little after we did. I just keep going over it all in my head. Maybe Alan told her we'd walked away, you know, quit?"

"What are you trying to say, Eric?" Grale asked.

"Alan must have told her before we went there. I mean, maybe he told her he'd broken up with his girlfriend and they decided to meet up that night. Maybe she knew he'd be there and they could hang out because he wasn't going home. She was in control, and we were stupid. I know they got together after that night," Indonal said. "I don't know if it even matters, but it's been bugging me, so that's why I'm calling."

"Where are you now?"

"At Indie."

"What? You and Ralin need to leave. Hasn't DoD talked with you yet?"

"We had a meeting this afternoon, and they said the risks have increased and they'll support whatever decision we make."

"No, you need to leave and not come back until we know it's safe. It's not worth it."

"Mark won't leave."

"Why not?"

"A lot of reasons, I guess. But I'll leave tonight. I get it. Talk to you soon."

After the call ended, Grale said, "That was hard for him."

"That's pretty much what he communicated last time."

"But he's seeing it more clearly. I hear grief and regret now. They worked together for so many years without knowing whether it would work, had to trust their instincts and look out for each other. They blew off DoD's warnings about strangers because they figured they weren't working for the government anymore. Indonal knows all of this."

"He feels guilt too," Jace said.

"Yeah, and he wonders the same as we do: Did Landis take part in Eckstrom's murder? We've got to keep him and Ralin alive." Grale caught sight of a road sign. "Three miles to Tonopah. What do you want to do for dinner? Want to check in first then find a place?"

"I found one already. So. How can we protect them? How can anyone unless they're put someplace secure?"

She looked over at him. He didn't have an answer. No one did.

54

AUGUST 16TH

We left Tonopah heading south before dawn with a full tank of gas and paper cups full of coffee. The outside range of the missiles was seventy-five miles, so in some ways it made the most sense to stay in Las Vegas. The city of Tonopah was a little over two hundred miles to the north, so farther away, but after we studied the unpaved desert roads we planned to get on, Tonopah had made more sense. We drove south on 95 until exiting and following GPS onto a dirt road headed east.

Overhead there was starlight but along the horizon the sky lightened with the new day. My gut said we needed to find them today. It made me hyperaware and nervous. We drove east toward sunrise watching for recent tire tracks and referred often to the list of locations aerial surveillance had flagged.

It was all open desert country with dry mountain ranges and few buildings. Among the rock abutments and narrow canyons were places capable of hiding a portable missile launcher. The site would likely be camouflaged, so we had to be cautious. We bounced and tossed on the rough, unused roads.

Some were no more than long-abandoned tracks, and others had crossings washed out by flash floods where we needed to navigate through strewn rocks and soft sand.

As the sun rose further, we were visible from a long distance away with a plume of dust rising behind us. We were a target slowly crossing empty desert plains and conscious of it.

I drove, and Jace scanned ahead with binoculars. We checked in with the command center by cell and then radio as we entered the circumference of the missiles' range. If access to an area looked unused or the road to it washed out by a flash flood, we crossed that site off our list. We kept in constant contact with spotter planes as satellites and drones also scoured from overhead.

But most of all we watched for recent tire tracks. Approaching the seventh location in barren country where the white baked hills were streaked with mineral deposits and dotted with alkaline volcanic rock, we found new tracks below a rock abutment.

"Cover me, and I'll walk up the road past that higher outcrop," I said.

"Okay, but we switch up on the next one."

My gear was a floppy desert hat with a wide adjustable brim, sunglasses, a bandanna, and a desert-camouflage coat of the type desert rats wear loaded with gear no matter how hot the sun is. There were mineral hunters out here too, and I looked enough the part of either, not that anyone guarding three missiles would bother to check.

A third of a mile up an unpaved road, the new tracks ended. I saw where they'd turned around at a building half buried, much like Indie, with yellowed concrete walls, a metal door and roof, a Cold War relic. The driver who'd left the tire tracks was just up here having a look, I decided, but we logged coordinates and took photos before heading to the next possible site.

We moved and moved again, and we were near the edge of the seventy-mile missile radius when I scanned with binoculars a rough road across a flat plain in the distance that disappeared into low, rounded hills. I handed the binoculars to Jace.

"It's hard to picture anything carrying missiles up that wannabe road," Jace said.

"Yeah, and it would take us a while to get there."

"Part of the road looks blocked."

"Let me have a look again," I said then focused in on a white object. I handed the binos back to Jace and pointed. "I think I see the back end of a vehicle. It's white."

"Oh, yeah, I see that," she said and asked, "What's that doing there?"

"Could be anybody or anything, but I think we check it out."

As we got closer, we realized there were more tire tracks, so we called in a spotter pilot. My heart rate picked up a little. There were tracks that looked recent and ran along the road into the hills. Jace got on the radio. I focused on two straight lines where it looked as if a helicopter had landed. With the naked eye, the marks were barely visible but easy to see through binoculars.

I handed the binos to Jace and said, "Off to the left just past that tallest red-gray rock. Tell me what it looks like to you."

She said, "Well, if I don't overthink it, I'd say they look like helicopter skids."

"Could be mineral exploration or something, but that's what I see too. Which would be the way to get people and whatever else ferried up. Let's get closer but put on our vests and check our guns first."

"I'll cook to death with the vest on."

"Let's do it anyway. This one is a possible."

The pilot's estimate for arrival had been twenty minutes. It took us fifteen minutes to drop down and drive across the valley. We moved closer to the hills and saw more tire tracks and drove past cactus and climbed through dead mesquite whose hardened branches clawed paint off the Suburban. We came up over a soft rise and went left around rocks, then bang, a heavy slug with a loud, hard sound punched a hole in our bulletproof windshield.

Another went through just left of my head, and we got out and down fast behind the back of the Suburban. Two more bullets tore through then lesser gunfire, an automatic weapon with a shooter advancing as I pulled out a shotgun and shells from the rear of the Suburban.

The shooter kept at it, so they made the mistake of giving away their position. When we had the shooter placed, we worked sideways to a rock outcrop. Jace radioed for help, and I watched and waited for a clean shot. Problem was I could hear another vehicle coming out of the hills. More reinforcements. More shooters. We wouldn't have much time.

Then the initial shooter stepped into view. He was much closer than I'd guessed and still targeting the Suburban. He was dark haired, tall, and looked experienced to me. He was watching everything everywhere and knew how exposed he was.

In a low voice Jace talked to the spotter pilot, giving coordinates. "You'll spot a Suburban. We're in the rock outcrop to the left about fifty yards."

I heard a crackle and the pilot asked, "Can you move farther away?"

"No," she said. "We have multiple assailants on the move toward us. We need firepower. And we need it now."

The car engine noise died, so there was a good chance more shooters had arrived. A moment later the dark-haired shooter came into clear view. I waited with my left knee in rocky sand and my weight on my right ready to stand. He'd pivot as soon as he saw movement. I might only get one chance. I saw him spot Jace first and bring his rifle up as I yelled, "FBI, drop your weapon!"

Without hesitating he swung toward me and fired. I reacted almost as fast but missed him with the first blast of the shotgun. My second round hit home as his fire sprayed rocks near me. I saw him jerk sideways, half turning, blood spraying from his neck, his weapon falling with a clatter as he slumped to the ground.

The new shooters, and there were at least two, were putting out more rounds than I could count, but they didn't have a good angle, and I heard the jets before I saw them. We saw white streaks in the sky and heard the whistling. An explosive concussion vibrated the air seconds later. Smoke rose and another missile hit, and I heard multiple explosions and saw a tall plume of black smoke rise back higher in the hills then a much louder, heavier explosion.

No more shots came our way. We watched the fighter pilots climb and turn and heard their turbo whine. Two more missiles hit in the same area in the hills above and a black pickup roared down and out into open desert after it appeared the fighters were flying away.

They got a third of a mile out before being struck by something powerful enough to toss the pickup burning and tumbling, its fuel tank exploding, the remains a ball of flames as it landed. Overhead a third fighter circled as we talked with the FBI spotter pilot.

An hour later helicopters and combat soldiers in Humvees arrived. After the road was cleared, we drove up and through the spotter pilot communicated with Mara that we were looking at the remains of three missiles. Later, we headed out to the highway with two soldiers following in case our shot up FBI Suburban stopped cold. We'd needed to switch out vehicles then resume searching, but we were ready to go. We were upbeat, almost euphoric, knowing we got three of twelve missiles and were still alive.

When we reached the highway and had cell coverage I listened as Mara asked Jace for details of the shooting and the man I killed. When he told Jace he'd call back soon, I knew something was up.

"Wait at the highway," Mara told me ten minutes later. "I'll send a tow truck for the Suburban, and we'll pair Agent Blujace with another team. You stay there, Grale, and I'll send a DT squad agent to pick up Blujace. There's an agent within ten miles of you. Grale, you'll go back out with two other agents and do a shooting report."

"A shooting report right now?" Jace mouthed. "That's crazy."

"Grale, are you hearing this?" Mara asked.

"Yes."

"We can't stop for a shooting report," Jace said as I put him on speakerphone. "You've got to be kidding. That's nuts."

"Watch yourself, Blujace," Mara said.

Smoke was still rising into a clear sky when I returned to the missile site with the two agents to do the report. I didn't say anything unless asked. But, in truth, I understood, and they were efficient and thorough. That the shooting got such weight when it was clearly defensive—and I doubted anybody questioned that—was because it was my fourth career shooting resulting in the death of a suspect. That stat put me among a small percentage of FBI agents. A decision was made years ago to scrutinize more closely agents falling into that category. It was automatic that a shooting report would be initiated the same day.

I'm sure Mara was against and chafed at the absurdity but wasn't going to risk defying that.

"Did you yell a warning to the shooter?"

"I yelled, and he fired."

"He shot first?"

"He did."

I'd already showed them the rocks hit by his sprays of bullets, and they'd already seen the Suburban.

"He shot at you, and you then returned fire?"

"Yes. I missed with the first shot but the second took out half of his neck, so that was good."

"Good?"

"Okay, it was great."

"You liked killing him?"

"I like living."

One smiled.

We started the slow ride back along rutted road, stopping at the burned carcass of the pickup, which smelled heavily of burned plastic and melted rubber. The bodies of the two men were broken and torn and separated by about forty yards. Both were facedown in the desert and not yet bagged. We rolled them and took photos of their faces with the hope we'd be able to identify at least one of them.

Another crew was on the way with body bags and went past us before we reached the highway. I called Jace from there. By now it was late afternoon. She was with a team of agents a hundred miles to the south acting on a credible tip that might lead to another of the missile launch sites.

The agents I came out with had driven separate Bu-cars. They gave me the keys to one and said good-bye with an apology about the forthright questioning.

They got in their car and waited for me to go first. I called Ralin as I drove and checked text messages Mara sent hours ago, after assuming the shooting report was finished. His string of text messages became more urgent when I'd failed to respond.

I typed, Shooting report just finished and back to the highway. Missed your messages, no phone coverage. I wrote,

Heading your way. Then I erased that and sent no reply. I'd call Mara but not yet. I took the exit for Independence Base and called Ralin instead.

55

At the guard gate, as I waited for Ralin, I called Steve Akaya, who said, "I'm not really a tactical guy, but I can tell you what I'd do after losing three out of twelve missiles. I'd launch the remaining nine missiles ASAP and do it first from one site then wait for the defenses to focus on those missiles before launching the rest. A twenty-five percent loss says your defenses and tactics for hiding aren't up to the task. I'd launch everything."

"That's the bottom line, launch everything?"

"Yes."

As the call ended, I saw Ralin get out of a military vehicle near the guard booth. He looked thinner, his face gaunt, eyes shadowed with fatigue. He spotted me as I got out and walked toward him.

"I'll give you a ride to wherever you want to go," I said.

"I don't know where to go."

"Then let's drive and talk. Where's Indonal? Is he still at the Indie building?"

"He's finishing something up, but he'll be out soon and off the base. Indie has one hundred percent control." After a deep breath he added, "I'm very nervous. Everyone is."

"Let's drive to where we can get an overview," I said and took us up Highway 157 toward the mountains and then out to Desert View Point.

We were there at sunset when two missiles came in from the east. At first they appeared as bright objects, high enough to catch sunlight, and then we saw the exhaust trails. Less than a minute later the southern sky lit up as five missiles rose. We watched their arcs climb and bend and the red and green trails they left as they streaked through the sunset sky above Las Vegas. Two more came from the northeast.

One of the northeast pair exploded near the eastern spine of the mountains bordering Indie, then one of the southern missiles veered off and exploded. Fragments from it glowed as they fell.

"One gone," I said.

"And three arcing down," Ralin said softly as the missiles to our right from the south began their descents. Simultaneously, bright sparks lit as missiles rose from behind the building housing Indie.

"Go, go, go," Ralin whispered, as multiple launches, almost too many to count, came from in and around the Indie building. One of the incoming southern missiles exploded with a bright flash and a dull roar. In the last of the golden sunlight, glittering drones enveloped the Indie building.

"They're making the building seem larger," I said and handed him binoculars. "Take a look. Will that matter if they're tracking on a GPS heading?"

Ralin waved away the binos. "I don't need to see; I know what it looks like. The drones will also broadcast electronic chaff."

"What does that do?"

"The missiles *may* read the drones as part of the building. That's the hope, but we're about to find out. Here we go."

A missile struck the building, and seconds later another made a partially deflected strike at the southwest corner. Through my binoculars it appeared vehicles parked near the building took the brunt. The remaining missiles flew through the drone cloud then struck the desert behind the building.

And just like that it was over. We stood in darkness listening to civil air-raid sirens sounding in Vegas, and Ralin told me what he couldn't say earlier.

"Indie has replicated itself as a defensive measure. It hijacked computers and created a copy."

"One or more than one?"

"We don't know yet."

"It didn't manage to do that on its own, did it?"

"No, we gave it what it needed then let it replicate."

"How long did it take?"

"Six hours or less."

"Shut it down."

"There's a conversation about slowing down until all the implications are understood, but if you're reading something nefarious in the speed of replication, you shouldn't—it's actually a great step forward. It's another defense. If missiles had destroyed the building, Indie would still have survived."

"Great step forward toward what?"

"Whatever we want to do with it. The issue isn't the speed of replication. The issue is our ability to keep up without ceding chunks of programming control to the AI." He glanced over at me and started to say more but checked himself when he saw my face. On the drive down we talked very little after word came that there were casualties. Ralin was unable to reach Indonal.

I thought of the red exhaust trails streaming in the sunset and what Jace had said about the murmurations of starlings the first time we saw the small drones in formation. Indie taught itself that. Indie saved the building tonight. But Indie was self-replicating itself, albeit in a slower form as it strung together computers across the world. I didn't believe that was a good thing, although admittedly I didn't know. I didn't like how it felt.

Nor did I like the idea of dropping Ralin at the Independence Base guard gate. I tried to talk him out of it. Rather than argue with me, he made a call and confirmed two DoD agents were waiting at the gate for him.

"They're going to take me someplace secure."

When he got out of my car, he leaned back in and said, "In the end, AI will be a force for good. In the end, it may save us. But nothing has turned out as Eric, Alan, or I hoped. This is a nightmare, but the potential . . ."

"I'll look forward to that day," I said and got a sad smile from him.

For my own reasons, I thought it unlikely our paths would cross again. Mara was narrowing the scope of what I investigated and worked on. I could see where that was going. I reached across and shook Ralin's hand. He was a complex man driven by inner winds.

"Make time for your kids, Mark."

"I plan to."

"Make it happen."

He let the door fall shut, and I waited until the DoD agents got out of their car and guided him over.

My phone rang as I pulled away.

"I'm with Agent Blujace. We're on our way to Boulder City," Mara said. "There's a credible tip that helicopters—possibly three of them—flew below radar down the river south of Boulder City. All air traffic was grounded right after the missile launches, but these helicopters flew anyway. If it's an actionable tip, and it appears to be, Blujace and I will get on an FBI helicopter there. We've got twenty agents in the area and more coming."

"And where do we think they're going?"

"Down the river and across the Mexican border. You really ought to be here for the takedown."

I didn't respond to that. Mara asked, "Where are you, Grale?"

"On my way to the fusion center."

"To do what?"

"Several things."

"Okay. We also got word that Ralin is safe."

"I was with him. He's fine. Two DoD agents are taking him someplace safer."

"Good on Ralin, but there's bad news on Indonal. The building was hit twice. He was struck by debris as he was running to his car. They got him to a hospital, but he didn't make it. I'm sorry to have to tell you that, Grale."

"Are you certain about Indonal?"

"Yes, but we will get the terrorists."

He sounded upbeat and confident, but I was thinking about Indonal. I didn't say anything until Mara asked, "You still there?"

"I'm here. Be careful how you capture them," I said. "Bring Dalz in alive."

I tuned out Mara's questions and leaned back with a deep wave of sadness flowing through me. I thought of Indonal hiding in the cabin of a woman he met as a teenager and how they came together again. When I was younger, I accepted collateral damage more easily. I've lost that acceptance, but maybe I've gained something else. Indonal's death filled me with true grief, and I couldn't help thinking of Weiss at Stanford talking about his "mathematical gifts that are once in a generation." I should have left him at the lake.

56

JACE

As Mara talked to Grale, Jace could tell their supervisor was choosing his words carefully. It said Mara brought her for more than the bust. He wanted her to hear him talk to Grale and be able to recount the tone. There was no question Grale was excluded from the takedown about to happen, and Mara was boosting her. In return he expected loyalty. She knew that, but had never been as uncomfortable with it as today. All kinds of thoughts spun through her head.

Grale once said to her that all good cases are built from evidence but that anything can be shaded, so nothing is more important than integrity. You have to have the integrity to honor evidence.

She listened as Mara maneuvered the conversation to Dalz tips. There was nothing malicious or wrong about it. It was Mara's way of working around to what he believed and what he'd probably try to convince Grale of.

"We got the predictable flood of tips when we went public with Dalz's face," Mara said. "In all of those tips nothing was solid, but he'll go down with the rest tonight. I'm sure of it. I'm sorry you won't be here for that, but you'll be first to interview him."

"Does SWAT know how much we want Dalz taken alive?" Grale asked.

"It's been talked through, and I'm confident everyone understands that the object is to capture as many alive as possible. There's also very high confidence they're all together."

"But specifically, Dalz?" Grale asked.

"SWAT has photos of him."

"But it's a night bust and anything can happen. If they're making a run for the border, they're not going to throw down their guns and surrender. Is there *any* confirmation Dalz boarded one of the helicopters?"

"Not specifically, but there are three helicopters, and they were organized and fast getting to the pickup area and loaded and gone. They'll be forced down if they resist."

"Shot down."

"They'll land. Overwhelming force will convince them."

"Will it?"

"What other choice do they have?"

"Dalz may not surrender," Grale said. "He'll have thought it through."

"Don't worry," Mara said. "You're going to get the call that we've got him and we're bringing him in."

Grale let that be. He didn't follow up, and Jace knew he'd picked up on Mara losing patience. *He's not challenging Mara,* she thought, *but he sees something else.*

"Whoever is behind this is trying to get everybody over the border to Mexico," Mara said. "That's what they were hoping, but they didn't anticipate all air traffic being grounded. We'll get him, Grale. We'll get him. I promise you that."

Jace heard the confidence in the way Mara's voice rose.

"Where are you now?" Mara asked Grale.

"At the fusion center."

"Take it on home. Jace will call you on the other side."

"I'm scanning through the Dalz tips."

That exasperated Mara. He glanced over at Jace and shook his head but managed to keep it out of his voice. "Like I said earlier," Mara told him, "we've had a nonstop stream of solo Dalz sightings, but it'll turn out he's catching the same ride out as the rest. The Air Force is tracking the three helicopters and will force them down at a spot downriver where SWAT is already on site. It's a SWAT show now, Grale. You're not missing anything. I'll text you a photo of Dalz in handcuffs."

"Do that."

"I will. Now get out of the office and go home. And congratulations on finding those three missiles today."

Of all people Grale should have been there, but the brass didn't want him in the media photos. No one had said that to Jace, and everyone would deny that was true. But everyone knew it was. And still she liked Mara. He was a good guy doing a complicated job. Being a supervisor was hard and mostly thankless, but it was Grale she admired most.

Mara shook his head as the call ended. "Grale will try to look through the tips, but he's still never really learned the new computer system. Every other agent on the DT squad has it down."

"If they had Grale's solve rate they wouldn't need to."

"He's got that," Mara said. "He does have that."

"No one else comes close, right?"

"We'll see how this year shapes up."

"He's pretty good on his laptop," Jace said. "He's got gaps, but I've seen him in action enough. I don't think he likes the new system, but I'm certain he knows it."

"I'm not. Those lights up ahead are Boulder City. That's where we're catching our helicopter."

Mara had taken a liking to her, and he said that on the drive here tonight. He complimented her on her discipline and attention to detail and said he saw great things ahead for her.

On the outskirts of Boulder City, they parked and waited. Maybe the escape plan made sense originally, before commercial flight traffic was grounded. Fly under the radar, down the river and across to Mexico. There were worse escape plans, but Jace knew what Grale was thinking. He was thinking, *With flights grounded why would you get into a helicopter?*

Maybe the terrorists didn't hear about it or figured they'd fly so low over the Colorado River they'd be below radar skimming. That didn't make sense either, and Mara hadn't been able to explain it in a way she believed. Making a run for Mexico made sense. Over the border to a cartel-controlled airport then out of the country and gone. Or maybe a cartel was getting paid to lose them in the desert after they land. No need to speculate about that part, she thought. Apache attack helicopters flying south, and fast, from Nellis Air Force Base will cut them off either way. She'd love to see their faces when they realize they aren't leaving.

Within ten minutes they were listening in on the back-and-forth with the Air Force pilots as a report came that the terrorist helicopters were verified to be south of the dam low over the Colorado River and nearing Lake Mojave. Mara turned and smiled. He held a hand up to high-five, and she slapped it.

"Got 'em," Jace said. "Or about to."

Mara and Jace climbed into an FBI helicopter then waited for the Air Force to bring the helicopters down so they could get airborne and get down there.

"You know they're celebrating," Mara said. "You know they are. They infiltrated the US, attacked a base, and damaged Indie. If they get out intact, that's a huge win."

Jace didn't say anything. A few minutes later the Apache attack helicopters made their move. Jace and Mara listened in on the calm cool of the Apache pilots making their presence known, first by radio then with warning flares. Two fighter jets arrived to drive home the point that the Mexico trip had just ended. The helicopter pilots didn't turn away, though—at least not at first. They dropped lower and kept flying.

More warning flares lit the sky, and the helicopters lowered, stopped, and hovered over the river. It was in that moment she realized they weren't going to surrender. Doors swung open, and men jumped into the water. As the helicopters disgorged, they split up, one flying downstream, one back up the river, and one due east.

"We need these guys alive," Jace said but might as well have been talking to herself. Gunfire had probably already started, and those who'd jumped in the water most likely were scattering. The smart ones would try to cross the river and get downstream as far as possible before daylight.

Jace and Mara listened as the go-ahead was given to shoot down the fleeing helicopters. She heard a pilot's acknowledgment then back-and-forth before missiles launched. The three helicopters were downed within minutes. She heard the phrase "not survivable" repeated as the pilots assessed the crashes.

Along the river SWAT was in a firefight half a mile a long, and inevitably that meant a mop-up operation that would continue through tomorrow. The terrorists in the river or out on the sand and in the brush probably didn't know Apaches had laser guided missiles and 30 mm automatic cannon fire. She'd worked around Apaches years ago. They were monsters. If one hit you, you were not only done but a mess to clean up. She continued listening, but it became almost impossible to follow. Then it became methodical as someone made a practical decision that capturing them alive wasn't worth the risk. Any terrorist who fired on the Apaches in the air above took massive return fire.

"They don't need us there," Mara said. "We may as well head home."

"What do I tell Grale? He's waiting on the call."

"He had a long day. He probably took a pain pill and is asleep and we don't have a confirmation on Dalz."

"No, he'll be waiting. You told him I'd call."

"Then say we don't know if Dalz was there or not. We'll know tomorrow."

"Did you see that coming, that they'd jump in the water?"

"No, but maybe we should have. We'll have information in the morning. You go home. I'll be in the office, and if anything significant happens, I'll call you."

"I'll stay with you."

"No, we need you rested tomorrow."

The drive back to the fusion center felt much longer than the drive out, and they didn't talk much. In the fusion center lot, she and Mara talked briefly before she went to her car. Mara was disappointed but shouldn't have been. The escape got shut down, and between dogs, helicopters, and summer heat, the stragglers wouldn't get far. There would be some survivors, and they'd be captured. But like Mara, she felt the failure. It left her down as she drove home. She almost called Grale but didn't know what she'd say. Who knows? Maybe Dalz was among the survivors.

57

I read through the Dalz tips then checked out an all-wheel drive from the vehicle pool. I lugged some gear out to it and was close to leaving the fusion center without having heard again from Jace or Mara. At that point I didn't really have a plan, I just wanted to be prepared, ready to follow my gut sense that Dalz would have broken away from the rest of the group. That was always his pattern after an attack—break away and disappear. Let the others leave the trail.

I was exhausted but amped up as I checked with our temporary front desk. They had little in the way of facts, only the blunt assessment that "it didn't go as planned." That was often code for "it went badly" but no conclusions could be drawn yet.

At a desk I flipped through some of the more likely Dalz tips, looking for any possible pattern of movement. But it was as Mara had said, too many tips and too varied to sort, so I fought fatigue and kept asking myself, *What is he going to do? What would I do? I've studied him. I* know *him at some level. What will Dalz do?*

That led me back to where I'd started. He would not be with the group. Other intelligence agencies, including Interpol, had interrogated captured terrorists who'd insisted Dalz was with them throughout, but later it turned out he was gone much earlier. Or in several instances he'd stayed for six months or more in the city where the attack had taken place.

Las Vegas has a large reputation, but the city itself isn't that large. It's not an easy place to hide in.

"He won't stay here," I said to an empty room. All air traffic into and out of Las Vegas was grounded. There were police checkpoints on the highways and main roads. On I-15 and the larger arteries, bumper-to-bumper traffic jams extended for miles. Dalz would have anticipated that. He's not at the airport. He's not in a line of cars on the highway waiting to show ID with a flashlight on his face. If he was escaping, we were losing the chance to apprehend him. I set aside the tips that made the most sense rather than those with the best description, then I left the office and headed home.

The roads were eerily quiet. Jo was at the hospital. I called her and left a message. She called back at midnight as I watched TV coverage. I told her what I was seeing. The media had learned about the river bust and was all over it, claiming the Independence Base terrorists were in three helicopters and had been captured or killed.

My view was more cynical. Whoever was behind this attack couldn't risk the United States identifying them. Three helicopters flying low over the Colorado River would draw immediate suspicion, and whoever planned that escape was highly aware of that fact. I hadn't argued the point with Mara, but the more I turned it over in my head, the more likely it seemed.

Yet another reason to have hired mercenaries for the attack. Hire the best but send them to their deaths and let the Americans kill and identify them after they'd boarded a sucker's ride to the Mexico border.

"You still there?" Jo asked.

"Oh, yeah, sorry, Jo. Just tired. And I'm thinking about this helicopter escape plan."

"Do you know you're in the news? You and Blujace, for finding the three missiles."

"We got lucky, and it was fighter pilots who took out the missiles. Are you at the hospital all night?"

"I am."

"Then I may miss you in the morning. I'll be gone early, checking a lead. It may be too late, but I have to take my best guess."

"But not alone, right?"

"At first, maybe, but there'll be a quick response if I get lucky."

"Paul, listen to me. Stay in close touch tomorrow, okay? This is one of those times we've talked about. I need to know you're okay."

"I'll do my best."

"Paul . . ."

"I hear you, Jo."

"And there's something else," she said in a slower, quiet voice. "We had a transfer to our trauma unit of a thirty-one-year-old male with severe head injuries from shrapnel at the Independence building. I was told he worked on the artificial intelligence project there. I thought you might know him. He died a few hours ago."

"Eric Indonal," I said. "I heard he was killed."

"He was the one you found?"

"Yes, and a good guy, I liked him."

I thought of Cindy Maldon and something she'd said to Jace. *"We were together that summer when we were sixteen, and I knew then he was the one for me."*

"I'll tell you more about him when I see you. Are you on ICU tonight?"

"Yes, and sticking with a patient who's having a tough time. So, you didn't tell me. Did Dalz get caught?"

"No. But I doubt he was there."

"Is Dalz the lead you're checking tomorrow?"

"One among many. Mara is sure they were all on board the helicopters. If I get confirmation Dalz was on one of the helicopters, well, then it's over, and I'll be home."

Jo paused, then said, "I'll never forgive you if anything happens to you."

"Didn't you hear what I just said?"

"Yes, and I've heard that before. I also know you're hurting."

After we ended the call, I slept four hours before heading to Mountain Springs, southwest of Vegas, up Blue Diamond Road and on toward the mountains. Higher up the road became Highway 160. Looking out over the valley I saw the lights of a passenger plane descending on Las Vegas and another right behind it. The flight ban must have been lifted.

Near Mountain Springs on the highway shoulder were two Nevada State Highway Patrol cars, but no checkpoint. I exited at Mountain Springs, which was small, mostly houses and people willing to live farther from the typical conveniences in a trade for beautiful views, clear air, and light. It was a very unlikely place for Dalz to be except for one thing.

I stopped at the Mountain Springs Saloon where a delivery truck was unloading and a woman who might be an owner or manager stood talking to the driver. I read a text from Jace before getting out and stretching a little as I stood in the early sunlight.

Her text read like a summary. All three helicopters had been shot down. Six terrorists were captured alive. Two of the six were in critical condition with bullet wounds. Nine others were killed, along with the three pilots. More bodies were still in a downed helicopter in the river, but the bodies had been checked out and Dalz wasn't among them. Jace called a few minutes later.

"You were right," she said. "He skipped the Mexico ride. Are you home? How are you feeling?"

"I'm in Mountain Springs checking on a tip. I'll call or text you if there's anything to it. I see planes in the air."

"The ban was lifted early this morning. What's in Mountain Springs?"

"One of the Dalz tips. I'll text it to you when we get off the phone."

I texted her, then talked with the woman receiving the delivery. I asked if she'd seen anything unusual the night before or this morning. I showed my creds and said we were looking everywhere. She hadn't seen anything but would ask around and wrote down my phone number.

I slowly drove the few roads in Mountain Springs as I turned over the reasons why Dalz might be here. Whoever called in the tip stayed anonymous. Nothing I could do about that, but I had hiking gear and danced around my initial idea of hiking up the Mountain Springs trail before calling Jace back.

"His decades-long habit is to leave alone," I said. "It's probably how he's survived for so long."

"Okay, but what do I tell Mara?"

"Give me a little more time. I'll call you back within an hour. I'll check around some more. If there's nothing more, I'll head to the office."

I didn't go unnoticed. People were nervous in the way they were after 9/11. A guy in a utility company pickup had eyes on me as I drove by. I turned onto a Williams Ranch Road and followed it past several houses. Straight ahead was a fenced utility yard with warning signs, but to the right and left of it were unpaved roads.

I took an unpaved fork knowing that soon ahead there was another fork I'd go right on. I took that second turn and the road steepened. I put it in all-wheel drive and climbed a short, steep grade to the trailhead. As the track leveled off, I saw the remains of a campfire with a lot of broken glass around it. A lone vehicle, an older model Jeep Cherokee with New Mexico plates, was there as well. Maybe it belonged to a backpacker or day hiker. It could be a geologist's vehicle, or even a developer scouting view lots, although the last made no sense given it was government land ahead. That was fatigue working against me.

I parked, got out, and gathered my hiking gear, then had a thought and made a call to a firefighter friend who'd once worked these mountains. He picked up, saying, "I figured you'd be down at the river pulling bodies out. Sounds like you guys got them all."

"Not all of them. Hey, I've got a question for you about Mountain Springs Peak and the surrounding mountains. How often are helicopters up on top?"

"Not often, but it does happen."

"Can land on top?"

"Oh, sure, it's flat enough. Usually it's someone scouting who isn't paying for the ride. Sometimes it's a rescue."

We talked more as I looked through the windows of the Jeep Cherokee. It was worn and tired. Nothing of note was visible inside—no wrappings, dirty coffee mugs, sunglasses slipped onto the floor mat, gear, or anything—but maybe the owner tucked everything away out of sight to prevent a break-in or keep items marginally cooler.

When our call ended, I adjusted the straps on my daypack, still debating hiking up or just driving the unpaved road as far as it went before becoming trail. I decided to walk despite the physical struggle it might become. If I drove and Dalz was there, he might assume it was someone allowed to drive there, possibly law enforcement. I didn't want to send that signal. I walked the road then turned onto the summit trail. As I did, I called Jace.

"Can you make a couple of calls for me?" I asked.

"What's the huffing?"

"I'm on the Mountain Springs Peak Trail."

"There were hundreds of tips on Dalz yesterday. What was it about that one?"

"It's far enough away from Vegas and helicopters sometimes land on top of the peak."

"Helicopters can land on plenty of other mountains."

"Yeah, but the road to get here is clean and easy, and the trail up isn't long. Hardly anyone lives in Mountain Springs. It checks a lot of boxes, Jace. And since the ban is lifted, a helicopter could get up. There's a Cherokee parked near the trailhead that probably belongs to a hiker, but I'm going to hike up and take a look."

"Seriously?"

"I know it's not much to go on. But it's the combination that makes this a good jumping-off spot. This wouldn't be his first choice. It would be a fallback escape route. He'd have one. I had him trapped in Croatia, and he was ready."

"What about you hiking? That seems sort of crazy on such a longshot. Are you okay?"

"Going up will be fine, coming down will be harder. The hike won't take that long. I need your help with the helicopter companies."

"But with your back—"

"I know about my back, just make the calls."

"Give me the mountain again."

"Mountain Springs Peak. He would have booked ahead anticipating the missile launch might shut down air traffic, so there's a chance he called again early this morning when the ban was lifted, just to make sure his ride was still coming."

"You're saying he knew the helicopters would get shot down, so he came up with a plan of his own."

"What I'm saying is he wouldn't trust the people who hired him. From TV, Internet, whatever, he'll know the escape helicopters were shot down. We're still trying to identify bodies and searching for anyone we missed, so that makes this morning the day to escape."

"I'll make the calls and brief Mara, but he might pull you off," she said.

"He might, or I might be too far up the mountain for cell service."

The pain was strong down my left leg and sharp near my spine, but I'd brought a pair of retractable walking sticks, and they helped. About a quarter of a mile up the trail I spotted a man well ahead and above me. I didn't feel any surge of adrenaline, but his long, lean build could fit. I kept on slow and steady. At this hour Jace might be leaving messages on helicopter services' voice mail, but that wouldn't slow her. She'd figure out a way to get through. She was nothing if not tenacious.

I got several more glimpses of the man ahead. He was alone. I called Jace an hour later when I took a break.

"I told Mara," she said. "He said he hadn't heard from you, but he's okay with it as long as you do not engage if you spot anyone."

"He thinks it's a waste of time?"

"I don't know what he thinks this morning. He's not happy. He said to remind you that you have the active duty physical coming up and not to hurt your back hiking up since we can check the mountaintop in a few minutes with a helicopter."

"What did you learn from the helicopter companies?" I asked.

"There's a guy counting on a ride who called twice yesterday and again early this morning, but he's got a little dog and a wife with bad knees who can't walk downhill."

"Bad knees and a wife who can't walk downhill?"

"Yes."

"That's not a threesome that's going to hike up a mountain in August heat. What time is that pickup scheduled for?"

"An hour from now."

"Then it's got to be the guy ahead of me. He's well ahead, but he's about the right height. No dog. No wife with bad knees."

"How long before you're at the top?"

"Half an hour. I'll call you before I summit."

"I'm heading your way," Jace said, "in case this turns real. And I'll make sure there's plenty of backup."

I exaggerated fatigue by leaning into the poles as I got higher. I knew the man was watching. He'd tuned in to me but was clever about it. I stopped, turned around, and looked back down the trail as if contemplating giving up, then drank from a water bottle, doing my best impression of a hiker flagging from early heat and altitude. I took photos of Potosi Mountain then looked down at my phone to admire my artistry.

I turned and started up again knowing he was tracking my progress but guessing he still hadn't made up his mind about me. The pain was worst where the trail turned to loose rock and sand. I moved more slowly then stopped as Jace called again.

"How close to the summit are you?"

"Close, and no, I'm not going to close in. He's watching. He's wearing a green knapsack. It's not large but weighs something. He's got gear in it, maybe ammunition, maybe worse. It could be Dalz. I think it's Dalz, but I'm still too far away to say for sure."

"What are you wearing?"

"The same jeans as yesterday, a green, long-sleeved T-shirt, and the same hat and sunglasses. I've got a pair of walking sticks."

"We've only talked to four of seven helicopter tour services. I still want to check the others, just to be sure."

"Are other agents helping?"

"Yeah, we're on you, Grale. We're not going to let anything happen to you before Mara or Esposito can fire you."

I laughed. "You're not pulling any punches this morning."

"I like it when you don't feel sorry for yourself, so I'm coaching. I've never worked around anyone better than you."

"Save all that for my funeral. I'm not dead yet."

"Hang on," she said. "There's another message. Okay, uh, it looks like the helicopter is about ready to go up, and they don't want to wait or the pilot will be late arriving."

"After all flights were shut down last night? It's okay, he can be late. Ask him to leave fifteen minutes late and fly one mountain over and circle that one for a while when he gets here. He'll look stupid, but it'll buy me time. I'm almost to where I can say and be one hundred percent sure it is or isn't Dalz. I'm that close."

"Hang back, don't get close, and we'll get on the road to you."

The helicopter arrived thirteen minutes later. The hiker watched it fly past and circle the next mountain over, and I watched as he pulled his phone out in frustration. I moved closer, but I did it gradually, stopping several times to take photos. I slowed, stopped, rested, and then continued toward him. But adrenaline was kicking in. He was tracking my progress, and I was watching his every move. We were headed to a moment.

The helicopter pilot still circled the wrong mountain, but it wouldn't take Dalz long to figure out what was going on. By now he'd have given the helicopter service the correct coordinates. I called Jace with my back to him.

"Ask the helicopter service to call and say the pilot is circling because he's got a mechanical problem and doesn't want to risk anyone by flying over Mountain Springs Peak. They're sending another helicopter. It's on its way or almost. He might believe that. And yeah, it's Dalz."

"You're certain?"

"It's him."

"Jesus, you're right there with him?"

"I'm far enough away."

Her voice rose. "Don't do anything, we'll get it all rolling! Keep your distance."

Jace hung up, and I knew the wheels were in motion. I sat down on a large flat rock with my back to him and after a few minutes I turned to face him and lay back on the rock. The rock's warmth eased the pain. A breeze promising even stronger heat later in the day swept across the summit plateau, and I let my hat cover my forehead, resting it on my nose in a way that let me still see him. He'd slipped his backpack off and may have gotten something out before putting it back on. He did something, but I couldn't make it out without standing and staring.

Something else occurred to me as he moved out of view, and I sat up and scratched my back as I freed my holster clasp. Dalz had started down off the summit and was walking almost straight at me. He deviated away in the last fifty feet. He was long-legged and looked different than I'd remembered. More muscular and older but that made sense. I'd always thought we'd had the age wrong.

I didn't move from the rock, and he didn't look at me again until the big sweeping turn down off the mountain gave him a view of me again. He only glanced at me. But he did. A few minutes later he'd dropped out of sight.

I called Jace and said, "He knows. He made me and is on his way out, meaning he's given up on the helicopter ride. Where's the backup you've asked for?"

"Some are just arriving but asking for clarification on the directions. Others are en route."

"Straight up the paved road then right at the fork and round and up to where they see my Bu-car. They can call me."

"Don't hang up, I'll be right back." After a few minutes Jace clicked back on and said, "Lead vehicle is on the dirt road with three agents. We're getting a helicopter up. Mara wants you to confirm again."

"It's him. It's definitely Dalz."

"Hang back, there are a whole lot of agents on their way."

58

I didn't hang back but was slow coming down the trail. Dalz might hear the click, click of the walking poles. I hoped so. I hoped it worried and distracted him as he tried to focus on escape. If he'd recognized me, then he knew more FBI agents were on their way.

I lost sight of him as he rounded the curve that fell along the southwestern face, but up ahead was a rock overhang with a rock underneath and room enough to sit. I'd thought about resting there out of view on the way up. As I closed in, I stopped using the walking sticks. I carried them and approached as quietly as I could.

Ten seconds later, there he was. I was face to face with Frederic Dalz and asking, "Okay if I sit in the shade beside you for a few minutes?"

Talk about surreal, but that's where we were at, and I rolled with it.

"Sure, sure, okay," he said.

I knew he'd recognized me. He shifted away from me as I sat close enough that he wouldn't be able to lift his right wrist without me clamping down on it. I took a deep breath and said, "It was beautiful up on top. Tight under here, though."

"Yes, but it's you."

I saw the start of a smile, and he started to slide to his left, maybe readying to stand. Then he stopped. He was uncomfortable with the closeness. I felt that. It was visceral for him and the move away was almost involuntary. We went several seconds in silence before Dalz spoke. It was in a tone like we were two old friends encountering each other after a long absence. "How did you find me in Croatia?"

"Your mother."

After a moment he said, "Ah, of course."

His hair was darker, his face more lined than I'd expected. He was definitely older. He had an accent and a deeper voice than I'd imagined.

"Where would you go?" I asked. "What's left for you?"

He didn't answer but studied me. *Undecided still*, I thought.

"Let's not reach for guns yet," I said. "You know so much, there might be another way. And with a helicopter and sharpshooter closing in . . . On the open slope you wouldn't have anywhere to hide." I pointed below and down the slope. "You can see more vehicles coming. See the dust rising? They'll close the road, the pass, everything. What have you got that's big enough to trade? Who was behind this?"

"I don't know. I was told I had to go."

"Then you do know."

"I could make a guess, but where would that get me?"

"You would need names. There would need to be proof."

"They were very careful."

"I'm sure they were. No one made it to Mexico. Most died last night. A few are trying to get down the river, but they'll be captured. That makes you more valuable. But they'll want decades of everything."

"I can give a very long list of names that will never be found."

"Can you live in a prison cell without anything?"

He turned and looked in my eyes for the first time. I drew a very quiet breath. He was poised, getting ready. I'd have to be very quick. I felt the small movements, the shifts he made as he tried to hold my gaze.

"Why is it that after a bombing you return and watch the wounded dying?" I asked.

"I need to see it but not in the way you think. Do you want me to explain?"

"At some point."

I pulled off my sunglasses and placed them on a rock to my right.

"Did you kill Desault?" I asked.

"He knew I would wait and find him."

"Did he ask you if you were the devil?"

"He asked to pray so maybe. He was praying when I shot him."

Down on the dirt road, agents came into view, and Dalz's voice became a little faster as he watched them cross through sunlight.

I pointed at a black speck in the sky. "That's one of ours."

"How did you know to come here?" he asked.

"There was a tip call. Someone in the area recognized you and called in. I knew you wouldn't go out with the others. I decided it had to be a helicopter, probably off a mountaintop so we couldn't converge and trap you. The pilot who missed the mountain was directed to by us."

"It *was* you," he said.

"Yes."

"Desault needed to see my wrists to believe I was human. These scars on my left wrist are from the fire when the hotel burned in Lebanon."

Most likely he was trying to draw my eye, but I looked. He slowly lifted his left hand and exposed burn scars at the wrist and his ring finger holding down a button with a wire snaking from it. No doubt the other end of the wire was in the daypack he wore.

"If I lift my finger, we die. The bomb is quite powerful. I propose this: you drive me to Mexico, and I go away and you never hear of me ever again. I'll disappear. I'm going to stand now," he said before I answered.

I gripped him. We rose together. The finger holding down the trigger could easily slip, but some sort of safety lag would be built in, at least a few seconds, maybe more, to get his finger back on it.

"Call and warn the agents that if they shoot me, my finger comes off and the bomb explodes. We'll take your car. Our talk is done."

I yelled down to the agents who had been coming up as Dalz and I talked and were now within shouting range. They froze as I yelled, "He's got a bomb! Back away, *now*!"

The helicopter came from behind us, and Dalz demanded I keep moving and repositioning to block the sharpshooter's angle. He was all about not getting killed, even to the point of letting me be behind him. He was confident, perhaps because of my injuries.

I was to his side when I stumbled forward and threw myself hard against him. He half turned, almost caught himself, then went off the edge. He grasped my clothes, and if I hadn't jerked free, we would have gone over together.

Most of the trail was just loose slope, but here there was rock and a straight drop, forty feet to a ledge. I tumbled onto the trail, and he fell without a sound. The agents below watched and said he managed to stay upright and land on his feet. They heard bones snap, then he tumbled forward and the bomb detonated with bright, hard force.

I heard the blast and felt heat wrap up and over me. Rocks clattered down. Black smoke rose then bent in the wind, and only then did my heart pound. I saw tatters of cloth and blood on the rocks below and a torso without a head or legs. For a bit I just sat there then eased to my feet and walked down.

We closed off the trail, and the helicopter pilot circled then left. Then it sank in that Dalz was really dead. I felt the embraces, the clap of hands on my back. These are the people I've worked with for years. These are the ones in the field, the ones I'll miss the most. As I limped down, they were already joking about the cleanup.

When you get lucky you can laugh, but I'd seen something I couldn't get my head around. His left arm had been blown off and was a distance from the body. I made my way to it and looked at the wrist where he'd showed me his scars from the fire. There was no clothing, just his arm. And no scars. What do you do with that?

I couldn't make sense of it or even try. He must have used some visual trick, something. A rational explanation might come later. I transferred my gear to Jace's SUV and flipped my keys to an agent who could drive the all-wheel I'd checked out back to the field office.

We imagine grand endings, but many things end quietly. My days on the Vegas domestic terrorism squad and all those years in the field ended there. When Jace and I drove down from Mountain Springs, we talked briefly with Mara on speakerphone. After that I talked with her as we drove to my house. I didn't know when we'd next get the chance, so I told her how great I thought she was. We don't do that enough in life. We don't take care of each other enough.

"You're going to be among the best, Jace. You've got the skills that can't be taught."

"If you say so."

"It's really about you and believing in yourself. I told Mara you were the best young investigator I've ever met. I meant it."

"I would never have known to look for Dalz on some mountain."

"But you will. He operated alone. He trusted no one. He knew there'd be roadblocks and no air traffic, and that wouldn't last long in a city dependent on tourists. You'll learn to trust what you know. I don't know why some agents do, some don't. But you get people, you understand, you have that feel."

She argued against herself, and I listened without commenting. That was all up to her. Intercepting Potello after a cartel lawyer posted bail was on her, but it was up to her to learn and move on.

"I want your solve rate," she said.

"Then mix it up between sitting in front of a computer and talking to people. People are much more complex than computers, they change and what they're willing to tell you may have a lot to do with your relationship with them."

On the drive down from Mountain Springs, I resolved that I'd try to pass on everything I knew that was worth knowing. I didn't know what would come next, but if it came to turning in my gun and laying down my badge and creds, I wouldn't just walk away. I'd work with Jace and try to pass more on before our lives grew too far apart.

Maybe that was my way of making peace with my fears, but it felt bigger. It felt like the right thing to do, and it calmed me. Jace had told me that in all her years as an agent in San Francisco, she would always lay out her clothes for the next morning. She knew how long it took in seconds to brush her teeth, what she would eat for breakfast, and the minutes her commute to the office would take, plus alternate routes if there was an issue with the primary. I get that. I know the feeling and know the loneliness.

"Are you going to get to know your dad?" I asked.

"You know what? I am. I want to."

"All of that matters."

"You mean like finding someone to love?"

"Or they find you because you're open to it."

"Yeah, you're right. I know the difference."

"I know you do, and you don't need me to tell you that you need counterbalances and good things. You call, or I'll call you," I said. "We'll just keep that going. I'm in tomorrow to do my reports, but things are about to change and I want to be sure we keep in touch."

"I'm down with that," she said and got out of the car and came around and gave me a hug. I shouldered my gear and watched her drive away.

59

Mara called early the next morning and asked, "When will I see your report on Dalz and Mountain Springs?"

"Today."

"That's what I wanted to hear."

After our call I pulled out the rolled-up piece of carpet I use when working on the jeep and lay down on it and looked under at the rear axles. Both were leaking and needed rebuilding. I opened the garage door for better light and inspected the rest of the undercarriage, thinking I'd get it towed to a mechanic I knew in the next day or two.

After inspecting everything, I lay on the carpet a minute before getting up. I was pretty beat up, so in a way it felt good just to lie there as I replayed yesterday in my head. Jo had nosed up her little SUV close to the garage door so I could easily see under it as well.

I spotted a red plastic tie that caught my attention then several other ties and something attached to the underside. I took a closer look and saw a long magnet and a couple of plastic straps of a kind I'd never seen before. Rather than being cinched together, the ends of the plastic straps looked like they were glued together. *Could be epoxy,* I thought, not that it made any difference. I backed away, called the office, and asked for the bomb unit. Then I got Jo out of the house and over to the neighbors.

The bomb squad brought the robot. A signal jammer was turned on so a cell call or another electronic device couldn't trigger it as the ties were cut, and the robot pulled the magnet holding it to a steel strut free. It took a half hour of back-and-forth to get permission to take the bomb into open space a mile away, empty lots facing the desert, and detonate it.

Mara arrived in time for the blast and the concussive bang that followed. The bomb squad left, and Mara and I talked more about yesterday. Funny how our attitudes can shift and we can become more open when we know change is near.

We talked awhile, and I liked that we didn't have a what-comes-next talk.

In the early afternoon, I went into the office and wrote my reports and took an unexpected call that I'd guessed Mara knew was coming. The head of TEDAC, the FBI Terrorist Explosive Device Analytical Center, asked me if I'd be interested in applying for a job.

"I trust Kathy Tobias in all things," he said. "I'd heard of you, but if Kathy recommends you—and she does—that carries a lot of weight with me. We need someone who could play a significant role in our joint responsibilities. You wouldn't be pushing a bomber off a mountain, but we see some pretty interesting stuff. We're six to eight months out from hiring. You wouldn't have to move, but you would have to travel. I'll e-mail a description, and let's talk again in a month. I'll send everything today if you're interested."

"I'm interested."

I called Tobias to thank her, but really I called her to talk about Indonal. I'd been thinking about him all day. I told her how much I'd grown to like him. She stifled a sob then broke down. She apologized, but do we ever have to apologize for caring?

"What do you think of the TEDAC idea?" she asked as a way of ending.

"I like it."

"I knew you would."

Later in the afternoon after Jo got home, we called Dr. Yandovitch and put him on speakerphone. He'd heard my name in the news and opened with, "You don't need me if you can hike up a mountain and wrestle a bomber off a cliff."

"I had a pair of those collapsible trekking poles, or I never would have made it."

"I knew there was more to it," he said. "If you've still got those sticks, bring them to my office. I'll hang them on a wall as inspiration to patients. I've reviewed your X-rays and the MRI again and have re-evaluated what you can reasonably expect after surgery. You talked about returning to active duty."

"That's right," I said, and my spirits sank as I listened.

"That includes running if I remember correctly."

"It does. In fact, I'm supposed to run in the next few days."

"Well, don't." He paused. "Don't do any running just yet. I'm confident surgery is a good decision, but I can't make you whole again. You'll be a lot better and if you're diligent we can arrest the degradation, but I don't think you'll ever get back to meeting the requirements for active duty."

"Never?"

"I won't say never—every time I do, I'm wrong—but as I said, I've looked at everything again and I have to restrain what I may have led you to hope for. The human body is a remarkable piece of working art, and yours may surprise both of us. Another surgeon might be more confident, so you don't have to take me as the last word, but I felt I had to tell you. I know you've been thinking it over . . ."

"Will I walk and be active and fit?"

"You'll be fit. You'll stand straight, but you shouldn't wrestle terrorists on mountains. You'll have to do something different."

"Different than active duty."

"Most likely."

"If you were me, would you go ahead with surgery?" I asked.

"I would."

"I'm close to a decision. I'll call you later today or tomorrow morning."

"I'll watch for your call."

I leaned back and looked at Jo. "Want to go out somewhere?" I asked. "Go do something, maybe get dinner somewhere."

"Yeah, let's get out of here."

"What do you really think of Yandovitch?" I asked after we were in the car.

"Everything I've ever heard was good. And I like him."

"I do too, but I've arrested people I've liked."

"Don't make the decision without talking to me first."

"We're talking right now. I want to know exactly what you think."

"Then I'm going to tell you."

But she didn't just yet. We had a cocktail and a nice dinner, and I got a few thumbs-up and nods from people walking by in the restaurant. Somebody sent our table a bottle that we ended up giving to the waitstaff. For a day or two I'd be a minor celebrity.

The badge, the gun, the creds I carried, the job I loved—they were my identity. Jo and I kept talking, but it wasn't until early the next morning that she told me what she really thought.

"It's about us as much as you," she said.

"I know it is. I think a lot about that."

"It's a serious surgery and one without any guarantees. I've been around the good and the bad ones. Sometimes it's a tangled nerve or a cancer that's spread more than the scans showed. In yours it could be an atrophied muscle he can't do anything with."

"He's made that clear, and I get it."

"I know you do. Here's what I really think. If you go ahead, you go without hesitation. None. You go with your all. You leave the doubts at the door and accept the risks, and I don't mean just you. I mean, me as well. Us."

Her eyes watered as she said, "I know what can happen. I've seen it. But for us, for you, we don't do any second-guessing later."

"I hear that, Jo. No hesitation. I've thought about it and I'm there. I'm in."

"Are you?"

"I am."

"Then I am too."

The night before the surgery, Jo lay close to me, her hand on my chest, her warm breath on my shoulder, and the smooth, lovely curve of her hip against me. I felt her heart beating. Very early the next morning she drove me to the hospital, where they bent the rules and let her stay with me until the anesthesiologist put me out.

"Hey," she said just before.

"Hey yourself."

"It'll go well and everything will be fine," she said then laughed and changed that to, "I don't mean everything will be."

"I knew what you meant."

She squeezed my hand hard, and I smiled up at her. What she'd meant was that everything would be different, and some of it quite hard, but that we would be fine.

ABOUT THE AUTHOR

Photo © 2020 Shoey Sindel

Kirk Russell's eleven crime novels in three series have garnered many starred reviews. His previous novel, *Gone Dark*, featuring FBI bomb expert Paul Grale, was an International Thriller Writers finalist. *No Hesitation* continues the Grale series. Russell lives in Berkeley, California.